Palmetto Island

Lowcountry on My Mind

ASHLEY FARLEY

ALSO BY ASHLEY FARLEY

Boots and Bedlam

Lowcountry Stranger

Her Sister's Shoes

Magnolia Series

Beyond the Garden

Magnolia Nights

Scottie's Adventures

Breaking the Story

Merry Mary

ONE

Amelia circles the block three times before entering the parking garage and locating a vacant space on the top deck. Tucking her platinum blonde hair beneath a black baseball cap, she retrieves a small rolling suitcase from the trunk and rides the elevator down to the street level. She pauses on the sidewalk in front of the garage before heading north. She doesn't need a map. She committed the route to memory before ditching her phone in a trash can at a convenience store an hour outside of Boston. At the stoplight at the end of the block, she takes a right and walks a half mile to Newark Penn Station.

Amelia left her laptop at home on purpose, to throw her husband off her trail. Her browser's history will reveal a rental car booked for one-way travel to DC along with a search for hotels in the Georgetown and Dupont Circle areas. Traveling to her destination will take over twenty-four hours and involve bus transfers in Raleigh, Columbia, and Charleston. While her destination will be apparent to Nelson, he will never think to look for her on a bus. Such pedestrian means of travel are beneath him.

At the Greyhound station, Amelia studies the ticket agents before choosing a gum-smacking, bored-looking teenager. She provides a fake name and is relieved when the ticket agent takes her cash without asking for identification.

Amelia boards the bus and chooses a vacant row near the back. Stowing her suitcase in the overhead compartment, she slides over to the window seat. The weight of her pistol in her crossbody handbag is heavy against her belly. Years ago, she'd purchased the handgun and trained to use it without her husband's knowledge. She's been plotting her escape for as long as she can remember. When the opportunity presented itself sooner than expected, she put her plan in motion without hesitation. The hardest part is behind her. Freedom lies ahead.

She leans her head against the window and closes her eyes, thinking back to the last time she ran away from home, eight years ago when her mother broke her hip. Bebe, the family's long-time housekeeper, had called Amelia with the news.

"Miss Dottie had surgery two days ago. She's out of the hospital and recovering nicely at home. I'm taking good care of her, but I thought you'd wanna know."

"I'll be there as soon as I can get a flight," Amelia told Bebe.

Her husband had been none too pleased when he found her packing her suitcase. "Mama broke her hip, Nelson. I have no choice. I'm obligated to go see her."

He'd argued, "But we're hosting a sit-down dinner for a hundred on Friday night. Wait until next week, and I'll go with you."

But Amelia had gone anyway. She'd been at her mother's side for less than twenty-four hours when Nelson came for her. She still remembers the fury in his dark eyes.

"Get your things. You're coming back to Boston with me."

Amelia had held her chin high in defiance. Being in her childhood home had given her a false sense of security. "And if I refuse?"

Leaning in close, he'd threatened, "I will kill your precious mama. Then her blood will be on your hands."

Amelia had willingly returned with him to their townhome in Boston's prestigious Beacon Hill neighborhood where she'd suffered the worst beating of her life. For days afterward, as she lay in bed with fractured ribs and a battered face, she began contemplating her getaway. She wouldn't dare leave while her mother was still alive. Which, by the grace of God, wouldn't be for a long time. Miss Dottie was a vibrant seventy-two-year-old. Her broken hip resulted from an accident on the tennis court. But the day would eventually come. And Amelia would be prepared. Or so she thought.

She'd been deeply shocked and saddened when Bebe had called yesterday to inform Amelia of her mother's death. "Miss Dottie passed away in her sleep during the night on Tuesday. I found her when I came to work this morning. I'm so sorry, baby."

Amelia had gripped the phone. "I don't understand, Bebe. Mama was in excellent health."

"Mm-hmm. Miss Dottie went to the doctor for her annual checkup just last month. But she was still eighty years old."

The roar of a tractor trailer horn jars Amelia back to the present, and she opens her blue eyes wide. The bus has departed Newark and is now heading south on the interstate. Resting her hand on her purse, she finds the hard metal of her pistol reassuring. This time, when Nelson comes for her, she'll be ready.

Max reluctantly gives her last room away, which she has never before done on a busy summer weekend. "I had to move the Simpsons from the third floor to the first," she tells Agnes, her night guest services manager. "The air conditioner in 310 was blowing hot air. They are now in 128 which, as you know, is a far inferior room. I comped the room for the weekend, and the Simpsons were polite about it, but I could tell they were irritated.

At this rate, if things continue to break, we'll have to send our guests down the road to the Coral Sands Motel."

Agnes's red-painted lip curls up. "Not the flea-ridden roach motel."

"Come on, Agnes. The Coral Sands isn't that bad. Besides, what choice do we have? This old building is falling down around us." Max's deep blue eyes dart about, as though expecting the walls to crumble.

"Aren't you starting the renovations soon?" Agnes asks.

Max runs a hand across her cropped blonde hair. "After Labor Day is the plan. But that's four weeks away, and I still haven't gotten my loan approved. To make matters worse, I can't decide which contractor to use. Truthfully, I don't like either of the two I've interviewed. Their bids are outrageous. I understand enough about construction to know they're trying to gouge me."

"Can you get another bid?"

"If I can find another contractor. These two are rumored to be the best on the island." Max retrieves her bag from under the counter. "What a day. I'm going for a drink. I'll be at Shaggy's if you need me."

Agnes glances around the empty lobby. "Where's Ron? Isn't he going with you?"

"I'm texting him now," Max says, flashing her phone as she exits the hotel.

The outside world is teeming with activity. Children with cotton candy cones skip alongside their parents on the boardwalk while boats of all sizes zip up and down the creek. Down on the marina dock, commercial fishing boats, their diesel engines rumbling, return from a day on the ocean. At the railing, a young woman gazes up at her partner, and he lowers his head to kiss her lips. Max envies them their obvious love for one another. She shared that tender passion with her late husband, but she doesn't feel it for her current live-in boyfriend. What does she feel for Ron? In the beginning, she'd been taken with his fun-loving, carefree personality. But that infatuation has now waned. Perhaps he's not as fun-loving or as carefree as she'd originally thought.

Max pockets her phone without sending the text to Ron.

She strolls through the small park—a water fountain surrounded by palm trees that separates the north and south branches of the waterfront area. On the corner opposite her hotel is Birdie's Nest Cafe, owned and operated by Max's lifelong best friend. Birdie is expanding her operating hours to include dinner. She's sectioned off an area of the boardwalk outside the cafe for seating. The tables are set with crisp white linens in preparation for the soft opening tonight.

As she passes the window, she spots Birdie and her new chef, Sydney, at an indoor table, their heads close together as they study notes on legal pads in front of them. Max knocks on the window and waves, giving them a thumbs-up. Birdie places an imaginary gun to her head and pulls the trigger. Max laughs and, cupping her hands around her mouth, she yells, "You're gonna do great."

Continuing on to Shaggy's, she's greeted by a boisterous crowd of vacationers celebrating happy hour. Max slides onto the only available seat at the bar and scrutinizes the special drinks menu. Lewis, the bartender, calls out to her as he fills two pitchers with draft beer. "What will it be, Max? The usual?"

She shakes her head. "I'm not in the mood for wine tonight. I want something fresh. I'll have a blueberry mojito," she says, returning the laminated menu to its place between the napkin dispenser and ketchup bottle.

"Excellent choice," Lewis says. "Coming right up."

She's admiring Lewis's strapping biceps stretching the sleeves of his black T-shirt when Ron appears beside her. He snatches a napkin out of the dispenser and hands it to her. "You're drooling."

She takes the napkin from him and balls it up. "You're hilarious."

"Are you avoiding me?" he asks with a hint of suspicion. "Why didn't you tell me you were going to Shaggy's?"

Guilt prevents her from meeting his eyes. "I was getting ready to text you," she says, the lie slipping off her tongue before she can stop it.

Ron looks at the other patrons seated at the bar. "There are no empty chairs."

"Be patient. It's happy hour. Something will open up in a minute." Lewis slides her drink across the bar, and she takes a sip. She rewards Lewis with a smile. "This really hits the spot. It's so light and fruity."

Ron's voice cracks when he tries to mock her. "It's so light and fruity."

Max glares at him. "Why are you so grumpy? Tough day at the beach?"

"As a matter of fact, it was. The beach is getting old. This town is—"

When the guy next to her abandons his barstool, Max says, "Grab that seat before someone else does."

"Cool." Ron takes the vacated seat and orders a Miller Lite in a bottle from Lewis.

When his beer arrives, Ron turns his attention to the baseball game on the wall-mounted television over the bar. Max studies Ron's profile. His scraggly hair falls below his collar, his beard is scruffy, and he wears a gold hoop earring in his right earlobe. She usually prefers clean-cut men, but when they met at the end of June, after a string of disastrous blind dates, she'd been desperate to have someone, *anyone*, interested in her.

Lewis takes a break during a lull in business to chat with Max. "So, tonight's the big night. I saw Birdie earlier. She's a nervous wreck. I assume you're going to the soft opening."

"As soon as I . . ." Max casts a nervous glance at Ron. "I mean, *we* leave here. Poor Birdie. She's a nervous wreck, even though she's only having family and a few friends."

Lewis drags a rag across the bar. "Birdie's been bringing me samples all week. Everything I've tasted has been over the top. Her new chef is not only talented, she's hot. She can cook for me anytime. What's her name?"

Max laughs. "Her name is Sydney. And I agree. She's pretty and talented. But she doesn't have much of a personality. You might find her difficult to talk to."

"I'm not interested in talking to her, Max," Lewis says with a naughty glint in his eye.

"You're a bad boy, Lewis." Max balls up her cocktail napkin and throws it at him.

Lewis catches the napkin. "Just speaking the truth," he says and moves to the other end of the bar to fill an order for one of the waitresses.

Max drains the last of her mojito and turns to Ron. "Are you ready to go to Birdie's? We should be there when the other guests arrive."

"I guess," Ron says in a tone that lets Max know he's not at all interested in the soft opening.

Max drops a twenty-dollar bill on the bar, and they exit Shaggy's porch. She's making a beeline to the cafe when Ron pulls her aside. "You know, you really shouldn't embarrass yourself by flirting with a man half your age."

"Flirting? With Lewis? Don't be ridiculous. He's a friend. I've known him for years." Max wrenches her arm free of Ron's grasp. "Jealousy is not a good look, Ron."

His brown eyes turn cold. "Jealous? Of Lewis? I don't think so."

"It sure sounded like it to me." When Max stalks off, he catches up with her. "I'm sorry, Maxie. I was out of line."

Max stops walking and turns to face him. "I'm sorry too. I'm not myself tonight. My hotel is falling apart at the seams, and the bank won't lend me the money to make the improvements."

"Oh? I didn't realize the bank had declined your loan request."

"It hasn't yet. But the loan officer is taking her sweet time in getting back to me, which is not a good sign."

"Try not to jump to conclusions." Ron pulls her in and holds her tight. "The Palmetto Inn is the main attraction on this island. To lose the only decent hotel would crush the town. Give the bank a little more time. I'm sure they'll approve your loan."

Max rests her head on his shoulder. Ron's not such a bad guy. Every relationship has its difficulties, and Max isn't getting any younger. Time is not on her side. Isn't being with someone she doesn't love better than growing old alone?

TWO

There are no taxis waiting in front of the bus station when Amelia arrives in Palmetto Island at almost nine o'clock at night. The pay phone outside the station is broken, and since she ditched her cell in Massachusetts, she has no way of summoning an Uber. She'll have to walk home. But Point Pleasant is less than three miles, and after sitting on a bus for nearly twenty-four hours, she yearns for fresh air and exercise. Besides, she's in excellent shape, thanks to the personal trainer Nelson pays to torture them every morning at six.

Amelia starts off slowly down Ocean Avenue, the hubbub of activity in her small hometown. After her escape attempt eight years ago, her husband has kept Amelia on a short leash. She's been home only twice since then, both times accompanied by Nelson. He humors her by permitting weekly phone calls with her mother, but he insists on being present in the room, eaves-dropping on every word.

Little has changed in Palmetto Island during her absence. The mannequins in the window at Leslie's Boutique sport cute outfits —casual resort attire that appeals to Amelia. Nelson encourages her to buy expensive designer clothes, most of which she was eager to leave behind in Boston.

An oak writing table catches her attention at Island Antiques, and next door, a crowd is gathered for a wine tasting at Corks and Nibbles. At the end of the block, two young couples are enjoying a late dinner at a picnic table in front of the Sandwich Shack.

As she crosses over the causeway, Amelia smiles at two teenage boys fishing over the railing in the inky water. They cast strange looks at her in return. A woman walking at night along the side of the road wheeling a suitcase is an unusual sight.

On the ocean side of the causeway, the sound of waves crashing on the shore boosts her spirits. She inhales, filling her lungs with salt-tinged air. Home, sweet home.

A half mile down the road, headlights appear behind her, and seconds later, a police cruiser pulls up beside her. The driver's window is down and a uniformed officer with a chubby face says, "Evening, ma'am."

Amelia dips her head in greeting. "Hello, officer."

"You wouldn't be Dottie Fairchild's daughter now, would you?"

"I am. I'm Amelia Archer."

"I thought you might be." Swinging open the car door, he hoists his stout frame from behind the driver's seat. "I'm terribly sorry for your loss. Miss Dottie and I were good friends." He extends his hand to her. "I'm Toby Summers, chief of police."

Tears prick Amelia's eyelids as she shakes his hand.

He eyes her suitcase. "Are you just getting into town? If I'd known you needed a ride, I would've sent one of my men to pick you up from the Charleston Airport."

"Actually, I'm not a big fan of flying. I took the train to Charleston and a bus to the island. There were no taxis at the station, and I accidentally left my phone on the train, so I couldn't call an Uber."

"That's rotten luck." He gestures at his car. "Get in. I'll give you a ride to the house."

"I appreciate the offer, but I don't have far to go."

"I insist," he says, grabbing her suitcase and tossing it into the back. "I consider it my duty to see you home safely."

"In that case, how can I say no?" She goes around to the passenger side and climbs into the front seat. The car smells like fried onion rings and stale coffee. Country music plays on the radio and cool air blasts from vents in the dashboard.

Getting in beside her, Summers puts the car in gear and slowly drives off. "Where are you from?"

"Boston," she answers, and before he can further interrogate her, she asks, "How did you know my mama?"

"Gosh." Taking one hand off the steering wheel, he strokes the flabby skin under his chin. "I've known Miss Dottie so long I can't remember how we actually met. She was a generous woman, always contributing to our fundraising efforts." He chuckles. "Your mama was a true southern belle. She would smile at me, and then, in that sugary sweet voice of hers, give me a piece of her mind."

Amelia smiles. "That sounds like her. What did she give you a piece of her mind about?"

"Vacationers mostly. She was always complaining about them not cleaning up after their dogs on the beach and trespassing on her property."

"I don't remember her mentioning trespassers. Did it happen often?"

"Every now and then. Curious folks sneak up from the beach to get a closer look at your beautiful home."

It is a beautiful home, she thinks as Point Pleasant comes into view through the darkness. With the ocean on one side and the creeks and marshes of the inlet on the other, the sprawling ten-acre estate feels like the end of the earth to Amelia. Landscape lighting illuminates the exterior of the house—its cedar shingles, black shutters, and yellow front door a sight for her weary eyes. Presumably, all this now belongs to Amelia. But it's meaningless without her mother to share it.

Chief Summers pulls into the driveway and parks beside the back door. "I was here, you know, the morning after your mama died. When I heard the dispatch, I came right out."

Amelia knits her brow. "I don't understand. I thought she was in good health. Was there evidence to suspect foul play?"

"Nah. Nothing like that. Bebe was shook up pretty good. She didn't know who else to call. Miss Dottie was peaceful. She slipped away in her sleep."

"I'm glad of that," Amelia says in a soft voice.

"Your mama had a lot of living left to do. Her passing was a shame." Summers retrieves her suitcase and joins Amelia at the back door, waiting patiently while she unlocks it and punches in the code on the control panel to turn off the security system.

"I hate for you to be here alone at a time like this." Summers's eyes travel to the four-carat diamond on her left hand. "Will your husband come down for the funeral?"

"I don't think so. He's too busy at work to get away." Amelia reaches for the doorknob. "Thank you for the ride."

"It was my pleasure. If you need anything, please don't hesitate to call me. Miss Dottie has my number in her contacts. I'm sure her cell phone is here somewhere. If need be, you can call the station and ask to be put through to me."

"Will do. Thanks again, and goodnight." She closes and locks the door behind him.

Leaving her suitcase in the mudroom, she enters the kitchen and discovers a note from Bebe on the counter, which welcomes her home and tells her about the casserole and salad she left in the refrigerator for her supper. The nausea that has taken up residence in her stomach overpowers the hunger pangs. But a glass of wine would calm her nerves, and she selects a bottle of Whispering Angel from the under counter wine refrigerator and pours a glass. She circles the kitchen, admiring the changes her mother recently made—new stainless appliances, marble countertops, and navy cabinetry. A breakfast room with windows and doors overlooking the inlet is adjacent to the kitchen on the back of the house. Opposite it, on the ocean side, a Florida room occupies the space her family once used as a formal dining room. She passes through the Florida room to the foyer, which houses an oversized wood-and-glass front door and a wide staircase curving upward to the second floor. Beyond the staircase is her father's oak-paneled study.

Amelia flips the wall switch, and soft light from the overhead fixture fills the wood-paneled room. Growing up, she relished rainy afternoons spent curled on the sofa with her mystery novels. Entering the room, she lowers herself to the leather chair behind her father's mahogany desk. She fingers the engraved initials on his silver-plated lighter—CTF, Clayton Terrence Fairchild. An image of her daddy lighting his pipe comes to mind. She can hardly believe he's been dead for forty-five years. She picks up a framed photograph of her parents on their honeymoon in the Cayman Islands. Her mama and daddy had loved each other dearly. Amelia's earliest memories were happy ones. Then things changed around the time she went to kindergarten. There was so much tension in the house during the years prior to his death. She studies the photograph of her father more closely. She never noticed the resemblance between her father and Nelson. But her husband is nothing like Clayton Fairchild. Her father was a gentle soul, a pediatrician adored by his young patients and respected by their parents.

Setting the frame down, Amelia pushes back from the desk, leaves the study, and goes into the living room. Her mother's decorating handiwork is apparent here as well with a new knotty seagrass rug, comfortable seating upholstered in neutral shades, and accent pillows and lamps in the colors of the ocean. A portrait of a young Dottie hangs above the fireplace mantel. Staring up at the portrait, Amelia can almost hear her mother's laughter and smell the scent of her White Shoulders perfume. Her mother is gone forever, and Amelia never got a chance to say goodbye. Amelia chokes down a sob. She's been holding back a torrent of tears since learning of her mother's death forty-eight hours ago.

Throwing open the french doors, she steps out onto the wrap-around porch and collapses in a rocking chair. Comforted by the semidarkness, she finally allows the tears to flow. She cries for the loss of her mother. But she also cries for the loss of thirty years of her life. She's home now, and she's never leaving. She has reclaimed her freedom and will protect it at all costs.

Amelia remains on the porch long after the tears have dried up. After taking her empty wineglass to the kitchen, she makes certain all the windows and doors are locked before engaging the alarm. Retrieving her suitcase from the mudroom, she wheels it up the stairs. At the top, instead of retiring to her old bedroom, she turns in the opposite direction. Her mother's suite occupies the entire south end of the second floor with windows offering a 180-degree view of the ocean and inlet, including the wide channel where the two meet.

Fresh tears fill her eyes at the sight of her mother's king-size bed, the place where she died peacefully in her sleep here three nights ago. Amelia changes into her nightgown and climbs into bed, stuffing her pistol under her pillow. Exhausted from her trip, she falls fast asleep, but her bladder urges her awake again shortly after midnight. She's feeling her way through the darkness to the en suite bathroom when a flicker of light in the apartment over the garage at the rear of the property catches her attention. Her family's full-time gardener once occupied the apartment, but to her knowledge, no one has lived there for years. Amelia doesn't remember her mother mentioning a tenant, but it would be so like Dottie to offer the apartment, rent-free, to someone in need of a place to stay. Cold dread travels Amelia's spine as she remains at the window, waiting for another flash of light. She feels as though someone is watching her. She has a sneaking suspicious she's in imminent danger from someone other than her husband.

THREE

At six thirty on Saturday morning, Max meets Birdie in the park, and they cross the boardwalk together to the marina's floating dock. Back in June, when Birdie's daughter and three-year-old grandson moved to Charleston, Birdie took up paddleboarding to occupy the lonely morning hours before opening the cafe. Birdie insisted Max buy a board and join her. Max was skeptical at first. She didn't understand how paddling around on a fiberglass board could be enjoyable. But now she strictly adheres to the routine. Not only is she proud of her newly toned muscles, her favorite part of the day is being on the inlet at dawn, watching the sunrise and seeing the wildlife come alive.

Max and Birdie remove their boards from the storage rack and slide them into the water. Pushing away from the dock, they paddle away from the marina toward the inlet's main creek.

Gliding alongside Birdie, Max says, "Everything appeared to run smoothly last night. At least from my perspective as a customer. Were you pleased?"

Birdie flashes her a broad smile that lights up her face. "Very much so. Having a soft opening highlighted our weaknesses. We have a few minor kinks to work out, but overall, we're off to an excellent start."

"That's great, Birdie. You've worked hard, and I'm happy for you. When's the real opening?"

"On Tuesday. We'll start on a slow night and work our way toward the weekend."

"That makes sense," Max says.

The women are silent as they pass a heron feeding on minnows. Then Birdie says, "Ron seemed out of sorts last night. Is everything okay between you two?"

Max stares down at the water in front of her. "I'm not sure, honestly. I'm afraid our honeymoon is over. The fun has worn off."

"I'm not sure what you saw in him in the first place."

Max looks over at Birdie. "What do you mean? I thought you liked Ron."

"I liked him because you liked him. But you have to admit there's something fishy about his story."

"What's fishy about it?" Max asks in a snippy tone.

"Come on, Maxie. He's traveling around the country with no agenda. Who does that?"

"Someone who made a fortune in software development. He's touring the country, searching for his dream destination to live out his days."

"Don't you think it's odd he doesn't have any family? No children or siblings or ex-wives?"

"Not really, considering he devoted his life to his career."

"Did you even research him?"

"Of course, Birdie. Duh." Truth be told, Max had been too enamored with Ron in the beginning to question his background. She should've asked her nephew to conduct a police background check on him. Bare minimum, she should've looked him up on social media before she went out with him. When she finally got around to it weeks later, she found no

17

mention of a software developer from Philadelphia named Ron Morton.

A commercial fishing boat passes them, swamping them with its wake. Birdie and Max drop to their knees and wait until the water calms. When they're back on their feet, Birdie says, "I'm concerned at how fast you jumped into a relationship with him. You'd only had a few dates when he moved into your apartment."

"The progression was natural, even if it happened quicker than usual. Ron was a guest in my hotel. We hit it off. When he decided to stay on the island indefinitely, I suggested he move in with me." Max smacks the water with her paddle, splashing Birdie. "You're one to talk about moving too fast."

Birdie's face reddens. "I'll be the first to admit Stan and I got ahead of ourselves. But once we realized it, we slowed things down."

"All the way down to friendship," Max says. "How long are you going to keep up that charade?"

Birdie glares at her. "It's not a charade. We're just friends. At least for now. I promised Stan I'll reassess the situation at the end of the summer."

Max wipes sweat out of her eyes with the back of her hand. "How does Stan feel about waiting?"

Birdie hunches a shoulder. "He's trying to be patient, but I can tell he's ready for more. This may sound selfish, but I'm enjoying my freedom. For the first time in decades, since Cary and I got married, I don't have to take care of anyone."

"Freedom has a nice ring to it. I've been a widow for six years. I'm used to captaining my own ship. Having Ron around is cramping my style." Max pauses before continuing. "While I'm not ready to give him up just yet, when the time comes, I'm worried about how I'm going to get rid of him. He has gotten awfully comfortable in my apartment."

Birdie thinks a minute before responding. "Tell him you're moving into my spare bedroom during the renovations."

"That's brilliant, Birdie. Is that a legitimate offer?"

"Of course. I'd love to have you as a roommate."

Max's lips turn downward. "*If* the renovation actually happens. I'm still waiting for the bank to approve my loan, *and* I'm having trouble finding a contractor. I remember you raving about the builder you used for your kitchen. What was his name? I can't remember."

"Davis Watson. I can give you his contact information. He's new to town. He has plenty of experience, but he's working hard to establish himself on the island. I'm sure he'd appreciate the business."

Flutters of hope dance across Max's chest. "He sounds ideal. Send me his contact info. I'll call him today."

When they reach the end of the small creek, they maneuver their boards around, heading in the direction they've come. "I'm roasting. Let's get wet," Max says and steps off the paddleboard into the cool salty water. Birdie follows suit and they float on their backs while their body temperatures lower.

"I read Dottie Fairchild's obituary in the paper this morning," Birdie says, staring up at the sky. "Such a shame. I saw her in church last Sunday. She appeared in good health."

"Goes to show, you never know what tomorrow will bring. In truth, Birdie, I can't help but wonder whether I'm wasting my time by staying with Ron. Or whether I should be grateful for our relationship and make the most of it. Or whether I'm too old to hope true love will once again come my way."

"That's a morbid thought, Maxie. I wanna believe we have many good years left."

"I hope so, too. I'm just saying, you never know." Max climbs back on her board and waits for Birdie to do the same.

As they paddle off toward the marina, Birdie says, "Miss Dottie's funeral is set for Monday at eleven. We haven't seen Amelia since her wedding. I wonder if we'll recognize her."

"I'm sure we will." Under her breath, Max adds, "If she comes."

Birdie cuts her eyes at Max. "Why wouldn't she come to her mother's funeral?"

"The same reason she never comes home."

"Amelia's the wife of a successful businessman," Birdie says. "She has responsibilities. She's probably busy entertaining and traveling. But I'm certain she's been home for visits. We just didn't know about them. She probably didn't have time to spare and wanted to spend every minute with Miss Dottie."

"That's a logical explanation," Max says. "But it's not true. I run into Bebe all the time at the grocery store and farmer's market. She told me Amelia hasn't been to Palmetto Island in years."

Birdie shakes her head in bewilderment. "I don't understand. Amelia used to be so close to her mama."

"Maybe they had a falling out," Max suggests.

Birdie considers the possibility. "Maybe."

"Anyway, if Amelia is so social, why doesn't she have an account on Instagram or Facebook or Twitter?"

Birdie shakes her head. "I can't answer that. I've searched for her myself."

Max has thought a lot about Amelia over the decades. Amelia, Birdie, and Max were inseparable throughout their childhood and teenage years. The years have made them strangers. Time has changed them. Will they be able to pick up where they left off like old friends often do?

FOUR

Amelia wakes to bright rays of sunshine streaming through the semicircular wall of windows. Confused by the unfamiliarity of her surroundings, she sits up in bed and surveys the room. She'd been too distraught last night to notice her mother's redecorated bedroom in shades of gray and lavender. The bed's headboard is upholstered in tufted gray suede. The wool carpet sports a subtle pattern of gray hues. And a chaise lounge, positioned by the window, is covered in lavender velvet.

Swinging her legs over the side of the bed, Amelia stands, stretches, and wanders over to the windows. The sky is a brilliant blue above a calm ocean, a lovely morning to walk on the beach. She's changing into exercise clothes when the security alarm pings and the status button on the control panel changes from red to green. Is that Bebe? On a Saturday? Or is there someone else on the property? Amelia remembers seeing a flicker of light in the garage apartment window when she woke to use the bathroom during the night. She tucks her holstered gun in the waistband of her lycra training shorts, slips on her running shoes, and hurries downstairs to the kitchen. Bebe is standing at the sink with her back to Amelia. Her hair has gone completely gray since the last time Amelia was home, but her figure is still lithe and her caramel complexion wrinkle-free.

"Bebe! What're you doing here on a Saturday?"

The housekeeper turns to face her. "I came to see you. And aren't you a sight for sore eyes?" She spreads her arms wide. "Come. Give me some loving."

Amelia steps into Bebe's familiar arms. Her scent, like lemons and sunshine, brings back memories of her childhood, of picnics on the beach and rainy days spent working jigsaw puzzles. "I've missed you."

"And I've missed you, baby girl." Bebe squeezes Amelia tight. "I'm so sorry about your mama."

Amelia relishes the feel of Bebe's warm body against hers. "Me too, Bebe. I'm sorry about a lot of things." How long has it been since she experienced this kind of genuine human connection? She certainly never felt comforted by her husband's embrace. Nelson's touch repulsed her.

"Let me get a good look at you." Bebe holds Amelia at arm's length. "You are way too skinny, child. I'm going to fatten you up while you're home. You didn't touch the supper I left for you," she says in her scolding voice.

Amelia drops her arms from around Bebe. "I was too exhausted to eat after my long trip."

Bebe cups her cheek. "Then you must be starving. Let me fix you some breakfast."

"Maybe later. I want to walk the beach before it gets too hot."

"Alright then, I'll have an omelet ready for you when you get back. I always made your mama's omelets with goat cheese, arugula, and summer tomatoes. How does that sound?"

Amelia's stomach rumbles at the thought of it. "Delicious. Thanks, Bebe. I won't be long, maybe thirty minutes."

Exiting the front door, Amelia walks across the lawn to the boardwalk and through the sand dunes. There's not a soul in sight on the beach in either direction. She tilts her head back and stretches her arms toward the sky. "I'm home, Mama. And I'm planning to stay. I only wish you could be here with me."

She heads north, taking in the sights and sounds around her. The waves breaking on the shore. Seagulls flying low over the ocean and sandpipers feeding in the surf. She survived thirty years of marriage to an evil man, and she's grateful to be alive. She won't go back to Nelson under any circumstances.

She increases her pace and walks down to the causeway and back. Bebe is at the stove cooking her omelet when she returns. Amelia pours herself a cup of coffee and slides onto the banquette at the breakfast room table. She looks out the window and across the lawn. "Bebe, is someone renting the garage apartment?"

Bebe sets her breakfast plate on the table in front of Amelia. "Nah. No one has been in that apartment in decades. It's infested with mice. Maybe snakes, too. What makes you ask?"

"I thought I saw a flicker of light in the window last night. But it could've been my imagination." Amelia takes a bite of omelet. The combination of flavors hits the spot, and she forks off more.

Bebe pours herself a cup of coffee and sits down next to Amelia on the banquette. "I'm sure that's it. You were tired after your trip."

Amelia offers her a tentative smile. "How are you holding up?"

"I'm doing the best I can," Bebe says with a sad smile.

"You always do. I know this is difficult for you. I'm having a hard time myself, processing my mother's death. When we spoke on the phone, you said Mama had recently been for her annual checkup. Do you think maybe she was ill? Maybe she found out bad news from her doctor and was keeping it from us?"

A faraway expression falls over Bebe's face. "Now that I think about it, Miss Dottie was quieter than usual the weeks before she died. I doubt it had anything to do with her health. She looked wonderful and was active as ever. But she seemed distracted. Then again, she often kept her feelings close to her chest."

Amelia eats the last bite of omelet and pushes her plate away. "I should be grateful Mama didn't suffer from a long-drawn-out disease like cancer or Alzheimer's. But I feel robbed of time I could've spent with her. I only have myself to blame for that."

As though reading her mind, Bebe says, "Your mama worried your husband was mistreating you. Is that true?"

Amelia considers how much to tell Bebe. For her own safety, the housekeeper should be aware of the potential for danger. "My life with Nelson has been a living hell."

Bebe reaches for her hand. "I'm so sorry, honey."

"We got married too young. He swept me off my feet. I was too head over heels in love with him to see his dark side until it was too late."

"Why did you stay with him?"

With quivering chin, Amelia says, "Because he threatened Mama. He said if I went to the police or I tried to leave him, he would kill her. He's a powerful man. On the surface, he's a wealthy businessman and philanthropist. But his legitimate businesses are merely a cover for his underworld dealings."

"Does he know where you are?"

Amelia blots her eyes with her napkin. "I left without telling him where I was going, but I'm sure he knows I'm here. And he will be coming for me." Amelia removes the gun from her waistband and places it on the table. "But I'm prepared."

Bebe reaches for the weapon. Ejecting the cartridge, she slides the barrel back to confirm it's empty and aims the gun at the window, pulling the trigger. "I trust you know how to use this."

"I do. Obviously, you do as well."

Bebe sets the gun back down. "And you think this little pistol will protect you from the vicious man you described?"

"Whether it does or doesn't, I'm not going back to him. I will fight to my death if necessary." Amelia shifts on the bench to face

Bebe. "But I couldn't stand it if something happened to you because of me. Maybe you should take some time off."

"No way." Bebe puffs out her chest. "If you're in trouble, I aim to stand by you."

"I appreciate your concern, but you should discuss it with your husband before you make your decision."

"Claude won't let anything happen to me or you. He has an arsenal of weapons, and enough brothers and cousins and friends to field an army. We've got your back, baby girl."

Amelia relaxes a little as some of the tension leaves her body. "Promise me you won't take any unnecessary risk."

Bebe presses her hand to her chest. "I promise."

Amelia takes her plate to the sink, rinsing it before placing it in the dishwasher. She returns to the breakfast room. "We must keep our guard up at all times. I want the alarm on as much as possible during the day."

Bebe nods. "Understood."

"If you see anything or anyone suspicious, I want you to tell me immediately."

Bebe gets to her feet. "Don't you worry. I have eagle eyes."

Amelia laughs. "I remember that about you. You caught me in the midst of many mischievous acts when I was a child."

Amelia surveys the contents of her mother's walk-in closet for something suitable to wear for her meeting with the estate attorney. She brought only the necessities from Boston in her one small suitcase. She wears the same size and shared the same taste as her mother whose love of fashion never wavered in her later years. Dresses for every occasion hang from racks while built-in shelves house neatly folded sweaters and Bermuda shorts and jeans. Amelia chooses a simple khaki-colored sheath, feminine yet professional, from Tory Burch, one of her favorite designers. She punches the code on the keypad of the wall safe and rifles through the velvet boxes for her mother's Tahitian pearls. Fastening the strand around her neck, she runs her finger over the smooth surface of the pearls, remembering when her father gave the precious gems to Dottie on their tenth anniversary.

She unplugs her mother's phone from the charger on the nightstand, slips it into her clutch, and drives Dottie's navy sporty convertible to her eleven o'clock appointment.

The law offices of Stanly, Hart, and Reid occupy one of the oldest two-story brick buildings on Ocean Avenue. Jonathan Hart is waiting for her in the reception area downstairs. He greets her with a perfunctory kiss on the cheek. "You look wonderful, Amelia. You haven't changed a bit since high school."

"Liar," she says in a teasing tone. The pimply teenager she remembers from their younger days is now a distinguished middle-aged man, tall and fit with thick wavy dark hair. They were never close friends, but in a town the size of Palmetto Island, everyone knows everyone else.

His hazel eyes look past her. "Is your husband with you?"

Amelia shakes her head. "Nelson couldn't make the trip. How's Lisa?" No one was surprised when Jonathan married his childhood sweetheart. They'd dated all throughout high school and college.

"Lisa and I divorced two years ago."

Amelia frowns. "I didn't know. I'm sorry."

"Don't be. Our marriage ran its course. But we've stayed friends. She's living in Mount Pleasant with her new boyfriend."

How simple Amelia's life would be if Nelson would amicably agree to a divorce. "Thank you for meeting with me on a Saturday."

"Of course. We have some urgent matters regarding your mother's burial to discuss. Miss Dottie's requests were specific. I've done my best to honor them."

"I'm sure she would approve of your efforts."

He chuckles. "I hope so. She was not an easy woman to please."

"Isn't that the truth?" Amelia's mother wasn't difficult. She just preferred things a certain way.

"Let's go upstairs to my office." Jonathan leads Amelia up a flight of stairs and down a short hall to an office with a view of the boardwalk, marina, and inlet. "Please, have a seat." He motions her to a seating area consisting of a sofa and two comfortable chairs. She sits at one end of the sofa, and he lowers his tall frame to the chair next to her.

"I've arranged for the funeral to take place on Monday." Jonathan opens a file on his lap. "Miss Dottie wrote her own obituary, which was printed in yesterday's paper. I saved a copy for you. I knew you'd want to see it."

"Thank you," she says, taking the folded paper from him.

"I've also made the arrangements with the minister and funeral director. Miss Dottie wanted me to plan everything . . . in case you couldn't make it to the funeral."

This information cuts Amelia deep. What a lousy daughter she's been. "I'm grateful to have the burden taken off of me. Those would've been tough decisions to make." She toys with Dottie's string of pearls at her neck. "Can you give me a rundown of the details?"

He hands Amelia two pages of typed notes. "As you can see, your mother picked out everything, from hymns and Bible readings to the outfit she wishes to be buried in. She chose the pall bearers and organized the catered luncheon at Point Pleasant for afterward. She thought you'd be more comfortable with a reception than a funeral home visitation the night before."

Whether at the funeral home or a reception at Point Pleasant, a crowd is a gathering of people in which Nelson can easily hide. "Is it possible for me to see her?"

"Of course," Jonathan says. "The funeral home director is waiting to hear from you to arrange the private viewing." He sits back in his chair and crosses his legs. "Do you plan to stay in town long?"

"For at least a few days. Possibly longer."

"At some point, we should discuss your mother's estate. You are the primary benefactor. But we'll need to go over the details."

This neither surprises Amelia, nor does it ease her persistent nagging doubt. "Can you tell me when her most current will was drawn up?"

Jonathan thumbs through the pages in the file in his lap. "In October of 1976."

Months after the bicentennial celebration. And the tragedy that befell her family during the days that followed. "And there are no codicils?"

Jonathan shakes his head. "No codicils. Your mother was very clear about what she wanted. Other than a few bequeaths to her favorite nonprofit organizations and a sizable gift to Bebe, you inherit the bulk of Miss Dottie's estate."

"Thank you for all you've done. You've gone above and beyond the call of duty." Amelia stands to go.

Jonathan walks her back down to the lobby, and, with a heavy heart, she returns to the parking lot. Discussing the details of her mother's funeral has made her death all the more real.

Pulling out of the parking lot, she heads in the opposite direction of home toward the grocery store.

Amelia had struggled with bulimia in college. Her mother, who picked up on her abnormal behavior during her winter break her sophomore year, sent her to a residential program for six weeks. With years of subsequent therapy, she's learned to cope with the disorder. Nelson, a fanatic about healthy eating and exercise, maintains strict control over their caloric intake. They have a full-time chef who cooks their meals and a housekeeper who does the shopping. Their diet is gluten-free, high in protein, and low in sugar.

In the produce department at Harris Teeter, Amelia loads her cart with fresh fruits and vegetables before moving on to the seafood section where she asks for a tuna steak and a pound of steamed shrimp. She's passing through the bakery when a plastic sleeve of chocolate-covered donuts catches her attention. When was the last time she ate a donut? Years ago. Maybe even a decade.

Why not? she thinks. *Nelson isn't here to restrict my diet.* She drops the donuts in her cart and continues to the checkout.

Back at home, after putting away the groceries, she goes downstairs to the laundry room in the basement where Bebe is polishing silver trinkets, including her father's engraved lighter. "I appreciate your efforts, Bebe, but this isn't necessary."

Wiping a wisp of hair off her forehead with a gloved hand, Bebe says, "I'm just putting a shine on a few things. Your mother would want everything to look pretty."

"Don't overdo it. You've had a traumatic week, and I want you to be fresh on Monday. And speaking of Monday, be sure to come dressed for church. I'm counting on you to ride in the procession and sit with me at the church and cemetery."

Tears fill Bebe's eyes. "I'd like that."

"I'm going down to the beach for a while. I'll take my key with me. Please turn the alarm on and lock up when you leave."

Nodding, Bebe sucks in an unsteady breath. "You call me, now, if you get scared. Claude and I will come right over."

"I will. I promise." Amelia pats Bebe on the back before retracing her steps up the stairs.

Changing into her bathing suit, Amelia places her gun in a mesh bag along with a towel and sunscreen. Borrowing one of her mother's straw hats, she grabs a beach chair from the side of the porch and walks down to the ocean. The gentle breeze and lapping of waves against the shores do little to calm her nerves. She tries reading the mystery novel she took from her mother's nightstand, but her mind is preoccupied, and her eyes keep drifting up to the house. Nelson won't come for her until after the funeral. Her mother's friends, including members of the police force, will be suspicious if Amelia doesn't attend the services. Why, then, does she have an uneasy feeling of being watched?

After ninety minutes of restlessness, she gives up and returns to the safety of the house. Bebe has already gone, and she lets herself in, resetting the alarm from Away to Home. She goes to the kitchen for lunch, and she's standing at the counter, eating last night's casserole straight from the baking dish, when she notices the sleeve of chocolate donuts has been removed from the wooden bowl where she left it, and a donut is missing. *Strange*, Amelia thinks. Bebe has always cooked for them, but aside from a cup of coffee in the mornings, Amelia has never known the housekeeper to eat their food. Not even a peanut butter and jelly sandwich at lunchtime.

Amelia's mouth waters at the sight of the donuts. Removing one from the sleeve, she pinches off a bite and stuffs it in her mouth. To her disappointment, the donut is stale. Definitely not worth the calories. She drops the package in the trash can, returns the casserole dish to the refrigerator, and goes upstairs. After a long shower, she stretches out on her mother's bed for a nap.

Late that afternoon, when she returns to the kitchen, the sleeve of donuts is back on the counter with four more missing. The hairs on the back of her neck stand to attention. Is Nelson playing tricks on her? Probably not, since he detests sweets. He doesn't know the alarm code, anyway. Perhaps her mind is playing tricks on her. Deaths of loved ones affect people in bizarre ways. Maybe she ate the donuts, and her mind is blocking the memory. Is the bulimia coming back? No, her gut instincts warn her there's something more.

Amelia removes her handgun from the soft holster inside the waistband of her shorts at the small of her back. Gun in hand, with arms braced in front of her, she searches the house from bottom to top. She finds nothing of concern, but in the attic, she discovers a box of her old things, including high school year-books. She takes the yearbook from her senior year back to her mother's bedroom and curls up under a mohair blanket. Flipping through the pages, she notices a picture of herself with her best friends, Birdie and Max, in front of the gymnasium after a basketball game. She runs her finger over the photo. What good times they had together. From first grade on, they were inseparable. How she's missed them over the years. She has plenty of acquaintances in Boston, most of whom are the wives of Nelson's friends and business associates. But no one she considers a true friend.

She closes her eyes as memories from the happiest days of her life come rushing back.

FIVE

Birdie's contractor agrees to meet with Max on Sunday afternoon after her weekend guests have departed. Davis is tall with broad shoulders, graying dark hair, and an infectious lopsided smile. Max reminds herself she's in a relationship, although more and more she wishes she weren't.

Moving from room to room, top floor to bottom, Max provides her thoughts on remodeling. Davis asks dozens of questions and takes pages of notes on his legal pad. They conclude their meeting with a glass of sweet tea at the bar in the lounge.

"When were you hoping to start construction?" Davis asks.

"Right after Labor Day if possible." She doesn't tell him the bank hasn't yet approved her loan. "I'd like to finish in time for the Festival of Lights in early December."

Davis flips through his notes. "That's a tight schedule, but we can make it happen by placing orders for fixtures and tile in advance." He tosses his pen on his legal pad. "I'm a straight shooter, Max. I hope you don't mind me being up front with you."

Max smiles. "Not at all. I appreciate honesty."

He settles back in his barstool. "I'd really like to win this project. I only have a couple of small jobs at the moment, and I can easily accommodate your schedule. You have excellent vision. And I think the results of your efforts will make the Palmetto Inn one of the premier destinations in the Lowcountry. Since I'm new to town, a project of this magnitude would help boost my reputation."

Max wraps her hands around her sweating glass. "I like to know who I'm doing business with, Davis. If you don't mind me asking, what brought you to Palmetto Island? Our small town is out of the way. Most people move here to be near family or to get away from the stresses of city life. You're taking a big chance starting a new business, especially at your age . . ." She flashes him a grin. "I mean, our age."

He laughs out loud. "I admire a woman who speaks her mind." His smile fades. "I lost my wife several years back to cancer. I'm originally from coastal Maine, but my wife, a native South Carolinian, refused to move up north. I willingly moved to Columbia, and I fell in love with the South. After Elizabeth died, I needed a fresh start. Both my children are living in New York, and, with nothing keeping me in Columbia, I began looking for a new home. I really missed being on the water, and well . . . here I am." He holds his hands out in front of him. "I'm an open-and-closed book, Max. No skeletons in the closet. You can trust me to always tell you the truth."

Something in his warm brown eyes tells her he means it. "I appreciate that."

"I can provide a list of referrals from past clients in Columbia."

"That would be great. You should know that I'm talking to other contractors. So far, neither has wowed me. Their estimates are way over my budget, and they both insist I hire an architect. Which I don't think is necessary and will only drive the costs up further. I believe we can accomplish the objective without breaking the bank."

"I agree. I'm a draftsman by trade. You don't need an architect to move a few non-load-bearing walls."

"A draftsman, huh? That's good to know. I imagine those skills come in handy."

"Yes, ma'am. Nearly every single day."

Max straightens. "Sounds like we're on the same page. How soon can you get me an estimate?"

Davis drains the rest of his tea. "If you don't mind me poking around a little more now, I can get you something by tomorrow afternoon."

Max slides off the stool to her feet. "By all means, make yourself at home." She walks him back to the elevator. "You have my cell number. Call me if you have questions. I'll be around."

Max feels as though the weight of the world has been lifted from her shoulders as she steps outside for a breath of fresh air. Standing at the boardwalk railing, she watches the boats zooming past on the creek, locals enjoying a lazy summer Sunday afternoon.

Davis emerges from the hotel twenty minutes later. He waves his legal pad at her and calls out, "I've got what I need for now. I'll be in touch as soon as I have some numbers for you."

Max gives him a thumbs-up. "Thank you!" Entering the hotel, she takes the elevator to her fourth-floor apartment. She needs a nap. She and Ron stayed out way too late at Shaggy's last night and then came home for several hours of drunk sex. Her face warms at the memory. What has gotten into her lately? She was never a party girl. Ron is a negative influence on her.

Hold the line, Maxie. You can't blame him. You're in control of your own destiny.

"I thought you were at the beach," she says to Ron when she finds him waiting for her in the living room.

"I came home. It's too hot. Who's your lover boy?"

Max can't gauge his mood. Is he angry? Or being flirtatious?

"You are, of course." When she cups his cheek, he grabs hold of her wrist.

"I mean the guy you were talking to in the lounge. Are you sleeping with him?"

Max narrows her blue eyes. "You mean Davis? Of course not. I met him for the first time today. Chill, Ron. He's a contractor. He's giving me an estimate on the renovations."

Ron tightens his grip on her arm. "I don't believe you. You haven't even gotten loan approval yet."

She glares at him. "Not that it's any of your business, but I expect it to be approved any day. Now let go of my arm. You're hurting me."

He twists her arm behind her back, bending it upward. "I'll break this arm and other parts of your body if you cheat on me. Do you understand?" he says, his hot breath near her ear.

Max kicks him in the shin with her heel. He screeches in pain, and she wrenches free of him. Darting behind the counter into the adjacent kitchen, she grabs a butcher knife out of the block and waves it at him. "If you *ever* touch me again, I'll stab you in the heart."

Ron's hands shoot up. "Sorry, Maxie. I didn't mean to upset you. I just saw you flirting with that guy—"

"I wasn't flirting with Davis. We were discussing business." Max brandishes the knife at him. "When I asked you to move in with me, we agreed we wouldn't get serious. This feels serious, Ron. I think the time has come for you to leave."

Ron cocks his head to the side. "Come on, babe. You don't mean that. We're good together. Remember last night? The mind-blowing sex we had on the floor where you're currently standing."

"That was sex, Ron. Not love. There will never be love between us. We're wasting our time."

His expression goes blank. "I'll need a few days to figure things out."

Bile rises in her throat. She'd been right to be concerned. He won't be easy to get rid of. "What do you mean? There's nothing to figure out. Time for you to move on." She points the knife in the direction of the hallway leading to her bedroom. "Pack your bags and go."

He hangs his head like a dejected puppy. "I need a plan, Max. I can't just get in my car and drive away."

"Why not? If you leave now, you can be in Savannah by nightfall. I assume this isn't a money issue. From what you've told me, you have plenty of it."

"It's not a money issue." He leans across the counter toward her. "Come on, Maxie. You're really angry. And I don't blame you. I was out of line. Let me buy you dinner. We can talk things out."

She shakes her head. "There's nothing to talk out."

Anger crosses his face. "Fine. Just give me until tomorrow. I'll be out by noon."

"You have until noon, and not one minute longer. But I want you to sleep in the guest room tonight." Coming from behind the counter, she holds the knife out as she passes him and hurries down the hallway to her bedroom, locking the door behind her. Bending over, she sucks in air. She catches site of the bruises materializing on her wrist. Why didn't she kick him out weeks ago when she first started having doubts about him? Because she was terrified of growing old alone. But no more. She'd rather be alone than with an abusive man.

SIX

Dottie Fairchild is as elegant as ever, prepared to meet her maker in her favorite summer tweed suit with her silver hair styled in a neat bob. In the private viewing room at the funeral home, Amelia spends more than an hour with her mother, confessing everything about her life with Nelson, including his strict rules and constant threats and frequent beatings. With tears streaming down her face, she begs her mother for forgiveness. "I'm sorry I neglected you, Mama. I was trying to protect you." She kisses the tips of her fingers and presses them to her mother's cold lips. "Rest in peace, lovely lady."

The funeral director is waiting for Amelia when she exits the viewing room. As he ushers her to the door, Mr. Bates explains, "A car will pick you up from your home a few minutes before eleven in the morning. You will have a police escort to the church, the cemetery afterward, and then back to Point Pleasant."

Even though Nelson would never approach her with so many people around, having a police escort sets Amelia's mind at ease. She thanks the funeral director and returns home to Point Pleasant, emotionally depleted.

Ignoring hunger pangs, she goes straight for the wine refrigerator. She's pouring a glass of red when she notices a banana missing from the fruit bowl. Surveying the kitchen, she finds the bag of pistachios she opened yesterday has disappeared from the pantry, and the bowl of strawberries she washed and sliced that morning gone from the refrigerator. Her mother had balked at the idea when Amelia suggested installing surveillance cameras with the security system. Dottie had said, "I understand the need for an alarm, Amelia, but I will not have cameras spying on me in my home."

The missing food has to be her husband's handiwork. Nelson is playing mind games with her. He wants her to know he's here, watching and waiting. But how did he get in? How did he get the alarm code?

Abandoning her wineglass, she circles the house with her gun but finds no evidence of an intruder. She spends thirty minutes on the phone changing the code with the security company and then retreats to her bedroom where she meditates for an hour before turning in early.

Amelia feels like an outsider at her mother's funeral. She studies the faces in the crowds at the cemetery. As expected, she sees no sign of her husband. But she doesn't see Max or Birdie either. While she recognizes many who have come to pay their respects to her mother, most of their names escape her. She smiles in response to their expressions of sympathy but says little.

Her mother would be proud. The funeral is vintage Dottie, a celebration of her life. Amelia manages to hold back her tears. Frequent beatings at the hands of her husband have taught her how to suppress her emotions. But her insides are churning. Her mother had a lot of living left to do. If only things could've been different between them. Despite their lengthy weekly phone calls, much was left unsaid. If she had to do it all over again, Amelia would've . . . She would've, what? She would've done exactly what she did. She protected her mother's life against her evil husband.

When she was in high school, Amelia had conducted in-depth research on the people buried in Palmetto Cemetery for a genealogy project. She enjoyed her time spent wandering the thirty acres of gravesites beneath live oaks dripping with Spanish moss. Her father, paternal grandparents, and an uncle who died in childbirth are all buried in the Fairchild plot. One day, hopefully later than sooner, she will be buried alongside her mother. With no children of her own, she is the end of the line for the Fairchild family.

Amelia knows little about her mother's background, only that Dorothea Christensen was originally from Alabama. Dottie's parents, Amelia's maternal grandparents whom she never met, died years ago. Her mother never spoke of siblings, and Amelia often wonders if she has aunts, uncles, and cousins out there somewhere.

As the minister is delivering his final comments, Amelia glimpses a woman standing by herself near the edge of the crowd. The woman seems somehow familiar. Her auburn hair is frizzy and unkempt and her pumpkin-shaped face full of wrinkles. Her long-sleeved black sheath is all wrong for an August funeral in the Lowcountry. But there's something else about the dress. Amelia has seen it before. Or one just like it on Saturday afternoon when she was searching in her mother's closet for something appropriate to wear today.

Amelia leans in close to Bebe. "Do you recognize the redhead at the back of the crowd?" Bebe follows Amelia's gaze, but the woman is now standing behind a tree with only a bit of her dress showing. "Never mind. You can't see her now."

As the minister announces the benediction, Amelia watches

for another glimpse of the redhead, but the woman is lost in the dispersing crowd.

Bebe and Amelia wait until everyone is gone to say their final goodbyes to their beloved Dottie. With bowed heads, they offer silent prayers and place single white roses alongside the spray of gorgeous blue hydrangeas fashioned by Dottie's garden club.

Seated side by side in the back of the limousine, they ride in silence back to Point Pleasant. As they're pulling into the driveway, Amelia says, "You're a guest today, Bebe. Don't you dare lift a finger."

"All right. But first I need to check on things in the kitchen," Bebe says before slipping out of the limo.

Amelia makes her way around to the ocean side of the house where an enormous tent provides shade for banquet tables of food and drink. She's swarmed by her mother's friends, who wait patiently in line to express their condolences. Most are brief but some linger to tell a funny story or share a special memory about Dottie.

Amelia is grateful to have a moment alone with her mother's doctor. "Were you surprised when Mama passed away in her sleep?" she asks Dr. Green.

"A little. But it happens. The last time I saw Miss Dottie was at her annual checkup a month or so before she died. She was in excellent spirits and perfect health." Dr. Green squeezes her hand. "Consider it a blessing, my dear. I see too much sickness these days."

While she considers it a blessing that her mother didn't suffer, Amelia can't shake the feeling there's something more to Dottie's death.

After greeting guests for nearly thirty minutes, Amelia spots Birdie and Max at the end of the line, and can hardly take her eyes off them as they inch toward her. The years fall away, and the memories come rushing back. When they are finally face-to-face, Birdie and Max smother Amelia with hugs and kisses.

"You have no idea how thrilled I am to see you two," Amelia says. "I was looking through our old high school yearbook last night. I've missed you both so much."

"And we've missed you," Max says. "We're so sorry about Miss Dottie. I saw her in church just last week. She looked wonderful."

Amelia nods, unable to speak past the lump in her throat.

Birdie hands her a glass of sweet tea. "We figured you'd be parched."

"I am. Thank you." Amelia accepts the glass and sips the lemony sweet beverage. She studies her friends. "You both look amazing. You haven't aged a bit."

Max snorts. "Liar."

Birdie ignores Max. "And you look lovely as ever, Amelia. You're the spitting image of Miss Dottie."

"I take that as a compliment," Amelia says with a sad smile. "I have so much to tell you, I don't know where to start."

"We definitely have a lot of catching up to do," Max says, and Birdie adds, "How long are you in town for?"

"I'm not sure yet. For the rest of the week, at least. Hopefully longer." She will invite them over for a day on the beach or a picnic supper once Nelson is no longer a threat.

Chief Summers approaches her. "Amelia." He kisses her cheek. "Lovely service. You did Miss Dottie proud."

"I can't take the credit. Mama planned everything herself." Amelia gestures at her old friends. "Chief Summers, I assume you know Max and Birdie."

Max hip-bumps the chief. "Toby is my nephew, my late-husband's brother's son."

"What a small world." Amelia takes Max's hand. "Mama told me you lost your husband. I'm so sorry."

Max's eyes glisten with tears. "Daniel died way too young."

When an elderly woman waiting patiently to speak with Amelia clears her throat loudly, Amelia says, "I'm sorry."

"We understand," Birdie says. "We'll talk soon."

Summers rests a hand on Amelia's back. "You know where to find me."

She offers him a warm smile.

Amelia watches Max and Birdie cut across the lawn to the driveway. She envies them their friendship. She's missed out on so much over the years. She's looking forward to starting her life over. But first she must face her past.

"Amelia is awfully thin," Birdie says to Max as she eases her station wagon out of the gravel driveway onto the road.

Max looks at her over the top of her sunglass frames. "I noticed. Do you think something's wrong with her? Maybe she's sick. Maybe that's why she never comes home." She muses out loud. "Could be cancer. Or some autoimmune disease."

Birdie shakes her head. "She's a healthy thin. Not a sickly skinny."

"I guess you're right. She looks amazing." Max stares out the window as they cross the causeway. "Do you ever think about Amelia's sister?"

Birdie hesitates before answering. "I barely remember her. What was her name? She smelled funny."

Max barks out a laugh. "She smelled like marijuana. Her name was Robin."

Birdie snaps her fingers. "Robin. That's it. If I remember correctly, she was a troublemaker."

"That's an understatement," Max says. "Robin was always causing problems for their parents. She disappeared the night Amelia's father died."

"Didn't Dr. Fairchild die of a heart attack?" Birdie asks. "Do you think Robin is somehow responsible?"

"I'm sure of it," Max says. "I never once heard Amelia mention Robin after she disappeared."

"Come to think of it, I didn't either."

They ride for a minute in silence, each lost in her own thought. "I think I'll take Amelia dinner tonight," Max says. "Wanna come?"

Birdie glances over at her. "I can see the wheels spinning in your brain. What're you up to? Are you playing Nancy Drew again?"

"I'm being a friend. Amelia just lost her mother. I'm taking her dinner. That's what friends do." Max is surprised when her throat swells. "I've missed Amelia. I'd hate for her to leave town again before we have a chance to catch up."

"Me too. And I wish I could go with you. But I have to get ready for the grand opening tomorrow night." Turning on her blinker, Birdie drives down the alley beside Johnson's Pharmacy and parks behind the cafe.

Max spots Davis on a bench in the park. "Davis is early for our meeting." She checks her watch. "Correction, I'm late."

"Are you going to hire him for the renovations?"

"I hope so. He's presenting his bid today. He's by far my top pick." Max gathers her belongings. "I forgot to tell you. I got a call from the bank this morning. My loan has been approved."

"Yay, you!" Birdie offers Max a high five. "I'm sure that's a load off your mind."

"You have no idea." Max gets out of the car and walks down the short alley to the park. Davis rises to greet her. "I'm sorry I'm late. I was at a funeral."

"No worries." He cocks his head to the side. "Was it someone close to you?"

"She was an old friend's mother." She motions him toward the hotel. "Let's go inside to my office."

Davis follows her through the lobby to her cramped, untidy office. Leaving the door ajar, she removes a stack of files from the chair opposite her desk. "I wish there was a way to add a window to my office."

He laughs. "You could add a window, but I'm not sure you'd have much of a view."

Max sits down behind her desk, and Davis hands her a copy of his bid proposal. For the next thirty minutes, they discuss the details as they go through page by page. When they get to the last page, he draws her attention to a certain line item. "You'll notice the estimate for electrical is quite high. I did a little poking around yesterday. Your systems are antiquated."

She looks up at him. "Neither of the other contractors mentioned it."

Davis arches an eyebrow. "I'm not sure how they missed it. I'm surprised you haven't had a fire."

She returns her gaze to the estimate. "Even with the high electrical estimate factored in, your bid is still much lower than the others. Should I expect an exorbitant bill at the end of this project for all the expenses you forgot to include?"

Davis's jaw tightens. Max hit a nerve, as she intended. She's sending him a message. She's a shrewd businesswoman who isn't easily fooled.

"I told you yesterday, I'm a straight shooter. I'm comfortable with my proposal. It's fair and realistic. And I'm confident in my ability to deliver."

"As am I." Max places her folded hands on the desk. "I checked out your references. Your former clients gave you glowing reviews. If you're in agreement, I'm ready to proceed."

"That's excellent news." Davis catches sight of the bruises on her wrist. "What happened to your arm?"

She rubs her wrist. "I was walking a friend's dog. He took off after a squirrel with the leash wrapped around my wrist."

Reaching across the desk, he gently takes hold of her hand and examines the bruises more closely. "Those look like finger marks to me." He looks up at her. "Did someone do this to you, Max? Is someone hurting you?"

"It was the dog." She retracts her arm and hides her hand beneath her desk. "What are our next steps?"

He hands her another document. "After you sign the contract and mail it to me with your retainer, you'll need to get busy making the selections for your tile and bathroom fixtures. As I mentioned before, I like to place orders in advance to avoid potential delays during construction."

She gets up from her desk. "I understand."

Davis shuffles his papers into his file, and Max walks him to the door. She opens the door and then turns back toward her desk. "Wait. I should give you a key. Once construction begins, I'll have a spare key made for you that controls the exterior doors." She opens the top drawer and hands him a magnetic card. "But for now, this controls all the interior doors in the building. Feel free to come and go as necessary, but please be mindful of the guests."

"Got it." He takes the key card from her. "I look forward to working with you, Max."

When they step out into the hallway, she's surprised to find Ron standing just outside her office. "Hey, babe." He leans in to kiss Max's cheek. "I've been looking everywhere for you." He turns his attention to Davis. "You must be the contractor. I'm the live-in boyfriend."

Davis gives him a curt nod. "Nice to meet you."

Ron ignores him, drawing Max in for a half hug. "Wanna go to the beach?"

Max's head swivels. *The beach? Why is he still here? He should be halfway to his next destination by now.*

Davis casts a nervous glance at the lobby. "Well, then. I'll be off. I'll talk to you soon, Max."

She waits until Davis reaches the lobby before digging her elbow into Ron's side. "Get off of me."

Ron tosses his thumb over his shoulder. "Did you hire that guy to do the renovations?"

"Not yet." Max has no intention of discussing her business with him.

"That's what I thought. You're still waiting for your loan approval."

She glares at him. "Why are you still here? You should be halfway to your next destination by now."

He looks at her with sad puppy dog eyes. "I was hoping you'd give me another chance."

"Ha. That's not happening."

"Can I at least have a couple more days to get my act together?"

His pitiful tone tugs at her heartstrings. "I'll give you forty-eight hours. But I want you gone by Wednesday at noon."

Relief crosses his face. "Thank you. Let me show my appreciation by cooking dinner for you tonight."

"Sorry, but I'm going out." She leaves Ron standing alone in her office. Why is he so hesitant to move on? She made it clear it's over between them. Did he lie about having money? Has he been mooching off her all this time because he has nowhere else to go? Is he a leech, preying on one unsuspecting single woman after another?

Max intends to make good on her word. She'll give him until Wednesday. But if he doesn't leave on his own, she'll . . . what? Call her nephew? Admit she allowed a man she hardly knows to move in with her and now she can't get rid of him? Involving Toby would be too embarrassing. She'll have to figure a way to handle it on her own.

SEVEN

The party rental company workers bring the tent down, and the caterers clear platters and fold tables. Within an hour of the last guest's departure, it's as though none of the three hundred plus mourners were ever at Point Pleasant today. Amelia and Jonathan stand with their backs to the ocean at the edge of the property where the lawn meets the sand dunes.

"Now what do I do?" Amelia asks, more to herself than to him. "How does one move on after the death of a loved one?"

"One minute at a time," he answers. "I'll be in touch later in the week, and we'll go over the terms of your mother's will. Until then, get some rest and enjoy the beach."

"I'm not sure relaxation is in my future, but I'll try."

They stroll together back across the lawn to the driveway. When they reach his car, Jonathan turns to her. "Miss Dottie was worried about you, Amelia. I promised her I'd look out for you in the event of her death. You have my number. I'm here for you." He opens the door and folds his long legs into the car.

As she waves goodbye, Amelia wonders how much her mother confided in him. *Miss Dottie was worried about you, Amelia.* While her mother didn't know the whole story, she knew enough to suspect Amelia was in danger. If she reaches a point she needs a confidant, Jonathan seems like someone she can trust.

Amelia strolls about the yard, picking up trash—a wadded napkin on the grass and a plastic wine cup in the sand dunes—before making her way inside to the kitchen where Bebe is storing away leftovers. "I told you not to work today," she says, eyeing the apron Bebe is wearing over her yellow dress.

Bebe ignores her. "We have so much left over. What do you want me to do with all this?"

"Goodness," she says peering over Bebe's shoulder. "That is a lot of food. Why don't you leave a little for me, take some home for your supper, and give the rest to your friends and neighbors?"

"All right. I'll put some in your freezer as well." Palming Amelia's cheek, Bebe asks, "How're you holding up, baby?"

Amelia kisses Bebe's hand. "I'm okay, I guess. I'm exhausted. Talking to all those people wore me out. I think I'll lie down for a while. Be sure to lock up when you leave."

"Yes'm. Call me anytime."

Amelia drags herself upstairs and changes into yoga clothes. Returning the funeral dress to her mother's closet, she notices the long-sleeved black sheath like the one the redhead was wearing at the funeral is missing. She flips through the hanging clothes but it's not there. Perhaps she's mistaken. Maybe she didn't see it in the closet. Maybe she saw it in a catalog instead.

Amelia lies down on the bed, but when she closes her eyes, her mind races. How long before Nelson comes for her? Maybe he's already here. Maybe he dressed in disguise at the funeral, hiding amongst the crowd. Or maybe he sent one of his henchmen, someone Amelia would never recognize.

She clicks on the television and tunes into an afternoon talk show on her favorite twenty-four-hour news channel. She closes her eyes, letting the sound of their voices lull her to sleep. When she wakes again, the evening news is on. She blinks open her eyes and is stunned to see a reporter standing in front of her Boston townhome.

"I'm Linda Vogel, reporting live from the home of wealthy entrepreneur Nelson Archer, who, just minutes ago, announced his plans to run for Congress next year."

Amelia sits bolt upright in bed. *Congress? Nelson?* There must be some mistake.

The camera pans to Nelson, who looks dashing in a navy suit and striped tie.

"What does your wife think of your decision to enter politics?" Vogel asks.

"This is the first I've heard of it," Amelia says out loud to the television.

Nelson flashes his most winsome smile. "She's thrilled, of course. I'm fortunate to have an extremely supportive wife."

"What choice have you given me?" Amelia says to her husband. "I either support you or else?"

"We'd love to have a word with her," Linda says. "Is she home?"

Amelia watches Nelson closely for his response. He doesn't flinch. "Not at the moment. She's down in South Carolina. She's had a death in the family. I'll be joining her at the end of the week."

Nelson's message to Amelia is clear. He knows about her mother, which she already suspected. And he's giving her a few days before he's coming to take her home.

"Your wife is an accomplished woman, Mr. Archer. The public will adore her. We'll extend an invitation for an interview at a later date."

"She'll be flattered," Nelson says.

An accomplished woman. She's spent years organizing charity events and presiding over boards of directors at nonprofit organizations. But leaving her husband has been her biggest accomplishment to date.

Amelia clicks off the television. Staring at the black screen, she says, "Politics, Nelson? Really?" Then again, he's achieved fame and prosperity. Why not politics? But why has he never mentioned his intentions to Amelia? Because he expects her to *support* him in all his endeavors, even though he knows how much she despises being in the limelight. But what does this mean for their relationship? He can't very well have his wife making public appearances with black eyes.

Amelia gets out of bed and crosses the room to the window. She inhales a deep breath and exhales it slowly as the tension leaves her body. At least she can relax knowing he's in Boston tonight, not sneaking around Point Pleasant stealing her food. But who is stealing her food, if not Nelson?

She freshens up in the bathroom—brushing her teeth, washing her face, and pulling her blonde hair back in a ponytail. Slipping a comfy knit top on over her leggings, she goes down to the kitchen where she finds breadcrumbs and bits of ham on the counter near the sink. Bebe must be the food thief. There's no other explanation. The housekeeper is getting careless in her old age.

Amelia uncorks a bottle of Pinot Grigio and fills a glass to the brim. She's headed out to the porch when she hears someone knocking on the back door. Retracing her steps to the kitchen, she sees Max waving at her through the mudroom door window.

She swings open the door. "Max! This is a surprise."

Max holds out a casserole dish. "Chicken tetrazzini. Put it in your freezer. I'm sure you have plenty of leftovers from today." She reaches into her shoulder bag and presents a bottle of wine. "I was hoping we could catch up. But I understand if this is a bad time."

Amelia isn't in the mood for company. But perhaps company is exactly what she needs. "Not at all. Now is a perfect time." She steps out of the way. "Come on in."

Amelia places Max's bottle of wine in the ice maker to chill and pours her friend a glass of Pinot Grigio. "I was just headed out to the porch. Let me make us a snack."

She throws together a tray of nibbles from the funeral leftovers and leads Max out to the porch.

Seated side by side in rocking chairs, Max rattles on about her life. And Amelia lets her talk. She enjoys hearing about Max's marriage to Daniel, their son Kyle who lives in New York, and the waterfront hotel she owns and operates.

When she empties her glass, Max goes to the kitchen for a refill and returns with the bottle. "I've been doing all the talking," Max says. "I want to hear about you. Are you still married? Do you have any children?"

"Still married. No children."

As the sun slips below the horizon and darkness falls over the porch, the conversation turns to memories from childhood. They share many laughs, and by the time they've polished off the second bottle of wine, they are more than a little tipsy.

"I don't know about you, but I'm starving." Amelia jumps to her feet. "What say we have an old-fashioned raid on the refrigerator?"

"I'm in!" Max says, scrambling to locate her discarded flip-flops.

They take the empty glasses and bottles and neglected tray of nibbles to the kitchen. Amelia opens the refrigerator door and removes plastic bags of boiled shrimp, satay chicken, slices of beef tenderloin, and ham biscuits.

Amelia digs in. She doesn't ever remember being so hungry. She's home, with old friends, where she belongs. Once she takes care of Nelson, she'll be able to let the healing begin.

"This is like old times." Amelia jabs a shrimp tail at Max. "I've missed you, Maxie. It's good to be home."

"Why did you stay away so long?" Max waves a chicken wing at her. "Never mind. I'm being nosy."

Amelia's eyes fall to the floor. "I'd rather not talk about it. My life is complicated. Suffice it to say, my husband is not an easy man."

Max's face falls. "Oh. I see. If you ever want to talk about it, I'm a good listener."

"I remember that about you." Amelia notices the bruises on Max's wrist. All-too familiar bruises. "Is there a special man in your life, Maxie?"

"Not anymore." Max drops the chicken bone in the trash. "I just got out of a relationship with a guy who turned out to be all wrong for me."

"Good for you for ending it. Life is short. Why waste your time on someone who doesn't deserve you?"

Max raises an eyebrow. "This from the woman who just admitted her husband is not an easy man."

"Touché." Amelia is a fraud, giving the very advice she's been too much of a coward to take herself. Until now. That's all going to change. Isn't it? Will she be able to stand up to Nelson when the time comes?

"It's getting late. I should be going." Max pulls her phone out of her pocket. "Give me your number. Even if you end up going back to Boston, we should make a pact to stay in touch."

"Agreed. But I'll have to give you Mama's number. I lost my phone on the way to South Carolina. I'm using her phone until I get a new one." Amelia recites Dottie's number as Max enters it into her phone. "We should do this again soon. Next time we'll invite Birdie."

"I asked Birdie to come with me tonight, but she's expanding her cafe hours to include dinner, and her grand opening is tomorrow night. If you'd like to go, I'll ask if she can fit us in."

The idea of having dinner with old friends appeals to Amelia. But coming home to an empty, dark house doesn't. "Maybe. Can I see how tomorrow goes?"

"Sure. I'll ask Birdie to save a table for us just in case." Max closes one eye and stares down at her phone. "I need to call an Uber—if I can find the app."

Amelia takes the phone from her. "If you go home in an Uber, you'll have to worry about getting your car in the morning. Why not spend the night with me?"

Max grins. "Can we have a sleepover in your mother's bed, like back in high school when she went out of town?"

Amelia laughs at the memory. "Mama was crazy to leave us unchaperoned. We had some wild parties, didn't we?"

Max holds her hand up for a high five. "Did we ever!"

Amelia slaps her hand. "The good old days."

After returning the leftovers to the refrigerator, the two women traipse up the stairs to Dottie's bedroom. Amelia locates a spare toothbrush in the linen closet and gives Max an oversized T-shirt to sleep in. Max stands at the bedroom window just outside the bathroom while Amelia washes her face.

"What is that building at the back of your property? I've never noticed it before."

"A garage, although I don't think my parents ever parked their cars in it." Amelia dries her face and joins Max at the window. "We use it as a garden shed, a place for the riding lawn-mower and yard tools."

A flicker of light appears in the upstairs window of the garage. "Did you see that?" Max asks.

Chill bumps break out on Amelia's arms. "I did. And that's not the first time. I witnessed the same flash of light my first night back in town. There's an apartment above the garage. But no one has lived there in years. I hope we don't have poachers."

Max squints into the darkness. "I love a good mystery. Let's go check it out!"

Amelia cuts her eyes at Max. "You mean now? In the middle of the night?"

"Yes, now. And it's not the middle of the night. It's only eleven o'clock." Max sends an elbow crashing to Amelia's ribs.

"What happened to your sense of adventure? You were always game for excitement when we were young."

A wave of sadness washes over Amelia. "I lost it, along with everything else about my youth."

"Then we need to see what we can do about finding it again." Max drags Amelia over to the bed. With arms spread wide, she falls face first into the soft mattress. Amelia follows suit, and they burst into hysterics.

When they stop laughing, Amelia says, "That felt good. You're right. I need to be more adventurous. We'll put on our Sherlock Holmes hats and check out the apartment tomorrow."

Max and Amelia crawl to the head of the bed, and Amelia pulls the heavy down comforter over them. Max lifts a framed photograph from the nightstand. Amelia was a toddler at the time the picture was taken. She's on the beach with her parents. Her father has Amelia on his hip and her mother's arms are wrapped around an enormous beach ball. "Your father was my pediatrician. I remember he used to hand out those lollipops with the loops sticks." She returns the photograph to the nightstand. "It's none of my business, and don't answer if you don't want to, but whatever happened to your sister?"

Amelia's gaze shifts from Max to the ceiling. "I have no clue. We never heard from her again after she ran away. I don't even know if she's still alive."

"Did Miss Dottie ever hire an investigator to try to find her?"

"Not that I'm aware of. Although I never asked Mama. The subject of Robin was strictly off limits."

Max rolls onto her side. "Don't you find that strange, considering Robin was her daughter? I'm sorry. I'm being nosy again."

"I don't mind." Amelia turns off the lamp on the nightstand, preferring to talk about her sister in the dark. "I don't remember much about Robin, except that she was a troublemaker. The arguments she had with our parents were dreadful. I was distraught when Daddy died. But I was also enormously relieved that Robin was gone. I didn't care where she went. I just didn't want her to come home. That's a terrible way to feel about one's sister. But I was so young. My sister and I were on different planets because of the ten-year age difference between us."

Amelia goes silent, and within minutes, she hears Max snoring softly beside her. Why didn't her mother ever try to find Robin? Or maybe she did and chose not to tell Amelia. Robin ran away forty-five years ago, a long time to be out of touch with one's family. She's probably dead. Maybe she's been dead all this time. She left home with only the clothes on her back. Hitchhiking was an accepted practice back then. Maybe she got in the car with the wrong person. On the other hand, what if she is still alive? Should Amelia try to find her, to notify her of their mother's death?

Placing her back to Max, she curls up on her side and stares out the darkened window. She fantasizes about a reunion with her sister. Ultimately, she decides that opening this can of worms is the last thing she needs at the moment.

EIGHT

A storm rages beyond the porch where a little girl with pale hair is crouched down in the shadows of light spilling through the french door. From inside the living room comes the sound of angry voices yelling at one another. She can't make out what the voices are saying, but their tones are hostile. A flash of lightning is followed by a loud crash. Peeking through the window, she covers her mouth to stifle her scream.

Amelia wakes from the nightmare gasping for air.

Max sits up beside her in bed. "Amelia? What's wrong?"

"I can't breathe," she says, clutching her chest.

Max massages her back. "I want you to inhale and exhale slowly while I count to ten. One. Two. Three . . ." By the time Max reaches five, Amelia's pulse has slowed, and she's able to take shallow breaths.

"Did you have a bad dream?" Max asks.

Amelia nods, and she's relieved when Max doesn't press her for details.

Max glances at the alarm clock. "Geez. It's eight o'clock already. I never sleep this late." She swings her legs over the side of the bed. "I need to get to work." She disappears into the bathroom and comes out a minute later dressed in yesterday's clothes. "I'm sorry for overstaying my welcome."

"You didn't overstay your welcome. I enjoyed the company." Getting out of bed, Amelia slips on her robe and turns off the alarm. "I'll walk out with you."

On the way down the stairs, Max says, "I'll check with Birdie about dinner reservations for tonight and let you know."

"Max, about tonight . . . I'm not sure—"

"Let's see if she can fit us in first. Then, you can decide."

They stop short in the doorway at the sight of the ransacked kitchen. Empty plastic bags, dirty utensils, and partially eaten bits of food litter the counter and floor. "What on earth?" Max says. "I thought we cleaned up after raiding the refrigerator."

Amelia fakes a laugh. She specifically remembers putting away the leftovers, but she doesn't want to alarm Max. "I guess we didn't. We definitely drank a lot of wine."

"Now that you mention it, that part of the night is a little blurry." Max begins gathering up the plastic bags.

"Put those in the sink, Max. I can take care of this. You need to get to work."

Max does as she's told. "Are you sure?"

Amelia hurries Max to the door. "Positive. Have a good day."

"I'll be in touch about tonight," Max calls, waving as she climbs into her car.

Amelia closes the door and faces the kitchen. Whoever broke into the house left this mess as their calling card. They wanted Amelia to know they were here, that they'd easily gotten into the house during the night while she was sleeping. Nelson is in Boston. She saw him on television with her own eyes. He sent her a message during his interview. He'll be joining her at the end of the week.

Once she's restored order to the kitchen, she brews a pot of coffee and drinks it while staring at the garage through the break-fast-room window.

She remembers Max's words from last night. *What happened to your sense of adventure?*

Amelia has survived thirty years of marriage to an abusive monster. That's enough adventure to last a lifetime.

No one is living in the apartment above the garage, Amelia. You imagined the flickers of light. Like you're imagining the break-ins. No one is stealing your food. You're terrified of what lies ahead, and you're letting your mind play tricks on you. You're stronger than this. Get yourself together.

———

Ron is waiting for Max when she enters her apartment. He steps in front of her, preventing her from proceeding down the hall to her bedroom. "Well, now," he says, crossing arms over chest. "Look who finally came home. Where did you spend the night? With your new contractor?"

Max owes Ron no explanations, but she doesn't want to risk him doing or saying anything that might embarrass her in front of Davis. "I spent the night with my girlfriend. She recently lost her mother, and we haven't seen each other in years. We had some wine. I didn't want to risk driving. Now get out of my way."

His arms shoot out, hands planted on the walls. "Not until you agree to have lunch with me."

"I'm not having anything with you. I recommend you spend the day packing and organizing the next stage of your trip, because you're checking out of here tomorrow."

"Please, Maxie. Give me another chance. I promise you won't regret it."

"It's over, Ron. Time for you to move on," she says and barrels past him.

Locking herself in her bedroom, she showers and dresses in white jeans and a loose-fitting pink top. She packs her toiletries and a few items of clothing in a small duffel bag, and when she emerges from her room, she's relieved to see that Ron has left the apartment. She takes the elevator to the lobby, and seated at her computer in her office, she books herself one night in the least desirable room on the first floor.

Emerging from her office, she spends a few minutes with her guest agents who report no leaking faucets or broken air conditioners. Exiting the building, she notices Birdie sweeping the boardwalk of her outdoor seating area. "Morning," she calls out. "Sorry I missed paddleboarding."

Birdie stops sweeping and waves at her. "Me too. Being on the water at dawn isn't nearly as fun alone."

Max moseys over to her. "I'm sorry. I spent the night at Amelia's. I'm embarrassed to tell you this, but we got into the wine, and I didn't want to drive home."

"You don't have to keep things like that from me," Birdie says. "Drinking is part of life. Most people can do it responsibly. I just don't happen to be one of those people."

Max pulls her in for a hug. "I'm proud of you, Birdie Fuller. You get stronger every day."

"I'm proud of me, too," Birdie whispers. "I have so much to live for—my business, Stan, my family, and friends. I'm terrified I'll lose my grip. I don't want to be that pitiful alcoholic anymore."

"You won't. I have faith in you. You're a completely different person now." Max drops her arms from around Birdie. "Are you ready for the big night?"

Birdie returns to sweeping. "I think so. Say a prayer for me. The food critic from the Charleston newspaper is coming."

Max's mouth falls open. "Tonight. On your first night?"

Birdie gives a one-shoulder shrug. "I couldn't very well decline his offer."

"That's so exciting, Birdie. Given the circumstances, I hate asking you this, but is there any chance you have room for two more?"

"Of course. I was counting on you and Ron. I have you down for seven thirty."

"Actually, the reservation is for Amelia and me. Ron and I are over." Birdie's face lights up, and Max knows her mind is reeling with questions. But Max is in no mood for an inquisition. "Long story. We'll talk later. Gotta run."

Max takes off up the sidewalk toward Atlantic Avenue. She's rounding the corner into the hotel parking deck when she collides with Davis. Max stumbles backward, and Davis grabs onto her, righting her. "Geez, Max. I didn't see you coming. Are you okay? I didn't hurt you, did I?"

Max's head spins, more from her hangover than the collision. "I'm fine. I'm glad I ran into you, though. You've saved me a trip to the post office." She removes an envelope from her pocketbook and hands it to him. "Your retainer and signed contract."

He takes the envelope and folds it into his pocket. "Thank you. Looks like we're in business. I was on my way to finalize a few measurements."

"And I'm on my way to pick out toilets."

The yellow flecks in his brown eyes sparkle in the sunshine. "Cool! Can I tag along? I might be able to offer some guidance."

Max tilts her head to the side. "Do you always get so excited about toilets?"

He chuckles. "What can I say? Bathroom fixtures are part of the job." Aiming his remote key at a black pickup truck, he clicks the doors unlocked. "I'll drive."

Davis proves to be an enormous help in selecting toilets, sinks, and faucets. He knows which brands perform best at affordable prices, and Max is content to let him do all the talking to Casey, the sales associate. Max admires the easy way he communicates with her. His gentle manner reminds her of her late husband. Davis is far more her type than Ron with his rough-around-the-edges personality. She'll never find a man like Daniel with the likes of Ron hanging around. With any luck, this time tomorrow, Ron will be out of her life for good. Then, if the right man comes along, she'll be available to pursue a relationship. If the right man never comes along, she'll be okay. She has Birdie, and now Amelia is back in her life, hopefully to stay.

Ninety minutes later, Max and Davis have made their choices, and Casey has confirmed that everything is in stock and available for shipping.

As they're exiting the parking lot, Max says, "You were an enormous help with that process. I'm even worse at picking out tile than I am bathroom fixtures. I have a meeting with the tile distributor tomorrow at one o'clock. Any chance you're free?"

"Sure! I can make myself available. Although, I confess my motives are selfish. Helping you helps me establish relationships with these vendors." He glances over at her. "Are you okay? You look a little pale, like you don't feel well."

"I have a horrible headache. It's self-inflicted, so I can't complain. An old childhood friend's mother passed away. That's the funeral I attended yesterday."

"I remember," Davis says.

"Anyway, Amelia and I haven't seen each other in a long time, and we had a lot of catching up to do."

"A reunion with an old friend is cause for celebration, regardless of the circumstances. A hangover is easier to cure than a broken heart. I thought maybe you and Ron had a fight."

"I ended my relationship with Ron. And my heart is definitely not broken over it. We were never serious. Palmetto Island was simply a stop along the way of his extended tour of the country."

"So, he's moved on to his next destination?"

"Not yet, but he will be soon," Max says, showing him her crossed fingers.

"In that case, let's do something about that hangover." Davis whips his truck into the parking lot of a Sonic Drive-In. Locating an empty space, he rolls his window down and orders two Super Sonic double cheeseburgers and two banana shakes.

"Why banana?" Max asks. "Not that I mind. I love bananas."

"Alcohol depletes your electrolytes. Bananas are rich in potassium."

"Ah-ha. Good to know." Max understands his concern for her well-being is nothing more than friendship. He's that kind of man, always looking out for others. He's honest and good. A true gentleman. A dying breed.

NINE

After spending the day alone on the beach, Amelia is thrilled when Max texts about dinner. *Reservations at 7:30. No excuses. Meet you at the cafe.*

Earlier in the day, she was flipping through channels while eating a salad for lunch when she saw Nelson on a news talk show discussing his candidacy for Congress. He's miles away in Boston. Why shouldn't she go to dinner with friends?

She texts Max back. *Looking forward to it.*

Amelia spends longer than usual preparing for her evening out. Tonight is the first time she's dressed for herself in years. Nelson always chooses her attire for parties and public events. He prefers for her to wear clothes that show off her slim figure, her long legs and high round breasts. He lavishes her with expensive jewelry, not because he loves her but because he wants her to look the part of a successful businessman's wife. Now a political candidate's wife.

From her mother's closet, she selects a simple black linen sundress and low-heeled, strappy sandals. She twists her hair into an elegant chignon and fastens her mother's pearls around her neck. She places her phone, wallet, and gun in a metallic clutch and leaves the house, making certain to activate the alarm on her way out.

Max is waiting for her at an outdoor table when she arrives at the cafe. Amelia surveys her surroundings. Strands of fat light-bulbs crisscross the outdoor seating area where tables are dressed in creamy linens. The waitstaff wear black pants and starched white shirts with gray aprons tied around their waists.

"I'm impressed," Amelia says. "This is very elegant."

"Not bad for little old Palmetto Island," Max says.

A server appears with a bottle of sparkling water. "The menu is prix fixe with wine offered for every course," he explains.

Amelia and Max exchange a knowing look. After overindulging last night, they'll only be sipping tonight.

"Are there any dietary restrictions?" the server asks, and both women shake their heads.

"In that case, I'll be back in a minute with your first course, a pickled beet salad, which is paired with a sparkling brut." After a slight bow, he scurries off.

"Birdie has really outdone herself," Amelia says.

"She's raised the bar high," Max says. "I hope my renovations measure up."

"I didn't realize you were remodeling the hotel. Tell me more. I'm a sucker for a construction project."

The waiter brings their salads, and while they eat, Max lays out her plans for transitioning the Palmetto Hotel from a rundown inn to an upscale boutique hotel.

"I have an interior design degree," Amelia says. "If you need help with anything, let me know."

Max's blue eyes grow wide. "I'd forgotten you studied interior design in college. Do you still work as a designer?"

Amelia shakes her head. "I haven't worked in years. Although I manage my own projects. We have houses in the Hamptons, Aspen, and Palm Beach. I've maintained my relationships with

many of the more established fabric and wall covering manu-
facturers."

"I could definitely use your help," Max says. "I have a vision.
But I have no clue how to obtain it."

Amelia holds her champagne flute out to Max. "Count me
in. I'm always up for a project."

Max clinks her glass. "Does this mean you're planning to stay
on the island indefinitely?"

Amelia is saved from having to answer when Birdie joins
them at the table. "Everything is lovely, Birdie. And delicious.
Can you have a glass of wine with us?"

Pink dots appear on Birdie's cheeks. "I don't drink. I had a
problem a while back."

Amelia's lips spread into a sympathetic smile. "We all have
problems in one form or another."

"So true," Birdie says. "I've instructed your server to bring
dinner for three. I hope you don't mind if I eat with you."

"Not at all," Amelia says. "I'd be honored."

Within minutes, the server brings out the second course—
seared scallops with a sweet corn risotto paired with a rosé wine.
While they eat, Birdie tells them about the food critic from the
Charleston paper who dined at the cafe earlier. "There were no
glaring issues," she says. "Now we wait for the review in next
Sunday's paper."

Amelia takes a bite of scallop. "Are you and Cary still
married?" she asks Birdie.

Birdie looks over at Max, who answers for her. "A few years
back, Cary cleaned out their bank account and ran off with
another woman."

"Which is when the drinking got out of control," Birdie
explains. "But Max saved me from myself. Cary is back in town,
but we're divorced and he's someone else's problem now."

"When did you buy the cafe?" Amelia asks. "Do I remember
correctly that it used to be a bakery and coffee shop?"

Birdie nods. "The Island Bakery. Two months after Cary disappeared, after Max helped me sober up, I took the equity from the sale of our house and bought the building and the business. We added a lunch menu, and when that proved successful, I decided to include dinner."

"Do you have children?" Amelia asks.

Birdie's features soften. "Yes. I have an amazing daughter, Hannah, who has a three-year-old son, Gus. They were living with me until a couple of months ago when Hannah's work took them to Charleston."

Birdie's love for her daughter and grandson are obvious. Not being able to have children has been her greatest disappointment in life. Even greater than her marriage to Nelson. She wanted to adopt, but Nelson wouldn't consider it. He refused to raise another man's child.

Out of the corner of her eye, Amelia notices Jonathan waiting with an attractive brunette at the hostess stand. Spotting them, Jonathan and the woman come over to the table to congratulate Birdie on her opening night. He introduces the woman as his sister. "You may or may not remember Frances. She was several years ahead of us in school. She's visiting from Texas."

Max's face lights up. "Wait! I *do* remember you. You were a cheerleader. I had a serious girl crush on you," she says, and they all laugh.

"What part of Texas are you from?" Birdie asks.

While Birdie and Max compare notes with Frances about mutual friends in Austin, Jonathan turns his attention to Amelia. "How're you holding up? I'm glad to see you out on the town."

"Thanks for asking. I'm doing as well as can be expected. I've enjoyed catching up with Birdie and Max after all these years."

"I meant what I said at the funeral. If you need anything, you let me know." Jonathan sets his gaze on her, his eyes as green as the lawn at Point Pleasant. He stirs something deep inside of her, a feeling she doesn't recognize that both scares and exhilarates her.

After being in an abusive marriage for years, is it so wrong of her to daydream about being with a man who will respect and appreciate her?

She smiles up at him. "I will. I promise."

The hostess comes for Jonathan and Frances, seating them at the next table over. Minutes later, their server delivers dessert, a simple dish of peach crumble with homemade vanilla ice cream. Amelia devours every bite. "I rarely eat dessert, but that was heavenly. I don't know when I've enjoyed a meal so much."

Birdie beams. "Come back anytime."

The three friends are lingering over coffee when there's a commotion at the hostess stand, a drunk scraggly looking guy arguing with the hostess. The color drains from Max's face.

"What's wrong, Max?" Amelia asks.

Birdie answers for her. "That's Max's boyfriend."

"He's not my boyfriend anymore," Max snaps. "I told you we broke up."

When the loud arguing continues, Max jumps out of her chair, but Jonathan is already on his feet. "Let me deal with it."

Every eye in the cafe is on Jonathan as he takes Ron by the arm and hustles him away from the hostess stand and across the boardwalk to the hotel. They speak briefly and Ron stumbles inside.

"If you broke up with him, why is he still staying in your hotel?" Birdie asks.

"I gave him until tomorrow to get out of my apartment," Max says.

"Right," Birdie says. "He's using you, because he's broke."

Max cuts her eyes at Birdie. "What makes you think that?"

"I can just tell," Birdie says. "Look at him. He can't even afford to get his hair cut. Does he ever pay for drinks and dinner when y'all go out?"

"Sometimes. Not that it's any of your business." Max shifts

her attention to Amelia. "I'm sorry for boring you with our bickering. We sound like a couple of old biddies."

"You sound like lifelong friends." Amelia thinks about all they've shared. Holidays and birthdays. Heartaches and happy times. Decades of long walks on the beach, discussing their problems and talking about their dreams. She's never felt more like a third wheel. She may have missed the past thirty years with these old friends, but she damn sure won't miss the rest of her life.

It's nearly ten o'clock when she says goodnight to Birdie and Max and drives home to Point Pleasant. She left enough lights on to light up Manhattan, but she has an eerie feeling someone is watching her as she enters the house. In the kitchen, she discovers a trail of brownie crumbs leading across the counter and floor to the basement door. How did the food gremlin get in when the alarm was on? Unless he or she was already inside. Is someone hiding out in the basement?

Removing her gun from her handbag, she slips off her sandals and tiptoes down the stairs. The utility room is empty, and there is nowhere to hide. Turning out the light, she goes upstairs to her mother's bedroom. She's drawing the heavy linen drapes when she sees the flicker of light in the apartment window. Someone is in that apartment. And she'd be willing to bet it's the same someone who is breaking into the house and stealing her food. Enough is enough. She'll wait until tomorrow, during the light of day, to search the apartment above the garage.

She grabs the comforter and pillows off the bed and settles in on the chaise lounge by the windows. As she stares out at the garage, her eyelids grow heavy, and she drifts off to sleep, only to awaken during the night with a start. She jumps to her feet. Through the darkened window, she glimpses a figure dressed in a white billowy gown, floating across the lawn. She squeezes her eyes shut and opens them wide again. But the figure has disappeared. Did she witness a ghost? It's not unheard of in the South where ancestral homes are haunted by both friendly and unfriendly spirits. Was it her mother? If so, why is Dottie stuck between the real world and the afterlife? Is she trying to tell Amelia something important? A chill crawls across her bare arms, and she shivers. She escaped her abusive husband, only to be haunted by a ghost.

TEN

Returning to the hotel after dinner, Max stops by the front desk to speak with Agnes. "How is everything going? Do you have any drama to report?" While she doesn't ask specifically about Ron, his drunken display at Birdie's Nest Cafe is at the forefront of her mind.

"Everything is fine for the most part." Agnes pushes her cat-eyeglasses up her nose. "Although Ron came through here a while ago. He was stumbling drunk. Were the two of you out together?"

"Nope. Our relationship is over, and he's leaving town tomorrow. Do you know if he went up to my apartment?"

"I assume so. He got in the elevator."

"Good," Max says with a sigh of relief. "How many rooms are occupied tonight?"

Agnes punches a few keys on the computer. "Twenty. All of them doubles. So, forty guests. We have a large group coming in tomorrow for a long weekend."

"I remember. The Anderson family reunion." Max starts off and then turns back around. "By the way, I'm avoiding Ron for obvious reasons. You should know, in case of an emergency, I'll be staying in room 130 tonight."

"Got it." Agnes jots the room number down on a notepad.

"But I'm going to my office for a few minutes first."

Agnes gives her a thumbs-up. "Goodnight, Max. Try to get some sleep."

Max closes her office door and sits down at her computer. She might have saved herself some heartache if she'd dug deeper the first time she researched him. Then again, she'd been in a state of denial, too infatuated with Ron to accept the truth. She starts over with the most popular social media sights, but her search yields no results. She spends some time typing keywords into her internet browser. Ron Morton. Software developer. Philadelphia software company. But she finds nothing.

Locking her office, Max goes down the hall to her room, changes into her pajamas, and falls fast asleep. Sometime later, a shrieking alarm jolts her awake. It takes a few seconds for her head to clear, for her to remember where she is and realize the awful racket is the hotel's fire alarm. She clambers out of bed and runs to the lobby in her pajamas.

"What's going on?" she asks a bewildered-looking Agnes.

"I'm not sure. I dozed off. We must have a fire somewhere."

The door to the stairwell bangs open and a group of guests in nightclothes emerges. "The elevator's out," a tall man shouts above the noise of the alarm. The woman with him adds, "We smell smoke."

"What floor are you on?" Max shouts above the noise.

"The fourth," the woman says. "What're we supposed to do?"

"Exit the building in an orderly fashion and wait for further instruction." Max joins Agnes behind the desk. "I left my phone in my room. Print off a list of our guests and their room numbers while I call the fire department."

Max punches in 9-1-1 on the house phone and reports the

fire to the emergency operator. "Tell them to hurry! I have guests staying in my hotel. Some of them may be trapped."

The stairwell door opens again, and guests spill out into the lobby.

Slamming down the phone receiver, Max holds her hand out to Agnes. "Do you have that list?"

Agnes hands her the printed list. "Of the twenty rooms occupied, four are on the fourth floor, nine on the third, and seven on the second."

Max and Agnes come from behind the counter to direct traffic. Following the last guest outside, Max claps her hand to get the crowd's attention. "Listen up! I know this is unsettling, but the fire department is on the way. I need to make certain we account for everyone. Please answer or raise your hand when I call your name."

As the sound of sirens approach from the distance, she quickly goes through the list of names. "All forty guests are here," Max reports.

"Except Ron," Agnes says.

Max's hand flies to her mouth. "Oh, no! He's in my apartment. On the fourth floor."

Agnes's green eyes are wild. "He's probably passed out and doesn't hear the alarm."

The fire truck, followed closely by a rescue squad, eases down the wide sidewalk, stopping on the other side of the park. Two firefighters in bunker gear make their way through the crowd. The taller of the two calls out, "Who's in charge here?"

Max raises her hand. "I am. I'm Max Summers, the owner of the hotel. Guests reported smelling smoke on the fourth floor. I did a roll call. All the guests are out of the building except one. My friend is staying in my apartment on the fourth floor. He had too much to drink earlier. He may not hear the alarm. The room number is 417. It's the third door on the right off the elevator. Which isn't currently working, so you'll have to use the stairs."

"Okay, ma'am. We're on it." Cupping his hands around his mouth, the taller firefighter calls out to the guests. "Please, move away from the building."

The crowd follows his orders, moving as one across the boardwalk toward the cafe.

Birdie appears at Max's side. "I heard the sirens. What on earth is going on? Is there an actual fire? Or is it a false alarm?"

"Looks like a real fire." As the words leave her mouth, tears spill from Max's eyes. "And Ron is trapped inside my apartment."

"Oh, honey." Birdie hands Max a tissue. "The firemen are here now. They'll get him out." Confusion crosses her face. "Wait a minute. Why did you leave Ron in your apartment when the fire broke out?"

"I wasn't in my apartment. I checked myself into a room on the first floor, because I didn't wanna be near him."

Birdie hugs her tight. "I'm so sorry, Maxie."

They watch the firefighters scurrying about as they prepare their hoses to fight the fire. The waiting is agony. Another fire truck arrives and more firefighters enter the building. The tall firefighter finally emerges from the hotel. "We found the fire. Your guests were right. It's on the fourth floor."

"Where on the fourth floor?" Max asks.

"In an unoccupied guest room. We're working on extinguishing it now. There's a lot of smoke." His walkie-talkie crackles, and he holds it to his ear. After listening for a minute, he reports, "My men found your friend on the floor of the apartment with a gash on the side of his head. We're sending in the paramedics. He should be out momentarily."

"What about my hotel?" Max sobs. "Can you save the building?"

"We're doing our best, ma'am. We'll know more soon."

When the firefighter disappears back inside, the guests surround Max, barraging her with questions she can't answer. "Can we go back inside soon? What about our belongings?

Where will we sleep?" Most are dressed in nightclothes with bare feet. In a rush to escape the building, all the guests left behind their cell phones and wallets and purses.

"Quiet! Please!" Max raises her hands to silence them. "The firefighters are putting out the fire now. Please be patient while we wait for them to give us more direction."

The paramedics come out of the building with Ron on a stretcher. "How is he? Is he conscious?" Max asks, walking alongside the stretcher on the way to the ambulance.

"Not at the moment," a female paramedic says. "He's suffering from severe smoke inhalation. We need to get him to the hospital as quickly as possible. Do you want to ride with him?"

Max's eyes travel from Ron to her guests. "I can't leave yet. I'll be there as soon as I can."

The paramedics load Ron into the back, and the ambulance takes off with sirens roaring. Max returns to Birdie and Agnes. Watching the firefighters bustle in and out of the building, her imagination runs wild with visions of flames licking the walls as they blast water out of their massive hoses. Her beloved hotel is suffering smoke, fire, and water damage. What if it burns to the ground?

Birdie turns her back on the hotel. "We're not doing anyone any good just standing here. Let's go to the cafe. I'm sure your guests would appreciate a cup of coffee."

Max and Agnes follow Birdie across the park to the cafe. The three women work together silently as they prepare large urns of coffee and gather disposable cups, packets of sweetener, and pods of cream. They're setting up the coffee bar on the boardwalk when the tall firefighter delivers the news.

"We've extinguished the fire. There's significant destruction on the fourth floor, but aside from extensive smoke damage, the other floors are intact. No one will be allowed back inside tonight."

"I understand. Thank you." When he walks away, Max collapses against Birdie. "This is devastating. Financially, the summer is over for me."

Birdie pats her back. "Look at the bright side. You were planning to renovate, anyway. Now you can use the insurance money to cover the cost."

"That's true." Max lifts her head from Birdie's shoulder and wipes her eyes. "What am I going to do with my guests?"

"I guess you'll have to put them up at the Coral Sands."

"I was afraid you'd say that." Using Birdie's cell phone, Max places a call to the Coral Sands night manager, who begrudgingly agrees to accommodate her misplaced guests.

Max and Agnes speak with the guests individually, most of whom are sympathetic and understanding. Agnes volunteers to shuttle the guests to the motel in their passenger van, and after seeing off the first load, Max says to Birdie, "I need to get to the hospital."

"You can't go in your pajamas. Come inside and let me get you a change of clothes."

"I don't have time to worry about my clothes, Birdie." She pats the pockets of her pajama bottoms. "But I left my keys in my room. Can I borrow your car?"

"Of course. I'll go grab my keys."

Birdie is back in less than a minute with the keys to her station wagon and a yellow T-shirt bearing the Birdie's Nest Cafe logo on the back. Max slips the T-shirt on over her pajamas and gives Birdie a hug. "I don't know what I'd do without you."

"You'd do the same for me." They walk together to the parking lot behind the cafe. "Text me from the hospital. I'm here if you need anything."

There is no traffic on the roads at three o'clock in the morning, and despite not having her driver's license with her, Max speeds to the hospital, cruising through stop signs and red lights. A cross-looking woman at the reception desk in the emergency room motions her to the empty waiting room. "I'll let the doctor know you're here. Someone will be with you soon."

Max waits for over an hour before a young female doctor comes out from the examining rooms to speak with her. "Are you Mr. Morton's next of kin?" Dr. Hamill asks.

"As far as I know, Ron doesn't have a next of kin. I am . . . I was his girlfriend. It's complicated. How is he?"

"In serious condition. We're moving him up to ICU now. We're placing him in a hyperbaric chamber. We need to run some tests, but we suspect considerable damage to his respiratory tract."

A wave of nausea washes over Max. "Can I see him?"

"Not yet. He's unconscious. Depending on how long he was deprived of oxygen, he may have suffered brain damage. But there is a waiting room on the fourth floor for families of ICU patients. You can wait there. We'll update you as we know more."

Max nods, fighting back tears. This is all her fault. If only she hadn't moved to the room on the first floor. If she'd stayed in her apartment, not only would she have discovered Ron passed out, she could've spared him the smoke inhalation. Even though they are no longer in a relationship, Max owes it to him to see him through. *If* he makes it through this medical crisis.

ELEVEN

Amelia wakes from a deep slumber in a cold sweat. Once again, she'd been dreaming about the white-headed little girl hiding on the porch. Closing her eyes, she plays the soundtrack over and over in her mind. She recognizes her mother's soft voice, and the deep one undoubtedly belongs to her father. She assumes the third voice belongs to her sister, Robin. But the voices are distorted, and Amelia can't make out what they are saying.

Frustrated, she gives up and throws back the covers. She's surprised to see it's past nine o'clock. Amelia typically rises with the sun, but after witnessing the *ghost* on the lawn last night, she had to take an Ambien to get back to sleep. She makes her bed, dresses in athletic clothes, and goes down to the kitchen where she finds a note from Bebe on the counter beside a fresh pot of coffee. *Gone to the farmer's market. Back soon.*

With her gun tucked in the waistband of her exercise shorts, Amelia marches across the back lawn to the garage. The double doors creak when she swings them open. Inside smells like gasoline and grass clippings, but the riding mower, wheelbarrow, and an assortment of yard tools are all in order.

Closing the double doors, she rounds the corner of the garage to a set of wooden stairs leading to the second-floor apartment. The apartment door is unlocked, and she lets herself in. The stench of cigarette smoke assaults her nose. The living room is empty aside for an ashtray overflowing with cigarette butts on the floor near the window. Beside the ashtray is her father's engraved lighter. This explains the flicker of light in the window. She thinks back to the last time she saw the lighter. On Saturday, when Bebe was polishing silver in preparation for the funeral reception. Whoever is staying in this apartment broke into the main house and stole her father's lighter. This squatter must be the food gremlin. She pockets the lighter and continues her search.

In the bedroom, an air mattress is laid out on the floor and clothes are strewn about, many of which she recognizes as her mother's. Amelia finds expensive face creams and cosmetics in the bathroom. Is it a coincidence the brands are the same as her mother's? Amelia doesn't think so. She moves on to the kitchen where trash litters the counter. The refrigerator door is propped open, and the interior is empty and dark.

Exiting the apartment, she takes the stairs two at a time on the way down and hides behind the garage to wait for the trespasser. The air is thick with humidity, and perspiration soon beads on Amelia's forehead. She's about to give up and go back to the main house when she hears someone humming. The sound grows nearer. She knows the song—a popular tune by Creedence Clearwater Revival—but can't remember the title.

Footfalls on the steps are followed by the opening and closing of the apartment door overhead. Amelia slips from around the corner and tiptoes up the stairs. Cracking open the door, she spots a woman standing at the window on the opposite wall. Fumbling to open a pack of cigarettes, the woman removes one and bends down for the lighter. But the lighter is gone.

Amelia opens the door wider. "Looking for this?" she asks, holding up her father's lighter.

The woman slowly straightens and turns toward her. Amelia recognizes her frizzy auburn hair and wrinkled face—lines etched into her skin from decades of smoking cigarettes. She's the woman who was hiding behind the tree at the cemetery.

Amelia steps inside the doorway to get a closer look. "Who are you? And what do you want?"

The woman tilts her head to the side. "You don't recognize me?"

"From the cemetery. You were at my mama's funeral. Do I know you?"

Disappointment crosses the woman's face. "I'm Robin, your sister."

Amelia gasps. "I don't believe you."

"And I don't blame you. It's been a long time, Mila."

The room spins as the past comes rushing back. Her sister is the only one who has ever called her Mila, which she pronounced as Mee-la. Amelia's memories of Robin are vague. She was so young when she last saw her sister. And Robin was only eighteen. She's now sixty-three, although she looks at least seventy.

"I don't understand." Amelia's mind reels with questions. "Why are you hiding out in the garage apartment? Why didn't you let me know you were here?"

"We haven't seen each other in a very long time. I didn't wanna freak you out. I was waiting for the right moment to approach you." Robin closes the gap between them. "Look at you. You're gorgeous, tall and thin and blonde. You're a walking goddess. Just like Mama."

"I . . . um."

Robin holds a hand out, palm facing Amelia. "I know what you're thinking. You wish you could say the same thing about me. I'm a wreck. Life hasn't been good to me, Mila."

"I'm sorry." Amelia studies her sister—searching for some

resemblance to their parents—but finds none. Maybe she's an imposter. Although there is something vaguely familiar about her.

Robin snatches the lighter from Amelia and lights her cigarette.

The smoke tickles Amelia's nose, and she coughs into her hand. "That's a nasty habit, you know?"

"Don't worry about it." Exhaling a stream of smoke, Robin drops the lighter in the pocket of her sundress.

"Why did you wait until Mama died to come home?"

"It's a long story. I could use some coffee. Am I allowed in the house?"

"Of course." Amelia curls her lip at the cigarette. "As long as you put that out."

"Fine," Robin says and snuffs the cigarette out in the ashtray.

With her sister on her heels, Amelia descends the stairs and crosses the yard to the mudroom door. Bebe is unloading her purchases from the farmer's market in the kitchen. When she sees Robin, the color drains from her face and she grips the countertop. "Oh, Lawd. Look what the cat done drug in."

"Bebe!" Amelia stares at the housekeeper in horror. She's never known Bebe to treat anyone with anything but kindness.

Robin gives Bebe a curt nod. "Nice to see you, too, Bebe."

Amelia's fingers graze Bebe's arm. "We'd like some coffee, please, and maybe a light breakfast. We'll be on the porch."

Amelia leads the way through the front hall and living room. She waits until Robin is seated beside her in a rocker before asking, "Where have you been all these years?"

A faraway look overcomes Robin's face. "When I ran away from home, I hitchhiked my way to California where I joined a religious commune. I'd rather not go into the details of my life. I had a few happy years, but most of them were pretty rough."

"Did you ever marry?"

Robin's expression remains impassive. "No. But I had a baby. She died as an infant."

"That's awful. I'm so sorry."

Robin tugs at strands of hair as she talks, giving Amelia glimpses of bald patches on her scalp. "I left the commune about fifteen years ago. I've been drifting around since then. I'm not trained to do much of anything, but I'm a hard worker, and I found odd jobs here and there. I slowly made my way back across the country to South Carolina. I'd arrived in Charleston, and I was on the verge of reaching out to Mama in hopes of making amends when I read her obituary in the paper."

Amelia questions whether her sister is telling the truth. Her story sounds too coincidental. "And you haven't spoken to Mama in forty-five years?"

"Not a word," Robin mumbles with downcast eyes. "She never tried to find me."

"You can't be certain of that," Amelia says. "She may have tried and failed. You, on the other hand, knew exactly where to find her. Did you ever stop to think about how hard it was for Mama, not knowing whether you were alive or dead?"

Robin lifts a shoulder in an indifferent shrug. "I doubt she lost much sleep from worrying about my whereabouts."

Bebe emerges through the french doors bearing a tray with coffee mugs and plates with slices of coffee cake. Robin digs into the coffee cake like a ravenous animal, not bothering with the fork, scraping up every crumb with her fingers. Is this how they ate in her commune? It certainly explains the mysterious crumbs in the kitchen.

"How have you been getting in and out of the house?"

Robin sets the empty plate aside and reaches for a coffee. "There's a window in the basement that's not hooked up to the alarm. You should get that fixed."

Chill bumps crawl across Amelia's skin. This woman, a virtual stranger, may have been spying on her in the shower and watching her while she slept. "Why did you feel the need to hide from me?"

"There's not a single photograph of me anywhere in the house. Mom obviously hated me. I figured you do too."

Amelia had often wondered about the missing framed photographs of her older sister. She assumed they were too painful for Dottie to look at every day. "Why would I hate you? I'm your sister. Whatever happened between you and our parents had nothing to do with me. And Mama didn't hate you. She might have been angry and disappointed, but she loved you." Amelia has no idea if this is true. But it's what she would want to hear if she were in Robin's shoes.

Her sister smiles, revealing a missing tooth, one of the smaller molars on the upper left side. "Thank you for saying that, even though we both know it isn't true."

Robin leaves the porch and walks over to the edge of the lawn to smoke a cigarette. Amelia watches her sister pace back and forth in front of the sand dunes, talking out loud to herself and jabbing at the air with her cigarette. Robin is homeless and mentally unstable, from the looks of it. But she's Amelia's sister, a Fairchild by birthright. It would be wrong for Amelia to let Robin live like a vagrant. She should invite Robin to stay in the house. But today is Wednesday, and Nelson will come for Amelia soon. She would hate for Robin to get caught in the crossfire.

When Robin returns to the porch, Amelia stands to face her. "We have a lot to talk about, a lot of catching up to do. Why don't we spend the day together on the beach?"

Robin rubs at the back of her neck. "I'm not a fan of sand. And I don't own a bathing suit."

"You can borrow one of Mama's," Amelia says, and thinks, *You've already been helping yourself to her closet.*

When Robin hesitates, Amelia says, "Come on, Robin. We're sisters. We should get to know one another."

"All right," Robin says reluctantly.

Out of the corner of her eye, Amelia notices Bebe hiding behind the drapery in the living room. What has gotten into her today? In all the years she's worked for their family, Amelia has never known Bebe to eavesdrop.

Amelia motions Robin inside. "Why don't you go on up to her room? I'll be there in a minute."

She waits until her sister has gone upstairs before pulling the drapery back, exposing Bebe. "What do you think you're doing?" she says to Bebe in a loud whisper.

Bebe straightens her boney shoulders. "Protecting you from yourself. You must be crazy letting that woman wear your mama's bathing suit. Letting her go up to Miss Dottie's room unsupervised."

"That woman is my sister."

"Humph! She's trouble is what she is. Miss Dottie never would've allowed her back in this house."

"Why do you say that? Why wouldn't Mama want her missing daughter to come home?"

"Not only did Miss Dottie not want Robin to come home. She lived in fear of her returning to Palmetto Island."

"You're scaring me, Bebe." Turning her back on the house-keeper, Amelia stands in the doorway and stares out at the mouth of the inlet. "I remember so little about her. What happened back then?"

Bebe comes to stand beside her. "Lots of bad stuff, baby. Stuff that shouldn't happen in a family."

"Stuff you witnessed, or stuff Mama told you about?"

"Both."

"What do you suggest I do about her? She's living in the garage apartment with no furniture, sleeping on an air mattress, and sneaking in the house to steal food. That isn't right. She's my sister. Maybe she's changed."

"A zebra don't change it stripes, honey." Bebe gives Amelia a half hug. "We'll come up with something. Take your sister down to the beach. See what you can find out about where she's been all these years while I figure out what to do about her living arrangements."

"Okay. But first I'm calling the alarm company." Retrieving Dottie's phone from the table on the porch, Amelia locates the security company's contact information and clicks on the number. After explaining her situation, the representative promises to send someone over this afternoon. Ending the call, Amelia says to Bebe, "Be on the lookout for the alarm company while I'm on the beach. When they get here, call or text me on Mama's phone."

"All right." They close the french doors and walk toward the stairs. "I got a bad feeling about this, baby. It ain't no coincidence that Robin showed up only days after Miss Dottie's funeral. She wants something. And you and I both know what that something is."

TWELVE

Max finds her nephew securing yellow crime scene tape across the front doors of her hotel when she arrives home from the hospital. "What're you doing?" she asks.

"Following orders from the fire chief," Toby says. "He's called in someone from the state's fire marshal's office to investigate the fire."

"Wait! Why would he do that?"

Toby continues with his task. "It's standard procedure for a small town when the fire department doesn't have a designated arson investigator."

Max shakes her head, as though failing to understand. "Arson? What're you talking about? The fire was caused by antiquated wiring. My contractor discovered that much of our electrical systems have gone bad."

Toby tears the yellow tape with his teeth, secures it to the door, and turns to face her. "And I'm sure they'll want to talk to him. But the chief has reason to suspect that someone deliberately set the fire."

"That's ludicrous. Who would want to burn down my hotel?"

His beady brown eyes become slits. "Why don't you tell me?" he asks in a suspicious tone.

Max brings herself to her full height. "What exactly are you implying, Toby?"

Toby mops the sweat off his brow with a folded red bandana. "I'm not implying anything. I'm concerned. You told me yourself you haven't gotten loan approval for your renovations. The insurance money would come in handy right about now."

"That's ridiculous. I haven't had a chance to tell you yet, but the bank notified me on Monday that my loan has been approved." Feeling a headache coming on, Max massages her temples. "I can't think about this right now. Forty of my guests are staying at the Coral Sands Motel. Agnes will be shuttling them back soon. They'll need to retrieve their belongings from their rooms. When the fire alarm went off, they exited the hotel in their pajamas. Many of them weren't even wearing shoes. They left their clothes and cell phones and car keys up in their rooms. Taking care of them is my main priority right now."

"I'll talk to Chief Vega to see what we can work out."

"Call him now, please," Max says, pointing at the phone hooked to his belt. "My desk clerks are on the way. I need them to help sort out our upcoming reservations. We're booked solid through Labor Day. I can't just cancel these reservations through the computer system. Many of the guests are long-time clients. They deserve an explanation via a phone call."

"All right." Toby steps out of earshot to place his call. She tries to listen in. She's hurt, angry, and bewildered that he accused her of setting fire to her own hotel. Is that what others are thinking? Is that what the fire marshal will determine?

Ending his call, Toby walks back over to her. "Okay, we have a plan. I'll tape off the elevators and stairs. When the guests arrive, keep them in the lounge. I will call in some of my officers to help with crowd control. We'll allow them to go to their rooms a few at a time."

"What about my desk clerks?"

"They may take care of business as long as they remain in the lobby and lounge." Toby takes down the yellow tape and steps out of the way for Max to enter.

She's unprepared for the overpowering stench. She covers her mouth and nose. "This is bad."

Toby waves his hand in front of his face. "Smells like my wife burned dinner again."

Max glares at him. "I'm gonna tell Brenda you said that."

"Lighten up. I'm only joking. We both know my wife is an excellent cook."

"Sorry if I'm not in a joking mood. I don't like being accused of arson."

He drops his smile. "I'm just doing my job, Maxie."

"And I'm trying to do mine. Now, get out of my way," Max says, brushing past him.

When she heads down the hall to her hotel room, he calls after her, "Where are you going?"

"To my room to change clothes and get my phone," she says over her shoulder as she continues walking.

"But your apartment is on the fourth floor."

Max stops in her tracks. She just walked into her own trap. She turns to face him. "I booked myself in a room down here last night. Ron and I broke up, and I didn't want to be in the apartment with him. It's not a big deal, so don't make it one."

Toby eyes the bruises on her wrists "Did he do that to you?"

She hides her hand behind her back. "Things got tense between us. But I was handling the situation."

"You were handling it so well, you let him run you out of your apartment. What happened between you two? Last I heard, you were in love."

Max shifts her weight from one foot to the other. "The chemistry between us fizzled. Ron asked for a few days to figure out his next move. He was planning to leave town today. Do I feel guilty about him getting hurt? Of course. Ron was upset with me. He went out on the town and drank himself into a stupor. If I hadn't been staying down here on the first floor, I could've gotten him out of the apartment."

"Shh!" Toby touches the tip of his finger to his lips. "This is serious, Max. You need to be careful what you say. Arson to get insurance money is one thing. This is an entirely different matter. I know you wouldn't hurt a flea. But from a stranger's perspective, this doesn't look good. A fire breaks out in the room next to your apartment, where your abusive boyfriend is lying unconscious on the floor from a head wound. Meanwhile, you've booked yourself into a room on the first floor."

"I told you, Ron was drunk. He fell and hit his head."

"Maybe. Or maybe someone clobbered him with a blunt object."

The bottom drops out of her stomach. "That someone wasn't me, Toby. Ask Birdie. Ask Amelia. Ask Agnes. I had dinner at the cafe. When I got home, I spent a few minutes at my computer before going straight to my room."

Toby thumbs his chest. "I'm not the one you have to convince. But it won't take long for the fire marshal to put two and two together. Being the owner of the hotel makes you the primary arson suspect. Whether you like it or not, your breakup with Ron will be a factor in this equation."

"What do I do?" she asks, her words barely audible.

"Go about your business as usual. And answer their questions truthfully. I'll make certain I'm informed on every aspect of the investigation. I'll know when to consult an attorney."

"Attorney? You really think it'll come to that."

He shrugs. "It might. Jonathan Hart has an excellent young criminal lawyer in his firm. I'll give him a heads-up that we may be needing his services."

"Now I'm officially terrified." She rests her forehead on his chest, and he pats her back.

"I don't mean to scare you. I'm trying to prepare you for what may lie ahead."

Max is setting up coffee dispensers in the lounge when Birdie arrives with an enormous tray of pastries, donuts, and croissants. "You're the best, Birdie," Max says, taking the tray from her. "My guests will appreciate these."

"What's with all the police officers?" Birdie asks. "They almost didn't let me in the building."

"They suspect arson. They think someone deliberately set the fire. Guess who's at the top of their list of suspects."

"You?" Birdie asks, and Max nods.

"That's ridiculous," Birdie says. "Why would you catch your own building on fire?"

"To get the insurance money to rebuild."

"I'm sure they're just doing their jobs," Birdie says in a dismissive tone. "At least you have Toby on your side."

"Thank heavens for small favors." Casting her eyes toward the ceiling, Max says a silent prayer that Toby doesn't turn on her. "Agnes should be here any minute with the first load of guests."

"I'll get out of your hair, then," Birdie says. "But let me know if I can help in any way."

Max walks Birdie through the lobby, and they step outside into the already sweltering morning.

"My offer still stands," Birdie says. "You are welcome to stay with me while you renovate."

Max considers the logistics. "I appreciate your offer. But where will Hannah and Gus stay when they come home to visit?"

"They can bunk in my room with me. But I'm not worried about that happening on a regular basis. I've only seen them once since they moved to Charleston."

"Aren't you worried an extended stay might cause more harm than good to our friendship?" Max asks.

"Not at all. Remember, I stayed with you for weeks when I hit rock bottom after Cary left me."

"True. And we had some good times." But Birdie was in a dark place back then. She needed Max. Things are different now. They are two independent women with their own lives. Max leans into her. "I'll at least stay for a few nights."

Birdie embraces her. "I'm here for you, Maxie. Whatever you need. Hannah and Ethan are coming for dinner tonight. Will you join us?"

Max smiles. "I always love seeing Hannah. And I've been eager to meet her young man. I'm not sure I'll be good company, but count me in."

"Perfect. Seven o'clock. I'll be here all day. Let me know when you're ready, and I'll help you move your stuff over."

"Assuming they let me back in my apartment," Max says under her breath as the women part.

Max is turning back toward the hotel when she notices Davis emerging from the parking deck.

He jogs over to her. "Max, I'm so sorry about the fire. It's difficult to lose your end-of-season business, but look on the bright side—we'll be able to start on the renovations earlier. And, depending on the damage, we may have to take the walls down to the studs, which will make rebuilding easier and quicker."

She glances around for anyone who might overhear them. "Don't say that too loudly. The fire chief thinks someone intentionally started the fire. They don't need more reason to suspect me." Max immediately regrets the words. She doesn't want to scare Davis off with her problems.

"Wait! What are you saying? Wasn't the fire a result of bad wiring?"

"It's still too early to tell, honestly. The fire marshal is sending someone from his office in Columbia to investigate."

"I'm happy to talk to him, to tell him about the bad wiring."

"Thanks. I'll pass that along."

Davis walks her to the front door of the hotel. "I'm here for you, Max. Both as your contractor and a friend."

"Thanks, Davis. That means a lot."

She'll need all the friends she can get if the police arrest her for arson. What if the case goes to trial? She could lose the hotel. Or worse. She could go to jail.

THIRTEEN

obin talks on about how terrible life has treated her and how lonely she's been all these years without her family. During their two hours on the beach, Robin doesn't ask Amelia a single question about her own life. When her sister finally falls asleep under the umbrella, Amelia returns to the house to make sandwiches for their lunch. She finds Bebe at the sink in the kitchen cleaning shrimp for her dinner.

"I packed a picnic for you. It's in that cooler." Bebe gestures at a soft cooler by the door. "What'd you find out from Robin?"

"Nothing important." Amelia retrieves a bottled water from the refrigerator.

Bebe deveins the last shrimp, rinses it, and places it in the colander. Drying her hands, she turns to face Amelia. "Your mama would roll over in her grave and come back to haunt me if she found out I allowed Robin to stay in this house with you."

"Then what do you suggest we do with her?"

"Ship her back where she came from. But we need to find out why she's here and what she wants first. In the meantime, I suggest we leave her where she is. There are some odds and ends in the attic, including an old mattress and box spring. We'll fix up the garage apartment for her. I've already called your mama's handymen. They're coming this afternoon to move the stuff over."

Amelia leans back against the counter as she considers the plan. "This could work. I'd rather not be under the same roof with her. We'll need to get the refrigerator fixed."

Bebe shakes her head. "The refrigerator ain't broken. We just need to plug it in."

With a snicker, Amelia says, "Easy enough. I'll have Robin over for dinner tonight and buy her some groceries tomorrow. After that, she's on her own."

Bebe pokes a finger at Amelia. "Better not let your guard down while she's around."

"Don't worry. I won't." Through the window over the sink, Amelia notices a white service van with the alarm company's logo on the side pulling into the driveway. "The repairmen are here to fix the security system. I'll go explain the situation to them."

Two uniformed service technicians are removing their tools from the back of the van when Amelia emerges from the house. "Morning. Thanks for coming on such short notice. I'm having trouble with an intruder entering and exiting my house through a window in the basement that isn't connected to the alarm."

"Yes ma'am," one technician says. "We'll get right on it."

"Out of curiosity, how long does it take to install security cameras?"

"We can't do it today, if that's what you're asking," the other technician says. "We have to follow a protocol. The first step is to have one of our salespeople come out and give you an estimate. I can have someone call you to schedule that appointment."

"Thanks, but I'm unsure of my schedule. I'll give them a call when I'm ready." Amelia shows the technicians inside to the basement.

When she comes back up from downstairs, she says to Bebe,

"I'm going to try to keep Robin on the beach until they're finished. I don't want her to know they've fixed the alarm."

Bebe furrows her brow. "Why not?"

"Now that we know she's here, she no longer has a reason to sneak around behind our backs. If she tries to break in, I want to know about it."

"Smart thinking. Do you have your gun on you?"

Amelia pats the pocket of her coverup. "Always."

She carries the cooler back down to the beach. Robin has woken from her nap and is smoking a cigarette. Amelia holds up the cooler. "Bebe prepared a picnic for us. Are you hungry?"

"I can always eat," Robin says and stuffs out her cigarette in the sand.

Her sister has a hardness about her that sets Amelia on edge. She feels Robin's eyes on her, watching her, judging her as they eat their ham sandwiches. "Bebe has been rummaging around in the attic," Amelia says. "She found some furniture to fix up the garage apartment for you."

Robin's jaw tightens. "Are you saying I'm not allowed in the main house?"

Amelia avoids her gaze. "We thought you'd be more comfortable in your own space. And you can smoke in the apartment as long as you promise not to burn the place down." She fakes a laugh, an attempt to break the friction.

Robin grunts in response.

"Anyway, Mama's handymen are coming this afternoon to help us move everything over."

Robin wads up her napkin and tosses it into the cooler. "Don't go to too much trouble. I'm not sure how much longer I'm staying in town."

"Where will you go?"

Robin shrugs. "I'm not sure yet."

She lights another cigarette. The smoke billows toward Amelia, but Robin doesn't bother moving from her chair.

The last thing Amelia needs right now is a cantankerous woman hanging around, polluting her air with cigarette smoke. She needs time alone to mourn her mother, time to prepare for her husband's arrival. What is wrong with her? Why isn't she jubilant over being reunited with her long-lost sister? Bebe's words ring in her ears. *Your mama would roll over in her grave and come back to haunt me.* Why? What happened between Robin and her parents all those years ago? *Lots of bad stuff, baby. Stuff that shouldn't happen in a family.* Dottie Fairchild was not one to hold a grudge. Especially not against her own child. She was the most reasonable woman Amelia has ever known. She would've forgiven teenage rebellion. There must be more to the story. Amelia can't have a relationship with her sister until she finds out more about the bad stuff.

Bebe texts Amelia, informing her that the security company technicians have gone and the handymen, Sammy and Nathan, have arrived.

In a chipper voice, she says to Robin, "The guys are here to move the furniture. Let's go set up your apartment."

"Yippee," Robin says in a sarcastic tone.

Gathering their belongings, Amelia and Robin traipse through the sand up to the house. While she's learned little about her long-lost sister over the past few hours, Amelia's gut instincts scream at her not to trust Robin.

FOURTEEN

Max's morning passes in a blur of activity. Her three most trusted desk agents make endless phone calls to cancel upcoming reservations. The current guests are understanding and patient about the drawn-out process of answering questions about the fire and being escorted to their rooms to retrieve their belongings. They take turns changing clothes and freshening up in the three rooms provided on the first floor. Max stations herself by the front door, bidding each of them farewell with promises of complimentary stays as soon as the hotel reopens in a few months.

Max says teary goodbyes to her desk agents, sending them home for an extended paid leave of absence. She's at the front desk making the last calls to her most valued customers when the inspector from the state's fire marshal's office arrives from Columbia around two.

"I'm Paul Reynolds." He flashes his credentials. "I'm here to investigate the fire." Paul Reynolds is a beast of a man with an angry scowl and faded burn scars up both arms and one side of his neck. Despite being sympathetic of the pain he's suffered in the past, Max is intimidated by him.

"I'm Max Summers, hotel owner. Please let me know if I can help in any way."

He nods. "I'm going up now to have a look around," he says and disappears inside the stairway.

Retreating to her office and wanting to keep her mind off the investigation taking place on the fourth floor, Max busies herself with tying up loose ends. Two hours later, Paul Reynolds knocks lightly on her open door. "May I have a word with you?" he asks in a tone of voice that matches his serious expression.

Panic tightens her chest. Is he going to arrest her? Where is Toby? She hasn't seen him in hours. Should she ask Reynolds if she needs an attorney present? *No,* she decides. That might make her look guilty.

"Of course." She pushes back from her desk. "But let's go to the lounge where we'll be more comfortable."

Max shows Reynolds to the lounge and offers him coffee, which he declines.

Setting his iPad on the table in front of him, Reynolds says, "I need you to walk me through the events of last night."

His penetrating gaze makes her uneasy, and she shifts her eyes to the window where the sight of a sailboat gliding across the creek calms her nerves. "Well, let's see. I had dinner with friends across the boardwalk at Birdie's Nest Cafe. Our reservation was for seven thirty, and we lingered after dinner over coffee. I didn't get back to the hotel until close to ten. I spoke with my night desk agent and spent a few minutes in my office." Max's stomach turns to stone. Will her internet browser history show she was researching Ron's past? With mind racing, she decides to keep quiet about that for now. "After that, I went down the hall to my room where I went straight to bed. I was awakened during the night by the fire alarm."

Reynolds finger taps notes into his iPad. "Did anyone see you go to your room?"

"Agnes did. She's the night desk agent. I waved to her as I passed by."

"And why were you sleeping in a room on the first floor when your apartment is on the fourth?"

Oh, boy! Here we go. Tell the truth, Maxie. You haven't done anything wrong. "I recently ended my relationship with my live-in boyfriend, Ron Morgan—he's the man who was injured in the fire. Because things were tense between us, as often happens after a breakup, I didn't want to sleep in the apartment with him last night. He was planning to move out today."

"I noticed two bedrooms in your apartment, Ms. Summers, each with its own lock." Reynolds eyes the yellowing bruises on her wrist. "Why were you afraid of him? Was he abusing you?"

Max sighs. "We rushed into a relationship before we had a chance to get to know one another. Turns out we're not compatible. Ron got rough with me once. He grabbed my arm, hence the bruises." She massages her wrist. "But once is enough for me. I asked him to leave. He was taking his time in getting out. I think he was hoping I'd forgive him and take him back."

"Did you ask the police for help? I understand Chief Summers is your nephew."

Max shakes her head. "It wasn't a big deal. I was handling it."

"Handling it how?" His menacing dark eyes make her squirm.

She glares at him. "I already told you. By avoiding him. By insisting he leave. By moving into the room on the first floor."

"Did you see Mr. Morgan when you were out at dinner?"

"I saw him, but I didn't speak to him. He stopped by Birdie's cafe on his way back to the hotel. I'm not sure where he'd been. Probably Shaggy's. He was drunk, and he caused a scene with the hostess. Jonathan Hart, a local attorney, escorted him back to the hotel. According to Agnes, Ron took the elevator up to the fourth floor."

"Did you see Mr. Morgan again after that?"

"I did not."

Reynolds shifts in his chair. "I understand you have plans to renovate in the works. Can you tell me about those?"

"Sure." Max spreads her arms wide. "As you may have noticed, the building is in a state of disrepair. Many of my rooms are currently uninhabitable. I'm working with a contractor, Davis Watson. I suggest you speak with him. He discovered outdated and hazardous wiring while he was assessing the property."

Reynolds types Davis's name into his iPad. "When is he planning to start construction?"

"After Labor Day."

"And how are you going to pay for the improvements?"

Max wonders again if she should have an attorney present. "With a loan from the bank. Which has already been approved. I'm happy to give you the name of my loan officer."

Max is relieved to see Toby striding across the lounge toward them. "What's going on here?" he demands.

Rising out of his chair, Reynolds flashes his badge at Toby. "Paul Reynolds. South Carolina State Fire Marshal. I'm asking Ms. Summers a few simple questions."

"Should she have an attorney present?" Toby asks.

"Not unless she's guilty of a crime." Reynolds looks from Toby to Max. "Are you, Ms. Summers? Guilty of a crime?"

"Don't answer that," Toby orders Max. He stares intently at the fire inspector. "Have you confirmed that there is, in fact, a crime?"

"We have. We are treating the fire as arson."

"And what evidence do you have?" Toby asks.

"I'm not at liberty to say yet."

"Then this interrogation is over for now. If you need to question Ms. Summers further, clear it through me first."

Max looks up at Reynolds. "When can I get my things out of my apartment?"

Reynolds slams the cover on his iPad and tucks it under his

arm. "We should finish our investigation by the end of the day today." He starts toward the lobby and turns back around. "Oh, and Ms. Summers, don't leave town."

Max falls back in her chair. "This is bad, isn't it?"

Standing behind her, Toby massages her neck. "Only if you're guilty. Which you're not. I spoke with Jonathan Hart earlier. He gave me the contact information for his criminal attorney. Jonathan claims Charles Sullivan is one of the best. He tries cases all over the state."

She cranes her neck to look up at him. "If he's such a hotshot lawyer, why is he living on Palmetto Island?"

"I didn't ask. I imagine that, like most professionals who make our charming island their home, he prefers to spend his free time in a relaxing environment." He drops his hand from her neck. "I'll contact Sullivan and explain the situation. That way, if we need him, and hopefully we won't, he'll be ready to jump in."

She straightens in her chair. "Thank you."

He pats the top of her head. "I don't want you talking to anyone about this fire without an attorney present, understood?"

Planting her elbows on the table, she buries her face in her hands. "Understood."

"You need some fresh air. Come on, walk me out," he says, helping her to her feet.

"All right. I should check in with the hospital, anyway." She rests her head on his shoulder as they exit the lounge together. "You believe me, don't you, Toby?"

"You are innocent until proven guilty."

"Which means you have doubts about my innocence."

With a chuckle, he gives her a squeeze. "You're a good person, Maxie. I don't believe you would ever intentionally cause anyone any harm."

After saying goodbye to Toby on the sidewalk, she retrieves her own car from the garage and drives to the hospital. She called several times throughout the day for an update on Ron's condition, but she kept getting transferred from one nurse's desk to another without ever reaching the ICU.

Parking in the main lot, she takes the elevator to the second floor ICU where she finds a young nurse with a perky blonde ponytail willing to speak with her about Ron's condition.

"He's in a coma, and we're giving him oxygen. The tests show severe damage to his respiratory tract, which will heal over time. The most concerning issue for now is his TBI, traumatic brain injury. He developed a subdural hematoma. The doctor performed burr hole surgery to drain the blood. We should see some improvement soon."

Beads of sweat appear on Max's forehead. *Burr hole surgery. That doesn't sound good.* "Can I see him? I'm the closest thing to family he has."

"Sure, but only for a few minutes." The nurse shows Max to Ron's room. The shades are drawn, blocking out the afternoon sunlight. Ron's face is covered with an oxygen mask and the right side of his head is bandaged. His skin is pale and his closed eyes are dark holes.

Max lowers herself to the chair beside his bed. As she watches his chest rise and fall, she reflects on the events of the past twenty-four hours. *Arson.* Max didn't set the fire. But someone did. Ron is the only person she can think of who'd want to hurt her. Whether a premeditated act or a reckless decision made in a drunken stupor, he did it to get back at her for breaking up with him. But she refuses to take the fall for a crime he committed. Her guilt ebbs away, replaced by a surge of anger.

FIFTEEN

For much of the afternoon, Robin stands off to the side watching Amelia, Bebe, and the handymen do all the work. Amelia directs Sammy and Nathan as they move chairs and tables and chests over to the garage apartment while Bebe locates extra bed linens and bath towels, boxes of dishes and cookware. Digging deep in the attic, Amelia finds an upholstered headboard, a few colorful rugs to scatter about the floor, and a couple of paintings for the walls. Under the window at the south end of the attic, Amelia discovers a locked steamer trunk. Curiosity getting the best of her, she attempts to pick the lock with a hairpin to no avail.

After everyone has gone home, when Amelia and Robin are alone in the apartment, Amelia says, "Feels kinda homey, don't you think?"

Robin glares at her as she sucks on a lit cigarette. Blowing out smoke, she says, "Since you like it so much, why don't you live here, and I'll move into the main house?"

Amelia ignores her. "We'll stock your kitchen with groceries in the morning, but Bebe made her fabulous shrimp creole for our dinner. I thought we could eat on the porch. How does seven o'clock sound?"

"Fine," Robin says, putting out her cigarette and lighting another.

Amelia returns to the house and engages the alarm. With a cool cloth draped over her forehead, she soaks in her mother's spa tub until the water turns cold. Wrapping her damp hair in a towel, she slips on her silk robe and flips through the clothes in her mother's closet for something to wear for dinner. She finally decides on a sleeveless blue linen dress with deep pockets that will hide her gun.

At seven o'clock, Amelia is setting the table on the porch when Robin, dressed in white jeans and a pink tunic with her hair tied back at the nape of her neck, strolls across the lawn from the garage.

"Welcome." Amelia positions a bottle of wine over a stemless glass. "Would you like some wine?"

"Yes. Please."

Amelia plans to ply Robin with wine to find out more about the past. And Robin falls into her trap, slurping down the expensive Pinot Grigio like water. She drinks two glasses during the salad course, and when Amelia goes to the kitchen for the shrimp creole, she returns with their plates and another bottle of wine.

As she's refilling Robin's glass, in a casual manner, she asks, "When did you say you arrived on the island?"

"I didn't say. I read the obituary in the Charleston paper on Friday and took the bus down early Saturday morning."

Amelia sips her wine as she watches Robin shovel the shrimp creole into her mouth as though she's never seen food before. "I don't remember much about the night you ran away. If you feel up to talking about it, I'd like to hear what happened."

Robin freezes, her fork an inch from her mouth. "You mean you don't know? I figured Mama brainwashed you against me."

"On the contrary. Mama refused to talk about you. I think it was too painful for her. I want to understand, Robin. You can trust me."

"I learned a long time ago never to trust anyone." She scrapes the food off her fork with her teeth and sets down her utensil. "My story isn't any different than thousands of others. I was a teenager constantly at odds with my parents. Mom and Dad rode me hard about everything. My grades weren't good enough, and they hated my friends. One night I finally snapped. I'd had enough. We got into a fight about something stupid. I don't even remember what. And they kicked me out."

Amelia sets down her wineglass and leans in closer. In a conspiratorial tone, she says, "Surely there's more to it than that."

"There's plenty more to it than that, Mila. Mama worshipped you. You're the spitting image of her. But she couldn't stand the sight of me, her unattractive oldest daughter who caused her nothing but heartache."

Amelia's jaw drops. "What? That's preposterous."

Robin rakes the last of her rice and shrimp onto her fork and stuffs it in her mouth. "Did she leave me anything in her will?"

Amelia remembers what Bebe said earlier. *She wants something. And you and I both know what that something is.* Robin is homeless. Of course, she wants money. Deep down, Amelia had hoped there would be something more to Robin's sudden reappearance. That maybe her sister wanted to reconcile with her family. Robin will be furious when she learns Amelia inherited Dottie's entire estate. Is her sister dangerous? The jury's still out.

Robin brings her fist crashing down on the table. "Damn it, Mila. It's a simple yes or no question. Did Mama leave me anything in her will?"

Amelia wraps her hand around the hard object in her pocket. "It may be a simple yes or no question. But I don't have the answer. We haven't had the official reading of the will. You should talk to Mama's lawyer. I can give you his contact information."

Robin pushes abruptly back from the table. "You're lying.

Mama didn't leave me a dime. I'm tired of playing second fiddle to you. Look at you." She sweeps her arm wide, wine sloshing over the rim of the glass. "Living in this big house all alone while I'm banished to the garage apartment. You've had a life of wealth and privilege, while I've been living like a pauper, struggling to make ends meet. I want what's rightfully mine. And I'm not going away until I get it."

Snatching the nearly full bottle of wine, Robin stumbles back to the garage. She's sending a clear message to Amelia. She'll take whatever she wants, whatever Robin deems as rightfully hers.

The tiny hairs at the nape of Amelia's neck stand to attention. On the one hand, Amelia feels guilty for all she's been given while Robin was forced out of her home at age eighteen. *Mama worshipped you. But she couldn't stand the sight of me. You've had a life of wealth and privilege while I've been living like a pauper.* On the other hand, her mother would never have cut Robin out of her will without good reason. Amelia's choices are clear. Either find out the truth about the past or share her inheritance with Robin.

Amelia stacks the dirty plates and takes them inside to the kitchen. After rinsing and placing them in the dishwasher, she secures the house, turns on the alarm, and retreats to her father's study. Seated at his desk, she combs through the contents of his drawers, including every single sheet of paper in his many files. She finds birth certificates—Amelia's and her parents' but not Robin's. Dottie's birth certificate shows her birthplace as Texas, not Alabama, where her mother claimed to be from. And she discovers something curious on her father's death certificate. The cause of death is listed as *pending investigation.* Why is that when her father died from a heart attack?

Amelia picks up the photograph of her parents on their honeymoon. *Why the secrets? What happened all those years ago? Tell me what I need to know.*

Amelia props her feet on the desk and turns on the television.

She doesn't have to wait long for news of her husband. Nelson's candidacy is still in the headlines. The attractive brunette reports, "In other news today, Nelson Archer announced that Richard Fletcher will head up his campaign."

Amelia rolls her eyes. No surprises there. Richard Fletcher is Nelson's right-hand man. But this is good news for Amelia. Nelson is focused on his campaign instead of her. At least for the time being.

Flipping to the local news, she's shocked to see a video of Max's hotel surrounded by fire trucks. The newscaster says, "The Palmetto Hotel is closed for the remainder of the season after Tuesday night's fire. The origin of the fire is under investigation. Sources tell WB12 News that a guest, a man identified as Ron Morton from Pennsylvania, is currently fighting for his life after suffering extensive smoke inhalation."

Amelia throws her feet off the desk and brings her chair upright. She thinks back to Ron's drunken display on Tuesday night. Had he passed out and somehow been trapped inside the burning building?

Poor Max. Amelia will check in on her in the morning. After she takes care of a little business. She sends Jonathan a text. *I have an urgent matter to discuss with you. Can we meet first thing in the morning?*

Despite the late hour, he responds immediately. *Is eight o'clock too early?*

Eight is perfect. See you then.

Taking her empty glass to the kitchen, she drags herself up to bed. She pauses at the security control panel to engage the motion detectors before continuing on to the bathroom. Amelia is brushing her teeth when the brass tray where her mother organized her beauty products catches her attention. The brass tray is empty now, and Amelia is certain the tray was empty when she arrived in town on Friday night. She thinks back to the expensive night creams and cosmetics she saw lining the counter in Robin's bathroom. Her mother's products. Her sister claims she came to Palmetto Island on Saturday morning. But this proves she got into town ahead of Amelia. Question is, how long has she been here?

She remembers what Bebe said about Dottie. *Miss Dottie was quieter than usual the weeks before she died. I doubt it had anything to do with her health. She looked wonderful and was active as ever. But she seemed distracted.*

What if Robin has been in town for a while? Did she see their mother? Did they spend time together? Did they fight? Did Robin threaten Dottie like she threatened Amelia tonight?

SIXTEEN

After unpacking her things in Birdie's spare bedroom, Max finds her way down to the cafe and joins her party already seated at a table on the railing. Birdie's daughter, Hannah, is like a daughter to Max, and Max finds Hannah's new boyfriend charming, but she struggles to stay focused on the conversation. Her gaze frequently drifts to the darkened windows in her hotel. Her heart aches for the dozens of guests whose annual vacations have been ruined because of the fire.

Hannah jerks Max out of her trance with an elbow to the ribs. "What do you think, Max?"

Max looks over at her, confused. "Huh?"

Hannah eyes Max's plate. "The soft-shell crabs. What do you think about the special?"

Max stares down at her untouched food. "Oh. Looks good." She forks off a bite and slides it into her mouth. The soft-shells are sauteed to the ideal level of crispiness, and the dab of tangy sauce adds the desired flavor. "Delicious. Your new chef is a genius, Birdie. Pay her whatever it takes to keep her."

All eyes travel to the attractive young woman in the chef's

coat working her way through the restaurant, pausing at each table to speak to the diners.

"Trust me," Birdie says, "I'm so blessed to have found her. Not only is Sydney creative, but she's also organized, efficient, and pleasant."

"She's so young to be so talented." Hannah studies the chef. "How old is she?"

"Your age," Birdie says of Hannah's twenty-five years.

"What's she doing working *here*?" Hannah asks, as though Palmetto Island were an undesirable place to work.

Ethan nudges Hannah. "I remember, less than two months ago, having to drag you off this island kicking and screaming."

Everyone erupts in laughter.

Sydney approaches their table. "Are you enjoying your dinner?"

They respond at once with praise.

"How are things in the kitchen?" Birdie asks.

"Running smoothly."

"Where are you from, Sydney?" Hannah asks in a friendly manner.

"All over, really. My father was in the military." Sydney glances at the next table over. "I'd better see to the other guests. Be sure to order the blueberry cobbler for dessert."

Hannah waits until Sydney is out of earshot. "The father-in-the-military story is code for she's hiding something," she says in a lowered voice.

Ethan laughs. "There you go again." He turns his attention to Birdie. "Your daughter missed her calling. She should've been a mystery writer."

Birdie smiles softly at Hannah. "She can do anything she sets her creative mind to. But don't go giving up your day job just yet."

Hannah's olive-green eyes light up. "No way! Everything is finally falling into place with my business. I have an amazing partner. And we're getting new clients every day. At this rate, we'll need to hire another graphic designer soon."

Max leans in close to Hannah. "Tell me about Gus. I miss his sweet little face so much."

Hannah pulls out her phone to show Max the most recent photographs of her son.

"What happened to his glorious curls?" Max asks, touching her fingers to her lips. "He's no longer a toddler but a little boy."

Hannah runs her finger over Gus's image on the screen. "I know. It's sad, isn't it? But I had no choice. He needed a haircut."

Hannah hands Max the phone, and she swipes through the photographs. "Where is the mischievous little bugger tonight?"

"Hope, my downstairs neighbor, is keeping him. Her four-year-old daughter, Sally, is Gus's new best friend."

Ethan chimes in, "Sally rules the roost. And Gus worships her. She keeps him in line."

Hannah laughs. "True. Gus has met his match in Sally."

When Ethan excuses himself to go to the restroom, Max leans across the table to Hannah. "He's adorable. I hope you're planning to marry him."

Hannah beams red. "We've only been dating a short time. We're enjoying the newness of our relationship. I don't wanna ruin it by prematurely talking about a future together."

Birdie winks at her daughter. "Smart girl. Take your time."

"What does Gus think about Ethan?" Max asks.

"Gus adores him," Hannah says. "And Ethan is really good with him."

"What's the latest from Ryan?" Birdie asks of Gus's biological father who recently came into his life. "Has he pursued a custody arrangement?"

"Ryan is getting married," Hannah announces. "I get the impression his fiancée, Danielle, isn't thrilled about being a step-mom. I don't know how much Ryan will be a part of Gus's life. Which makes me sad for Gus."

Ethan returns from the restroom, and the waiter delivers dessert. Max is eating her last bite of blueberry cobbler when she notices Paul Reynolds at the hostess stand. Max pushes abruptly back from the table and marches over to him. "What're you doing here?"

"Following up on a lead. I heard your boyfriend caused quite a scene here last night." He nods at Kathleen, the hostess. "I was asking this young lady to fill in the details."

"Do you have to do this now?" Max gestures at the bustling cafe. "As you can see, Birdie has a full house. Can't it wait until tomorrow?

"This is a matter of some urgency, Ms. Summers. I'm trying to wrap up this investigation. I would think you, of all people, being the proprietor of the hotel, would understand that. Unless you're trying to cover up something?"

Max's lips flatten and her nostrils flare. "I resent that, Mr. Reynolds. I want to find out who started the fire more than anyone. I assume Ron is a suspect as well. How can you wrap up your investigation until he wakes up from his coma?"

Taking Max by the arm, Reynolds leads her away from the hostess stand to the railing overlooking the marina. "I'll be honest with you, Ms. Summers. *You* are my primary suspect."

Max remembers what Toby said. *I don't want you talking to anyone about this fire without an attorney present.* She's had enough wine, she doesn't care what her nephews says. She's innocent. And she aims to prove it. "Why are you so certain I started the fire and not Ron?"

"Because he was passed out at the time."

"And I was sleeping in a room on the first floor. The scenario makes perfect sense to me. Ron had motive. He wanted to get back at me for breaking up with him. He fell and hit his head on his way back to my apartment after starting the fire. How was the fire started, Mr. Reynolds?"

Reynolds's dark eyes are black stones. "Why don't you tell me, Ms. Summers?"

"I have no clue. I wouldn't know how to go about starting a fire."

He lets out a grunt. "Cut the act and save us both some time."

"You're trying to pin this crime on me so you can go home to Columbia. Well, it won't work, because I didn't set that fire."

"Why don't you have surveillance cameras in your hotel, Ms. Summers?" Reynolds asks in an accusatory tone.

Max throws her hands in the air. "So now my lack of security cameras is part of my conspiracy to burn down my hotel. To answer your question, I haven't needed surveillance cameras until now. My guests are family-oriented, law-abiding citizens. But a security system upgrade is in the works for the renovations."

Before he can respond, Max turns her back on the fire marshal and storms off. Instead of returning to the table, she passes through the cafe and kitchen and climbs the back stairs to Birdie's apartment. She calls the hospital, and this time, she's put through to the ICU. When she inquires about Ron's condition, the nurse tells her there's been no change.

Max stays awake half the night, trying to figure out a way to prove her innocence. Even if he's guilty, Ron, if he ever wakes up, will deny starting the fire. What if his brain injury affects his memory? They may never know what happened on the fourth floor last night. If a prosecutor can prove Max is guilty, that she either set the fire for the insurance money or intended to get back at her abusive boyfriend, she could go to prison for the rest of her life.

SEVENTEEN

Amelia is standing at the window in Jonathan's office when he arrives on Thursday morning.

"I hope you haven't been waiting long." He hangs his saddlebag on his desk chair and joins her at the window.

"Only a few minutes." She glances over at him and then returns her gaze to the inlet. "Do you ever get tired of the view?"

"Never. Some may take the beauty of God's earth for granted, but I count my blessings every single day."

Amelia turns to face him. "Thank you for fitting me in. Something has come up and I need your advice."

"Certainly." He motions her to the chair opposite his desk, and they sit down across from one another. "Now, tell me, what's this about?"

"My sister," she says and watches closely for Jonathan's response.

He appears genuinely surprised. "Your sister? Miss Dottie never mentioned another daughter. Do you mean stepsister?"

Amelia shakes her head. "Robin is my sister, my parents' biological child. She's ten years older than me. She ran away from home the summer before she was to go off to college."

As the words leave her lips, angry voices fill Amelia's head. Robin's desire to go to college in California had been the source of many arguments with their parents. Her sister had been hell-bent on attending school on the West Coast while her parents had argued one of the southern SEC universities would be a better fit. Based on her fascination with California, the West Coast would have been the logical place for Robin to go when she ran away. Her mother knew where to look for her. Why didn't she? Or did she find her and choose not to bring her home?

Amelia feels Jonathan's eyes on her, waiting for her to continue. "We never heard from my sister again. At least I didn't. Mama may have. I always assumed she was dead. But she's very much alive and staying in our garage apartment."

"At Point Pleasant?" Jonathan taps the desk with his finger. "On Palmetto Island?"

Amelia nods. "She just showed up out of the blue."

"On the heels of your mother's funeral? I'm sorry, Amelia, but that's not a coincidence."

"I actually saw her *at* the funeral. I just didn't know who she was." Amelia fills Jonathan in on the details. She tells him about Robin hiding out in the garage apartment, breaking into the house to steal food, and insisting she came to the island on Saturday when the presence of the beauty products in the garage apartment proves she's been here longer. "Bebe says Mama was withdrawn the weeks leading up to her death. What if she knew Robin was in town? Or worse, if Robin had somehow threatened her? Are you absolutely positive Mama never mentioned Robin to you?"

Jonathan holds up three fingers in scout's honor. "I would not have overlooked important information like that."

"Did Mama leave any documents or papers with you for safe-keeping?"

He opens a desk drawer and removes a thick hanging file. "All the documents I have on file pertain to her estate. I was planning to wait until later in the week, but given the circumstances, we should go over the particulars of her will now."

Jonathan slides a stapled sheath of papers across the desk to Amelia, and for the next half hour, they discuss the disbursement of her mother's assets. Every bequest is straightforward. Aside from sizable gifts to Bebe and Dottie's favorite nonprofit organizations, Amelia inherits the bulk of the estate.

"Robin said last night at dinner that she wants what's rightfully hers." Amelia hooks her fingers in air quotes. "Which I translate to mean she feels entitled to a portion of Mama's estate. Normally, I would agree with her, but . . ." Amelia's voice trails off.

"But what, Amelia?" Her name is soft on his lips. She remembers how popular Jonathan was amongst their classmates in high school. Not because he was good-looking and athletic, but because he was a true friend, someone they could trust. No wonder he turned out to be a successful estate attorney.

"It was Mama's choice not to include Robin in the will. And it's her money. Who am I to go against her wishes? On the other hand, I have more money than I can ever spend, and Robin is penniless. She's my sister, my blood relative. How can I turn her away with nothing?"

Jonathan closes her mother's file. "You could give Robin a lump sum of money, a settlement of sorts."

"I thought about that. But what happens when that money runs out? What's to stop her from coming back for more?"

"You make her sign a legal document stipulating this is a onetime gift."

"Something tells me that won't be enough for Robin. I get the impression she wants Point Pleasant. And I refuse to give her my family's home. Then again, it's her family's home too." Amelia slides back in her chair. "What a mess. What do I do, Jonathan?"

"You figure out why your mother cut Robin out of her will. That should help you decide how to proceed."

"I'm working on that. I found our birth certificates, my parents and mine, but not Robin's, which is why I asked if Mama ever gave you any documents for safekeeping."

He frowns. "That's strange."

"And that's not all. There's more to the story of Robin's disappearance than Mama led me to believe. I need answers. And I intend to get them." A thought occurs to Amelia. "I wonder if your sister knew Robin in high school. Maybe Frances remembers something that might help?"

"Robin would've been older than Frances. But I have to drive Frances to the airport in Charleston later this morning. I'll talk to her about it then."

Amelia stands to go. "That would be great."

Jonathan comes from behind his desk. "I'm worried about you, Amelia. Is there any chance you're in danger? Do you think Robin might hurt you in any way?"

"I can take care of myself." She pats her handbag. "I have a handgun and a permit to carry. Speaking of which, do you know if there's a shooting range nearby?"

"Actually, I have one on my property. I live on a spread of land a few miles outside of town. I'm busy all day, but we can meet there after work."

"Perfect." She flashes Dottie's phone. "You can text me the address on Mama's phone." When he gives her a quizzical look, she adds, "I lost my phone. I haven't replaced it yet."

"Funny how addicted we are to our phones. I'm glad you're able to use Dottie's as a backup." He walks her to the door. "So, I'll see you around six?"

"That works. I'm off to check on Max. She must be devastated about the fire."

Jonathan drops his smile. "Unfortunately, Max is in a bit of a pickle at the moment."

"How so?"

"She . . ." He stops himself. "It's probably best if she tells you about it."

———

Max is stationed behind the coffee bar when Amelia enters the cafe. "Max, I'm so sorry about the hotel. I only learned about it late last night on the news."

Max's throat thickens. "Thank you. I'm trying to look at the bright side. This speeds up the process for the renovations."

Amelia studies the chalkboard menu on the wall behind Max. "I'd like to order a coffee. Can you get that for me?"

"Of course. Birdie put me to work. I was driving her crazy with all my nervous energy. What would you like?"

"A large black coffee, please. The hazelnut blend."

Max turns her back on Amelia while she pours coffee into a to-go cup. She slides the coffee across the counter.

Amelia removes her credit card from her wallet. "How much do I owe you?"

"Nothing," Max says. "It's on the house."

"Thank you," Amelia says, and returns her wallet to her bag. "Will your boss allow you to take a break? I'd like to hear more about the fire."

"Birdie and I were talking about going for a walk, if you care to join us."

"Of course," Amelia says. "Do you have someone to cover the coffee bar for you?"

"Heather's here," Max says, gesturing at the teenager behind the pastry counter. "Let me grab Birdie, and we'll meet you out front."

Max pours two more coffees and goes in search of Birdie. She finds her in the small office off the kitchen. "Amelia's here. Is now a good time for our walk?"

"Sure." Birdie comes from behind her desk. "I could use a break."

Birdie and Max join Amelia in front of the cafe, and the three women head west past the park toward Ocean Avenue.

"They mentioned an investigation on the news last night," Amelia says. "Do the police think it was arson?"

"Unfortunately," Max says. "And I'm their primary suspect."

"Why you?" Amelia asks. "What about Ron?"

"Ron is in a coma," she says, and explains the extent of his injuries. "The fire investigator claims I have more motive than Ron, that I need the insurance money for my renovations. You have no idea how terrifying it is to be accused of something and not be able to prove your innocence."

"I can't imagine," Amelia says, shaking her head. "Do you have an attorney?"

"Toby is working on that for me. Apparently, Jonathan has a good criminal attorney at his firm. Can we please talk about something else?"

They fall into silence as they cross over Ocean Avenue. When they stop to look in the window at Leslie's Boutique, Amelia says, "I have news."

"I hope it's good news," Birdie says. "We could use some."

"Depends on how you look at it. My sister is back in town."

Max's jaw hits the sidewalk. "Robin? Your long-lost sister, Robin?"

"She's the only sister I have," Amelia says. "She's been hiding out in our garage apartment. I'm not sure how long she's been there."

Max snaps her fingers. "That explains the flash of light I saw in the window."

Amelia nods. "My father's cigarette lighter. She stole it from his study. She's a chain smoker."

"What does she want?" Birdie asks.

"A portion of Mama's estate," Amelia says and starts walking again.

Max and Birdie exchange a look before hurrying to catch up with Amelia. "Did your mama not provide for Robin in her will?"

"Max!" Birdie says in a warning tone. "That's none of our business."

"I don't mind," Amelia says to Birdie and to Max, "Mama didn't leave her a dime. And I don't blame her. We've neither seen nor heard from Robin since the night my daddy died."

They reach the end of the block and cut back over to the waterfront. Amelia drains the rest of her coffee and tosses her cup in a nearby trash can. "I remember so little about that night. Mama always told me my father suffered a heart attack during an argument with Robin. And that my sister got scared and ran away. But I sense there's more to it than that. Do either of you remember anything about those events?"

"Let me see," Birdie says, tugging at her chin. "I remember going to your father's funeral. And being sad for you when I saw you crying. And I remember my mama telling me something really bad had happened to Robin."

Amelia narrows her blue eyes. "Something bad had *happened* to her. Or that she'd done something bad?"

Birdie repeats, "Something bad had happened to her."

Max says, "I don't remember specifics, but that was my impression as well."

Amelia stops at the railing to look at the boats in the marina. "What do you remember about Robin?"

"That she was a bully," Max says. "She used to call us names. I was twerp and Birdie was pipsqueak."

Birdie says, "I remember Robin hitting on you a lot. You always had enormous bruises on your upper arms."

Max looks down at her feet. "I'll admit it. I was downright afraid of your sister."

Birdie gives Max a playful slap on the back. "Which is saying something. I've never known you to be afraid of anyone."

"Except the fire marshal," Max says under her breath.

Continuing on to the park, the three old friends sit down together on a bench.

"How are you going to handle Robin?" Max asks.

"There's a lot I can't remember about the past," Amelia says. "Before I do anything, I need to learn as much as I can about my family's history."

Max spots Paul Reynolds emerging from the parking deck with two firefighters. Reynolds sees Max. "There she is!" he says, and the three men increase their pace, jogging toward them.

Max's body goes still. "Uh-oh. Incoming trouble."

Reynolds stops in front of her. "Maxine Summers, you're under arrest for first degree arson." Taking her by the arm, he pulls her to her feet and twirls her around. He's placing handcuffs on her wrists when a black unmarked car, a single blue light flashing through the windshield, whips around the corner and drives down the sidewalk to the park. Her nephew gets out on the passenger side, and the man Max knows to be his most trusted detective, Jared Carlson, crawls out from behind the wheel.

Toby yells, "Reynolds! Take your hands off her."

Reynolds hollers back. "I warned you, Chief. This is my case."

Toby lumbers over to the fire inspector. "And I warned you, this is my jurisdiction."

Reynolds glowers at Toby. "She's your aunt. You're obligated to recuse yourself from the case."

"I have recused myself," Toby says. "I'm placing my detective, Jared Carlson, in charge. He'll handle the booking. Handcuffs won't be necessary."

Max's heart skips a beat. *Booking?*

Jared steps toward her and removes the handcuffs.

Rubbing her wrists, Max says, "Are you seriously arresting me? What about Ron? He's still in a coma. How do you know he didn't start the fire?"

Toby hangs his head. "I'm sorry, Maxie. All the evidence points at you."

EIGHTEEN

Amelia and Birdie watch Max drive off in the back seat of the unmarked car.

"This is bad," Amelia says.

Birdie nods. "Really bad."

"We should do something," Amelia says. "Although I have no idea what."

Birdie swipes at her eyes. "She's in good hands with Toby."

They part with a hug, and Amelia watches Birdie walk slowly back to the cafe.

Amelia fights back her own tears as she drives home to Point Pleasant. Much has changed on Palmetto Island in her absence. But not her two best friends. Despite the decades that separate them, she knows Max and Birdie. They are two of the finest people she's ever known. Amelia doesn't need evidence as proof. She knows in her heart that Max did not start that fire.

Amelia unlocks the back door, disengages the security system on the panel in the mudroom, and goes in search of Bebe. She finds her dusting in the living room. "I'm glad you had the alarm on. We should utilize the security system as much as possible while Robin is staying in the garage apartment."

Bebe stops dusting. "Does this mean your sister has shown her true colors?"

"Enough for me to have serious concerns about her. Hopefully she won't be here long."

Bebe snorts. "She'll be here forever if she has her way about it."

"Trust me, Bebe. I'm not going to let that happen."

Bebe's chin drops to her chest. "What're you up to, baby girl?"

"Sit with me for a minute and I'll tell you." Dropping to the sofa, Amelia pulls Bebe down beside her. "I'm trying to figure out a few things about the past. What can you tell me about the night my father died?"

"Well, this is what I remember." Placing the duster in her lap, Bebe sits back against the sofa cushions. "Your mama called me shortly after midnight and told me to come pick you up. When I got here, the place was swarming with police cars and other rescue vehicles. The two of you were waiting for me at the end of the driveway. Miss Dottie asked me to take you home with me. She said for you not to watch the news, and she would come for you in a few days, after the dust settled."

Amelia stares up at the ceiling as the memories return. "I remember being at your house. You live on a creek, and we went fishing off your dock. You had a cocker spaniel named Millie."

Bebe grins. "That's right. Millie took an instant liking to you. She moped for days after you left."

"How long did I stay with you?"

"For four days. You were one sad little girl. Every night, you cried yourself to sleep and woke frequently from bad dreams. I'm not sure how much you witnessed that night. You refused to talk about what had happened to your father and Robin."

"Mama told me Daddy died from a heart attack, but the cause of death on his birth certificate says pending investigation."

"Mm-hmm. What did your mama tell you about your sister's disappearance?"

"That she ran away."

"I suspected as much." Bebe fingers the duster. "I did as Miss Dottie asked. I never once turned on the television while you were in my care, but I read the newspaper after you went to bed every night. According to the reporters, an intruder broke into your house, stabbed your father to death, and kidnapped Robin."

Birdie's words come back to Amelia. *I remember my mama telling me something really bad had happened to Robin.* But murder and kidnapping? "How can that be, Bebe? Surely I would've remembered something so traumatic."

"Not if you didn't see it with your own eyes. Your mama sheltered you from the truth. The day after your daddy's funeral, she swept you away to England. You two were gone for over a month. The scandal had blown over by the time you returned."

Amelia smiles. "We went several times to England to see Mama's friend, Miss Janie. I remember she lived on a beautiful estate in the country. She taught me to ride." Her smile fades. "But why would Mama leave the country if Robin had been kidnapped? Wouldn't she wanna be here if the kidnappers demanded ransom?"

"Not if there were no kidnappers." Bebe leaves the sofa and returns to dusting the books on the shelves on either side of the fireplace. "I have a theory. I think Robin stabbed your father and ran away. And Miss Dottie made up the kidnapping story to protect her daughter."

"That's a serious allegation, Bebe. Robin was only eighteen years old."

Bebe dusts with fury. "Robin ain't right in the head. She's dangerous. Which is why I want her off this property."

Looking through the french doors, Amelia notices Robin marching across the lawn toward the house. "Speak of the devil.

Here she comes. I forgot I promised to take her to the grocery store."

Bebe cuts her eyes at Amelia. "I don't like the idea of you being in the same car with her."

"I'll be fine." Amelia kisses Bebe's cheek, grabs her purse, and goes out the back door, heading Robin off before she reaches the house. "I was just coming to find you. Are you ready to go to the grocery store?"

"I've been ready," Robin snaps. "I've been waiting all morning."

"I'm sorry. My friend had an emergency. But we can go now."

"Fine," Robin says and takes off ahead of Amelia toward their mother's convertible.

Amelia gets into the car and starts the engine. She's no sooner left the driveway when Robin lights up a cigarette. "Please don't smoke in the car."

"Then I'll put the roof down," Robin says, and begins pushing random buttons on the dash.

Amelia brushes Robin's hand away from the dash. "Not in the midday sun."

"What-ever." Robin rolls down the window and flicks out the cigarette. After adjusting the seat for several minutes, she scans stations on the radio.

Amelia's nerves are raw. First Max's arrest and now her skittish sister. "Just pick one and leave it."

She lands on Y2Kountry. "I hope you like country."

Amelia manages a smile. "Anything is fine."

"Never mind. I hate it. Too many sad stories and sickly sweet voices." Robin fusses with the controls again until she finds a classic rock station.

Robin shifts in her seat, crossing and uncrossing her legs, and then rummages through her pocketbook for their father's lighter. She flicks it repeatedly until Amelia finally snatches it away from her.

"Give me that. What is wrong with you? Why are you so fidgety today?"

"I don't know. Just my nature, I guess."

Amelia makes a right-hand turn into the grocery store parking lot. "You should exercise more. It helps get rid of nervous energy."

"I don't like to sweat."

Amelia turns off the engine. "Who says you have to sweat? You could swim or walk on the beach or do yoga."

"No thanks. Not everyone likes to be in shape like you." They get out of the car and walk toward the store together. "I've known starvation before, Mila. It gives new meaning to being thin. While you may think it fashionable, I think you look disgusting."

"I wasn't suggesting you lose weight, Robin. I was merely pointing out that exercise might help calm your nerves."

"My nerves don't need calming. This is who I am. Like it or leave it."

Inside the store, Robin gives Amelia a cart and takes one for herself. "Why do we need two carts when we're only shopping for one?" Amelia asks.

"I have a long list."

They start in the produce section and work their way through the store. True to her word, Robin fills both carts with more food than one person can eat in a year, including three boxes of cheap wine and a carton of cigarettes. At the checkout counter, her purchases add up to over five hundred dollars.

Amelia holds her tongue as she inserts her credit card into the card reader. At least she won't feel obligated to invite Robin to dinner again.

Back at the house, she parks in front of the garage and helps her sister carry the bags of groceries to her apartment. She opens her wallet and removes two hundred dollars in cash. "Here, I want you to have this if you need anything else."

Robin snatches the wad of twenties. "You owe me a lot more than two hundred dollars. And I aim to collect."

"I don't owe you anything, Robin." Amelia points at the money. "That is *my* money. Not Mama's. And that was *my* money I spent at the grocery store. So, don't you dare threaten me."

Spinning on her heels, Amelia storms out of the apartment. Her world is closing in on her, and she's running out of time. Her husband could come for her as soon as tomorrow, and with Robin breathing down her neck about the inheritance, she needs answers now.

NINETEEN

Toby shifts in his seat to look at Max in the back. "You doing okay?"

"No, I'm not okay. None of this makes sense. Why are they arresting me?"

Toby lets out a sigh. "They claim they have evidence against you, Maxie."

"How can they have evidence, when I didn't commit a crime?"

"You had motive," Jared says, his eyes on the road. "The building is in a state of serious disrepair. It won't take much to prove you set the building on fire in order to get the insurance money for the renovations."

Through gritted teeth, Max says, "For the thousandth time, I don't need the insurance money. I've been approved by the bank for a loan that covers all the construction costs."

Jared says, "If you'll provide your loan officer's contact information, I'll be sure to speak with him."

"I'm texting Toby *her* contact information now." Max's fingers fly across her phone screen as she accesses the contact and forwards it to Toby. She looks up from her phone. "Ron had motive too, you know," Max says. "He was trying to get back at me for breaking up with him."

"That motive will be more difficult to sell to a jury," Jared says. "Who puts people's lives in danger because their feelings are hurt about a breakup?"

"Criminals. Have you done a background check on Ron?" When the two men remain silent, Max says, "I take that as a no. I've tried to find out more information about him. The man doesn't exist. At least not on social media."

"Maybe you should've checked him out before you asked him to move in with you," Toby says.

Max sends death daggers to the back of her nephew's head. "Whose side are you on, Toby?"

"The side of the law," he snaps.

Max asks, "How was the fire even started? No one will tell me."

Toby looks over at Jared who shakes his head. "Reynolds will talk about that during your interrogation," Jared says.

"So, you know, but you won't tell me," Max says.

"It's better if we don't talk about the case until after you've spoken to your attorney." Toby looks at her over his shoulder. "Look, Maxie. I promise not to throw you to the wolves. We *will* get to the bottom of this."

Max's stomach knots when they pull into the parking lot at the police station. "Will I have to spend the night in jail?"

"No. After you're processed, you'll meet with your attorney, and together, you'll talk to Paul Reynolds. Accompanied by your attorney, you'll appear in court this afternoon. You'll plead not guilty, the judge will suggest bail, and you will post it. You'll be home in time for dinner."

"I no longer have a home," she mumbles under her breath.

Her nephew may have her best interests at heart, but if Reynolds has evidence that points the finger at her, there is nothing Toby can do to save her.

The booking process runs smoothly. Two female officers, Campbell and Ward, having been told about her relationship with the chief, treat her with kid gloves. They fingerprint her, photograph her, and inventory the contents of her purse. Afterward, she's shown to an interrogation room where her attorney is waiting.

Charles Sullivan greets Max with a smile that lights up his green eyes. Max guesses him to be in his midthirties, which in her opinion is way too young to try hardened criminals in court.

Sullivan motions her to a chair opposite him at the rectangular wooden table. "Before we meet with the fire marshal, I'd like to hear your side of the story."

Max walks him through the events of the past week, beginning with the day Ron bruised her wrists and ending with being awakened by the fire alarm in the early hours of the morning on Wednesday.

Sullivan wears a serious expression as they discuss her case. He's articulate and knowledgeable, and Max's anxiety lessens as her faith in him grows. "How much wine did you have at dinner?" he asks.

"Not much. A couple of glasses over the course of several hours."

Propping his elbows on the table, he laces his fingers together. "And you're absolutely certain you didn't go up to the fourth floor after you returned to the hotel."

"I'm positive. My night guest services manager can confirm that."

Sullivan sits back in his chair. "The fire investigator believes someone hit Ron Morgan from behind with a blunt object. He's implying that *that* someone is you."

Max's brow hits her hairline. "That's absurd."

Sullivan holds his hand out. "Don't worry, Max. He has no proof. It's purely speculation at this point."

"I've visited Ron in the hospital. His wound is on the side of his head. Seems to me, if someone attacked Ron from behind, his injury would be to the back of his head?"

Sullivan considers this. "That would make sense to me."

"I've been in my apartment since the fire, Mr. Sullivan. I've seen the bloodstain on the carpet beside one of the sofa's end tables. That table has a marble top with a very sharp edge. Many witnesses can testify to Ron's drunkenness that night. I saw him myself. I'm telling you, he stumbled and fell and hit his head."

Sullivan is quiet for a long minute. "As your attorney, it's my responsibility to play devil's advocate. Was Ron too drunk to start a fire?"

"I wouldn't know, since no one has bothered to tell me how the fire started."

The door swings open, and Reynolds sticks his head in the room. "Is now a good time?"

Sullivan says, "Give us a few more minutes, please."

But Max jumps to her feet. "Actually, now is the perfect time. We were just discussing how the fire started. I'd like to know what it is I'm being accused of, because I don't have a clue."

Reynolds strides into the room with Jared on his heels. Sullivan moves to Max's side of the table and the detective and fire investigator sit down opposite them. Reynold says, "You can cut the innocent act, Ms. Summers. No one is buying it. According to the toxicology report, Ron Morgan was way too drunk to fashion the complicated device used to start the fire."

"Which was?"

"Two graphite pencils sharpened on both ends," Reynolds says. "A copper penny was held between the pencils at one end with a rubber band while the other ends were inserted into an electrical outlet located behind a bed in one of your guest rooms."

Max laughs out loud. "Are you kidding me, right now? If I

were going to start a fire, I would use gasoline. Devising some crazy gadget like that would never cross my mind."

Reynold's smirk is malicious. "The browser history on your iPad shows that you spent several hours researching different methods of starting fires."

"My iPad?" Max repeats. "I only use my iPad to read. And I've been so busy, I haven't picked it up in weeks."

"That's a likely story," Reynolds says.

"I resent your insinuation, Mr. Reynolds. I am not a liar." Max jabs her finger at him. "If you've done your homework, you're aware that Ron has been staying in my apartment for weeks. He had plenty of access to my iPad. I admit, I failed to create a password for the device. I never felt the need to. But that is the only thing I'm guilty of in this situation." She pushes back from the table, knocking her chair over. "I'm done here."

Reynolds leaps to his feet. "You're not calling the shots, Ms. Summers."

Max sets her eyes on him and holds her gaze steady. "Like hell I'm not."

Sullivan gathers his belongings. "Excuse us, gentlemen. We're due in court."

Thirty minutes later, as Max pleads not guilty to the judge, the enormity of the situation hits her like a ten-ton wrecking ball. This is real. Paul Reynolds is determined to pin this crime on her. She can't count on Toby and Jared to save her. She has to find a way to save herself.

TWENTY

Jonathan is waiting for Amelia in a rocker on the wraparound porch of his Lowcountry farmhouse. "Afternoon," he says, coming down off the porch to greet her. "Did you have any trouble finding the place?"

"None at all. This is spectacular." She turns in a circle as she takes in the house and dock extending over the marsh to a narrow creek. "How many acres do you have?"

"Twenty. I look forward to coming home to peace and quiet after a long day at the office."

She pauses, listening to the crickets chirping nearby. "Definitely relaxing. Point Pleasant is peaceful in a different way. The waves crashing in the background are our white noise."

"Point Pleasant is a unique property. Miss Dottie loved her home. I hope you'll have many happy days there in the years to come."

"That's a lovely thing to say." Amelia won't let herself think about a happy future. Not until she's dealt with her sister and her husband. "Are you ready to shoot?"

"I am. Did you bring your weapon? Or would you like to borrow one of mine?"

"I brought my own. Along with a box of ammo." Amelia retrieves her bag from the car. "Lead the way," she says, and follows him to the edge of a cornfield where targets of all shapes and sizes are set up. "Do you farm this land yourself?"

He chuckles. "No. I pay a farmer to harvest the corn. Planting the field in the summer makes for good dove hunting in the fall."

"I was right about you. I thought maybe you were an outdoorsman." Even when he's wearing a suit, there is something rugged about Jonathan's appearance—scruffy beard and tanned face with sunglass lines at his temples.

"Yes, ma'am. This may sound corny, but hunting and fishing are my way of being one with nature." He sweeps a hand at the target. "Go ahead. Show me what you've got."

For the next hour, they take turns shooting at targets. Even though the sun is hidden behind a blanket of clouds, the thick humid air causes Amelia to perspire. But she doesn't mind. For the first time since arriving on the island, she feels in total control.

Jonathan is an excellent shot with a large array of handguns. He lets her try out a few, but she prefers her own, a Sig Sauer P365 that fits perfectly in her small hand.

When they return to the house afterward, he offers her a cold beer.

Amelia licks her parched lips. She can't remember when she last drank a beer. But the idea of having a beer with Jonathan makes her feel uncomfortable. "I should probably get going."

"Come on. Stay for one beer. You have nothing to fear. After seeing you shoot, I'd be a fool to make a move on you. Besides, as pretty as you are, I don't go for married women."

"In that case, how can I say no? A beer sounds refreshing." She fans her face. "I'm still getting reacquainted with the Lowcountry's oppressive heat."

"After living in New England, I imagine the heat and

humidity are quite a shock to your system." He walks her to the rocking chairs on the porch. "Make yourself at home. I'll grab some beers and be right back."

Amelia drops her purse on the floor, the weight of her gun landing with a thud, and settles into a rocker. Tilting her face toward the overhead ceiling fan, she closes her eyes and imagines what it might be like to be married to a man like Jonathan. Handsome and successful and concerned about her well-being. A husband that doesn't insist she follow strict rules about nutrition and exercise and everything else *he* deems important.

Jonathan returns with an acrylic tray bearing two frosty beer mugs and a plate with cheese, crackers, and grapes. Setting the tray on the small table between their chairs, he says, "I'm not much of a cook. But I get by."

"This is perfect. Thank you." Her stomach growls, reminding Amelia that she's eaten little today. Nibbling on a chunk of cheese, she asks, "Did you live here with Lisa?"

Jonathan shakes his head. "She's a city girl, and I love the outdoors. Which ended up being the final nail in the coffin of our marriage."

"How so?" Amelia asks.

He looks out over the water. "We have twin daughters who are seniors in college. When Anna and Kayla were young, Lisa and I spent our weekends driving them to various activities, cheerleading and sporting events and dances. But once the girls left home, we realized how little we still had in common. I wanted to spend my free time fishing and hunting, and Lisa wanted to travel. I didn't blame her, nor she me. We'd reached a fork in the road and decided to take separate paths."

"All divorces should be so amicable," Amelia says, and takes a sip of beer.

Jonathan gives her a quizzical look. "I'm impressed with your marksmanship. You've clearly spent a lot of time target practicing. What are you afraid of, Amelia?"

Amelia thinks carefully about her answer before responding. "I'm afraid of fear. Someone important once said that."

"Franklin Roosevelt, in his 1933 inaugural address."

Amelia tilts her head sideways. "How did you know that?"

"I was a history major in college. And the truth in his profound statement has stuck with me throughout the years. Others may try to harm us, but if we overcome our fears, we can stand up to them. Many women I know have done that by purchasing handguns and learning to use them properly. With that being said, let me rephrase my question. Who's trying to harm you, Amelia? Your husband?"

Amelia longs to confide in him, to unburden herself with the problems in her marriage. She feels she can trust him. After all, he was her mother's attorney for years. Staring into her lap, she nods her head.

"Does he abuse you?"

She bites down on her quivering lip. "Both verbally and physically. He has total control over my life. He refused to let me come home to see Mama unless he was with me. The one time I sneaked away, he came after me. He gave me the worst beating of my life when we got back to Boston."

"Why not file for divorce? We have a divorce attorney, a real hard-ass, in our firm if you want to file in South Carolina. If you'd rather go through the process in Boston, I can help you find an attorney up there."

"I wish it were that simple. My husband has announced his candidacy for Congress. He wants his dutiful wife by his side. Nelson has some business dealings with the wrong sort of people, if you know what I mean."

Jonathan narrows his green eyes. "The mafia?"

"Yes," she says, her voice barely audible.

"Does your husband know where you are now?"

"He does. He's coming down this weekend to take me back

to Boston." Amelia looks away, staring out over the cornfield. "But I'm not going with him. I refuse to leave Point Pleasant."

"What if he attacks you? Are you going to shoot him?"

"It's the only way." She gets to her feet. "I shouldn't have told you any of this. I don't want to drag you into my problems. I can take care of myself."

Jonathan sets down his beer and stands to face her. "Don't do this, Amelia. There are other ways."

Unable to meet his gaze, she keeps her eyes on the floor. "That's easy for you to say. You've never been abused by your spouse."

"Get the police involved. Bring charges against him." Jonathan reaches for her arm, but she jerks it away.

She shakes her head. "I can't. I have no proof. No hospital records. Nelson never broke a bone, and I never needed stitches." Their staff witnessed plenty over the years, but they are loyal to Nelson. They would never rat him out for fear of retaliation.

"Chief Summers is a friend of mine. Talk to him. He'll look out for you."

"No way." She looks up at him. "And you can't tell him either, Jonathan. You were Mama's attorney, which makes you my attorney. Which makes you obligated to keep my secret."

Jonathan lets out a sigh. "I'll keep your secret. Unless you instruct me to do so otherwise. But I urge you to reconsider your options."

She picks her purse up off the floor. "I should go."

"Please don't leave angry, Amelia. Walk with me to the end of the dock. I have something I need to discuss with you. I promise I won't mention your husband again." He draws an *X* on his chest.

The breath she's been holding rushes out of her lungs. "Okay. I'll go with you out on the dock, but then I really need to head home."

"Fair enough." He motions for her to go down the stairs ahead of him.

They walk in silence across the lawn. When they reach the dock, Jonathan says, "I spoke to my sister about your sister. Even though Frances was only in middle school at the time, she was acutely aware of Robin's reputation as a notorious troublemaker. Frances remembers hearing some disturbing rumors about Robin."

Amelia stops walking. "What kind of rumors?"

"Rumors about Robin belonging to a satanic cult."

Amelia's mouth falls open. "That's disturbing. Is there any way those rumors were true?"

"According to Frances, Robin hung out with a small group of four friends, two boys and two girls. They dressed in black, spoke often about the devil, and walked around chanting indistinguishable words."

Amelia vehemently shakes her head. "That's just crazy. She must be mistaken. Kids always blow things out of proportion."

Jonathan's hands shoot up. "Don't shoot me! I'm only the messenger."

Amelia softens. "Thank you for asking Frances about her. And for telling me what she said."

They continue down the dock. When they reach the end, Jonathan extends an arm with finger pointed across the marsh. "If you squint, you can see your house way over there at the mouth of the inlet."

Her eyes follow his finger. "I don't need to squint. You could probably see in my bedroom window with a pair of binoculars."

"I happen to know your bedroom window is on the other side of the house."

She doesn't tell him she's been sleeping in her mother's room. "How do you know that?"

"Miss Dottie once gave me a tour." They sit down side by side on the wooden bench. "Frances told me about something else concerning your sister. She claims that on the night your father died, an intruder broke into your house, stabbed him with a knife, and kidnapped your sister."

"I learned this from Bebe today," Amelia says. "But Bebe doesn't think Robin was kidnapped. She's convinced my sister killed my father and ran away."

"That's Frances's theory as well. This afternoon, I spent an hour searching online, but I found nothing relating to Robin's kidnapping case or your father's death."

"I'm not surprised," Amelia says. "It was so long ago. I should go to the public library and check out the microfiche from that time."

"Or you can talk to Chief Summers. Maybe he'll show you the file."

Amelia cuts her eyes at him. "Why are you so determined for me to contact Chief Summers?"

He shoulder-bumps her. "You have a lot going on, Amelia. An abusive husband and a sister with a questionable background who wants your inheritance. Having a friend on the police force could prove beneficial."

Although she doesn't admit it to Jonathan, Amelia suspects he might be right.

TWENTY-ONE

After she posts bail, Max asks Toby to drive her back to the waterfront. He stops along the sidewalk on Ocean Avenue to let her out. "Try not to worry, Maxie. We're gonna figure this out."

She reaches for the door handle. "*Your* detective already has it figured out. Because I had the biggest motive, I'm the guilty party. Never mind that he hasn't done his job. And you need to do your job, Toby. Make Jared investigate Ron." She swings open the car door.

"I'm keeping close tabs on Jared. We're investigating every angle. I promise you, Max, I've got your back."

She gets out of the car and sticks her head back in. "If that's true, why does it feel like you're on Jared's side?" She slams the door before he can answer.

She experiences a pang of guilt. Deep down, she knows Toby will look out for her. With eyes on the ground, she's walking down the alley to the cafe's back door when Davis calls her name.

"Max! I've been looking for you." He jogs over to her. "I heard what happened. Are you okay?"

Max, afraid to speak for fear of breaking down, shakes her head.

Davis pulls her into his arms. When she tries to resist him, he tightens his grip. "Keep the faith. Everything will work out."

His concern eases her tension, and she rests her head against his chest. "I hope you're right." She relishes the comfort of his arms a moment before pulling away. "Sorry. I didn't mean to lose it on you. I'm just so furious. They are treating me so unfairly."

"Sounds like you need to talk. I've been hearing great things about Shaggy's. I was thinking of going there for a drink, but I don't want to look like a loser sitting at the bar alone. Any chance I can convince you to go with me?"

Max considers her options—spending the evening alone in Birdie's apartment or happy hour at Shaggy's. "I need to shower first."

A playful smirk tugs at his lips. "To get rid of the jail grime?"

Max laughs, despite her foul mood. "You're hilarious."

"I couldn't resist. I'm glad you appreciate the humor." He sweeps his arm toward Shaggy's. "Why don't I go on over and grab us a table?"

"I prefer to sit at the bar."

He salutes her. "Yes, ma'am. I'll see you in a few."

Max watches him disappear down the alley before entering the building. From the coatroom, she glimpses Birdie in the kitchen having a heated discussion with one of her servers. Max hurries up the stairs. She knows Birdie will want to hear what happened at the police station, but Max isn't in the mood to talk about it.

After a quick shower, she dresses in clean white jeans and a gray short-sleeved linen top. Towel-drying her short hair, she drags her eyeliner brush across her lashes and clear gloss over her lips. Staring at her reflection in the mirror, she feels more like herself and less like a convict.

She's headed back down the stairs when Birdie appears in the coatroom. "There you are! You poor thing, how're you holding up?"

Max shrugs. "I'm hanging in there."

Birdie hugs her, squeezing her hard. "Is there anything I can do for you?"

Max squirms free of her grip. "You can pray the fire marshal and detective discover the truth."

"I'm sure they will. Come have dinner with me. I've reserved a table for us outside. Sydney's scallops are out of this world tonight."

"Actually, I'm on my way to meet Davis for a drink at Shaggy's."

Birdie's face falls. "Isn't it a little soon after your breakup with Ron to be going on a date?"

"It's not a date, Birdie. Davis and I are friends."

Birdie casts her a skeptical look.

"It's okay for a man and a woman to be friends," Max says. "Aren't you and Stan friends?"

Birdie blushes. "Not anymore. We kissed last night."

Max offers her a high five. "You go, girl. You and Stan make a lovely couple." She brushes past her. "Gotta run. Davis is waiting for me."

Birdie calls out after her. "You're playing with fire, Maxie."

Max freezes, letting Birdie's words sink in. She swings back around. "Did you really just say that to me?"

Birdie's face is now red. "I'm so sorry, Max. The words just slipped out. I didn't mean it."

"You didn't mean what? That I make a habit of playing with fire? That I tried to burn down my hotel. That I tried to kill Ron, and Davis is my next victim." Max sounds irrational, even to her own ears.

Tears well in Birdie's eyes. "I would never think that, Maxie. I love you like a sister. I believe wholeheartedly in your innocence."

Crossing the coatroom in two strides, Max throws her arms

around Birdie. Swallowing past the lump in her throat, she says, "I'm sorry. That was uncalled for. I'm not myself right now."

Birdie strokes Max's hair. "I know, my friend. You have so much on your plate. You keep everything bottled up inside. It would help to talk about it. Why don't I make us some tea? We can go upstairs and have a nice long chat."

Max pushes away from her. "Maybe later. You have dinner guests to attend to. And Davis is waiting for me."

Max feels Birdie's eyes on her as she leaves the building and hurries down the alley.

Davis is seated at the bar, drinking a Stella in a bottle. She slides onto the vacant barstool next to him. "Sorry that took so long."

"No worries." He studies her face. "What's wrong? Other than the obvious. Did something else happen?"

Max dumps her bag on the bar. "I had a run-in with Birdie on my way out just now."

Davis angles his body toward her. "How so?"

"Something she said set me off. It's partially my fault. I'm overly sensitive right now."

"And understandably so." Davis signals the bartender. "This lady needs a drink."

Lewis tosses a paper napkin on the bar. "Hey there, Max. I'm sorry about the fire."

She smiles softly at him. "Thanks, Lewis."

"Can I interest you in a blueberry mojito?"

Max considers his offer. "Thanks, but I think I'll stick with wine tonight."

"Then I'll get you the usual," Lewis says and moves away from them.

She turns her body toward Davis. "Birdie means well. She and I have been friends since we were kids. We're closer than most sisters. We're always in each other's business, trying to tell each other what to do. Sometimes, I think we're too close. I've been worried that living with her during the renovations might negatively affect our friendship. What happened just now validates those concerns."

"I know of a place for rent," Davis says. "One of my customers owns an oceanfront house. She's looking for someone to rent her guest house over the winter. I've done some minor repairs on the small cottage. It's nothing fancy, but the view is nice. Would you like me to text Pauline, to see if you can look at it tomorrow?"

Max sits up straight in her chair. "An oceanfront guest house would be ideal." She eyes his phone on the bar. "Text her now, please!"

Chuckling, he thumbs off the text and sets the phone back down.

Lewis brings her wine, and she takes a sip. "I've been widowed for six years. I value my independence. Our relationship moved too quickly. Ron recently sold his software company. Having him hanging around all the time with no purpose really grated my nerves. Now I know how women feel when their husbands retire. I guess I'm destined to be alone."

"Or maybe you haven't met the right guy yet," Davis says with a glint in his brown eyes.

His comment strikes Max. Is Davis suggesting he's the right guy for her? She senses chemistry between them. The way he looks at her with that crooked grin stirs something within her. *Chill, Max. Why are you thinking about romance when your life is in turmoil?*

"Maybe." She runs a finger around the lip of her glass. "But after the way things ended with Ron, I'm taking some time off from dating."

"If you don't mind me asking, how did the two of you end up together in the first place?"

"He was a guest at my hotel." Wineglass in hand, she slides back in her chair. "Back in June, I joined a dating website. After a series of disastrous encounters, I was flattered when someone paid attention to me. And Ron's a fun guy. Or at least he was for a while."

"Until he set your hotel on fire."

Max presses her lips into a thin smile. "I'm glad someone believes I'm innocent."

Davis drains the rest of his beer and sets the bottle down. "How did the fire start?"

"You won't believe it," she says and tells him what she learned from Reynolds about the complicated device used to start the fire.

"I've never heard of such a thing." He signals Lewis for another beer. "So, Ron used this device to make the fire look electrical. Did you tell him that I'd discovered faulty wiring?"

Max's mind races. "I don't think so. We were on the outs and didn't talk much those last few days."

Davis's body goes rigid. "Hold on a minute. Remember, we caught Ron lurking in the hallway outside your office the day you and I were discussing the bid proposal? Do you think he overheard us?"

Max thinks back to that day in her office. "I left the door ajar during our meeting."

"That's right. And I told you the estimate for the electrical was high because your systems were antiquated."

"You're a genius, Davis. Would you be willing to tell this to the fire marshal?"

"I'll track him down in the morning."

Something else about their meeting nags in the back of Max's mind. She envisions herself walking Davis to the door and then turning back to her desk. "I gave you a master key card and told you the key controls every interior and exterior door on the premises. I have several copies of the master in my desk. Ron could've taken one at any time."

"I think you're on to something, Max. I think you should be the one to relay this detail to the fire marshal."

"Don't worry. I will. Although I doubt he'll listen. He's determined to pin this crime on me. Ron's in a coma, and Reynolds wants to wrap up this investigation as quickly as possible."

"I'll make certain he listens to me." Davis reaches for the laminated menu. "I'm starving. Wanna order some appetizers?"

"Sure thing!" Max says. "I recommend the calamari."

"Sounds good." Reading from the menu, Davis says, "Along with a dozen raw oysters and a half pound of steamed shrimp."

Max thinks this is too much food for the two of them, but they devour every bite, and order another dozen oysters. While they eat, they share much about their lives. Sadness falls over his face when he speaks of his beloved wife. He loved Elizabeth as much as Max loved Daniel. A love like that only happens once in a person's lifetime. Or is it possible for a person to find a second true love?

When they ask for the check, Davis slaps down his credit card but Max insists they go dutch. Davis's phone vibrates on the bar and he reads the text from the owner of the guest house. "Pauline says we can see the guest house tomorrow afternoon at four. Does that work for you?"

"I'm flexible. Aside from paddleboarding with Birdie, I have nothing on my agenda for the foreseeable future. Assuming I'm not locked up in Folsom Prison, of course."

Davis laughs as he types the text to Pauline. "Folsom Prison is in California, Max."

"The name just popped into my head. Isn't it from an old Johnny Cash song?"

Davis places his hand on his chest. "Indeed, it is. And I'm a fan."

Max's lips turn downward. "What *will* I do with myself while the hotel is under renovations?"

"You'll have plenty to keep you busy." He flashes his crooked grin. "If you'd like, I'll give you a hardhat and put you to work on my demolition crew."

She raises her hand. "I accept. I even have my own tool belt."

He bursts out laughing. "Why am I not surprised? You're an intriguing woman, Max Summers. I'm looking forward to working with you on this project."

"As am I with you," she says and gathers her things.

As they're exiting Shaggy's porch, activity on the marina dock catches their attention. "Let's go see what's going on," Davis says, and leads her across the boardwalk.

Down on the dock, a sport fishing boat has just returned from the ocean with a citation-size bluefin tuna. Standing out of the way of the crew, Max and Davis listen as one of them tells the story of their catch. "We were calling it a day, getting ready to pull the lines in, when we got the strike. We fought that sono-fabitch for four hours."

Leaning into her, Davis says close to her ear, "Do you like to fish, Max?"

Max nods. "My husband and I used to fish all the time. Do you?"

"Yes, ma'am. One day I'd like to own a fishing boat. Is it silly to have those kinds of dreams at our age?"

"To stop dreaming would be to give up on life. And we can never give up on life." As the words leave her lips, the enormity of what she faces with a potential jail sentence hits her. She can't give up fighting. She didn't start the fire. If she wants any sort of future, if she wants her freedom, she must prove her innocence.

TWENTY-TWO

Amelia speeds over the causeway, racing to get home before dark. Letting herself in the back door, she secures the house, grabs an apple from the bowl of fruit in the kitchen, and heads down the hall to her father's study. Turning the television on to the news network, she combs through the desk and bookcase while listening for updates on her husband's run for Congress.

She clears out all the drawers and checks to make certain no documents are taped to the bottoms. When this search yields no results, she turns her attention to the bookcases. Removing the books one by one, she fans through the pages before placing them in neat stacks on the floor. When all the shelves are empty, she examines the back of the bookcase for hidden panels. Again, she finds nothing.

Pouring a glass of brandy, she leans against the empty bookcase as she sips the warm golden liquid. She muses out loud. "Where else could those documents be? Where do people hide things?" A thought strikes her, and she pushes off the bookcase. "In safe deposit boxes, of course. Why didn't I think of it sooner?"

Returning to the desk, she brings the computer to life and clicks on the internet browser. Her mother's credentials are automatically stored for her online bank account, and Amelia signs on to the website with ease. She accesses the electronic bank statement for January and scrolls down the charges. About three-quarters of the way to the bottom, she finds the line item for the safe deposit box rental. *Yes!* She punches the air with her fist and falls back in her chair. *Now. Where's the key?*

She shifts her attention to the television. There has been no mention of her husband, which means he is likely on his way to South Carolina. But she's ready for him. She's determined to overcome her fear.

Amelia tunes into the local news channel while she reorganizes the items in the drawers and the books on the shelves to her liking. This is her study now. Her house. And she'll fight for it come what may. The meteorologist catches her attention with a report about a tropical disturbance off the coast of South Carolina. The forecast calls for a stormy weekend, which doesn't bother Amelia. She loves a rainy day at the beach.

Turning out the lights, she climbs the stairs to her mother's bedroom and stands in front of the window. The garage apartment is dark. She can't see Robin, but the red glow from the tip of a burning cigarette tells Amelia she's there. Watching her.

The idea of a former member of a satanic cult living in such close proximity sends chills down Amelia's spine. Was the commune where Robin lived all those years really a cult? Did she sacrifice animals? Robin claims her daughter died at birth. Was the child a sacrifice to whatever devils they worshiped?

Stop it, Amelia! You're letting your imagination get the best of you.

Half-drunk from brandy, she lies down fully clothed on the bed, intending to rest for a minute before searching her mother's room for the bank box key. She falls fast asleep and wakes from a nightmare around four thirty. She pads in bare feet to the kitchen for a cup of chamomile tea. While she waits for the tea to steep, the nightmare comes back to her. She's hiding in the shadows on the porch. Loud arguing comes from inside. But the dream was different this time. This time she can make out what the angry voices are saying.

"I hate you!" Amelia assumes this shrill voice belongs to Robin.

The next voice Amelia recognizes as her mother's. "Don't you dare speak to your father like that."

Robin screams, "He's not my—"

Amelia woke before her sister finished her sentence. He's not her what? He's not her father? Amelia brings a trembling hand to her mouth. Is it possible? This would explain why Robin's birth certificate is missing.

Her tea forgotten, Amelia flies up the stairs and tears her mother's room apart. Thoroughly searching the chest of drawers, she moves on to the walk-in closet. She checks the pockets of hanging clothes before dropping to her knees to inspect the neatly stacked rows of shoe boxes. She's getting to her feet when she notices her mother's jewelry safe. Why didn't she think to look here first?

Amelia spins the combination dial and turns the lever. She goes through every velvet box of jewels but turns up no key. She lifts the felt liner at the bottom of the empty safe where she discovers two keys—an old-fashioned skeleton key and a thin key with a long neck and jagged prongs that's etched with the number 133. She's certain the latter fits the safe deposit box. But what does the skeleton key fit?

Amelia is standing at the bank's front door when they open at nine on Friday morning. A customer service representative shows her to the vault where the safe deposit boxes are housed. She waits for the woman to leave before inserting her key into box 133. Inside are two documents—her sister's birth certificate listing her father as Joseph Boone and her father's official death certificate showing the cause of death as homicide.

Who is Joseph Boone? And who killed her father? It couldn't have been her mother. Dottie loved Amelia's father, and her mother was not a murderer. Which leaves either Robin or the alleged kidnapper.

Finding it difficult to breathe, she slams the safe deposit box shut, slips the documents into her bag, and leaves the bank. With more questions than answers, she drives straight to the police station. Chief Summers is exiting the building when she arrives.

"Amelia, this is a surprise. Is something wrong?"

"I was wondering if we could have a word in private." When he hesitates, she says, "I can come back later if now is not a good time."

"Not at all. I was just on my way out for bagels." With a chuckle, Summers pats his ample belly. "But I really don't need them." He holds the door open for her. "Let's go to my office."

She follows him through the small waiting room and down a short hall to a large room with desks lined up in rows. The chief's office occupies the space in the corner of the room, which is partitioned off with glass walls. Summers goes behind his metal desk, and Amelia sits down opposite him. "So, tell me what this is about."

"My father's death in 1976. I have reason to believe my older sister, Robin, was involved."

Summer's smile fades. "Miss Dottie never mentioned another daughter."

"Because she's been missing since 1976. No one has seen or heard from her until recently."

Sweat glistens on his forehead. "Until recently? Are you saying she conveniently showed up after your mother died to claim her inheritance?"

"That's exactly what I'm saying. Here are the documents." She shows him the birth and death certificates and tells him what she knows about her father's death and her sister's disappearance, including the rumored kidnapping. "Mama always claimed my father died from a heart attack and my sister ran away. I'm assuming she lied to protect me from the truth and Robin from going to prison. According to two different sources, there were rumors that Robin was kidnapped."

Stroking his turkey neck, Summers says, "Wow! This all comes as something of a surprise. I knew your mother well. She never hinted at such a colorful past."

"There's a reason Mama left Robin out of her will. Before I give up any of my inheritance, I need to know what happened that night."

"And you're hoping I can fill in the blanks." He swivels in his chair to face the computer. "We digitized all our records years ago. What was the date?"

"July tenth, 1976."

He pokes at the keys with his two pointer fingers. After a considerable amount of humming and tapping and drumming his fingers on the desk, he looks up at her. "There's nothing here. I've gone through the records for the entire year. I'll have one of my officers check the records room, but I doubt we'll find anything."

"What does that mean?"

"That means someone ditched the file. Darryl Swanson was police chief back then."

A memory flashes in Amelia's mind at the mention of the name. Swanson is pressing her eight-year-old self for details about what she saw from the porch that night. Amelia is crying hysterically. She either can't remember or doesn't want to tell him. "I remember Swanson. Tall, skinny man with a black beard. He looked like—"

"Abe Lincoln," Summers says finishing her sentence.

"Swanson was one of the good guys. He's the one who introduced me to Miss Dottie. They were close. I'm sure I don't need to tell you how persuasive Miss Dottie could be."

"Are you suggesting Mama convinced him to get rid of the file?"

He holds out his hands, palms up. "Stranger things have happened."

Disappointment sets in. Amelia may never find out the truth about the events of that long ago night in July. "What do I do, Chief?"

He hoists his rotund body out of the chair. "Why don't you go to the library, see what you can dig up on the microfiche files. I'm going to contact a buddy of mine at the FBI. They may have been called in to assist with the case."

Summers and Amelia exit his office and walk together to the front door. She offers her hand. "Thank you, Chief Summers. I'll let you know if I find anything."

He squeezes her hand. "And I'll be in touch when I hear back from the FBI."

Leaving her car in the police station parking lot, Amelia walks two blocks to the public library where the librarian, an older woman with a cap of gray curls and reading glasses on a chain around her neck, shows her how to use the microfiche machine. After what just happened at the police station, with Summers being unable to locate files regarding her father's death, she's not surprised to find the microfiche from all of July 1976 missing.

Amelia spends close to two hours searching through old copies of the *Palmetto Island Times* but she turns up nothing about her sister's disappearance or her father's death. Not even his obituary.

She leaves the library frustrated. She's driving home to Point Pleasant when Jonathan calls. "Good morning."

"*Bizarre* would be a more accurate way to describe this morning," she says and quickly brings him to speed on her discoveries.

He lets out a low whistle. "That is strange. How can I help?"

"You can search any files your firm has relating to my family. Let me know if you find anything out of the ordinary."

"I can do that." He's silent for a beat. "I hate to add to your troubles, but Robin called me a little while ago."

Amelia's blood runs cold. Robin doesn't have a phone. "What number did she call you from?"

"I'm not sure. Let me look at my call log." He reads off the number. "Doesn't ring a bell to me. Does it to you?"

Amelia tightens her grip on the phone. "That's the landline at Point Pleasant."

"No wonder I didn't recognize it. I always spoke with your mom on her cell phone."

"What time did Robin call?"

Another pause while he checks the time. "At eight fifty-one precisely. Is that important?"

"Yes. I left the house at eight forty-five to go to the bank. Bebe has a doctor's appointment this morning. She won't be in until around noon. Which means Robin got into the house somehow. What did she want?"

"She requested a meeting with me this afternoon. I told her I thought you should be present. I suggested we meet with you at Point Pleasant at five. Does that time work for you?"

"Five is fine." Amelia pulls into her driveway and puts the car in gear, leaving the engine idling and the air conditioning running. "How do you plan to approach this meeting?"

"I'm going to feel Robin out, see what she wants. I assume you're not ready to offer her a settlement."

Amelia considers this option. Giving Robin money will get rid of her. But for how long? Amelia is tired of living under someone else's thumb. Besides, her mother had her reasons for leaving Robin out of the will. And Amelia won't go against Dottie's wishes. "Not yet. Not until I get some answers to my many unanswered questions."

They speak for a minute more before ending the call.

Amelia turns off the engine and goes inside. She's drinking a glass of sweet tea in the kitchen a minute later when Bebe arrives. "You weren't here earlier, were you?"

Bebe shakes her head. "I told you, I had a doctor's appointment. Why do you ask?"

Amelia explains about Robin's call to Jonathan.

Bebe drops her leather sack on the counter. "She's the devil. Do you think she has a key?"

"I don't know how else she could have gotten in. But I'm going to call the security company. I'll be in the study."

She's halfway out the door when she remembers. "Oh, Bebe." She shows her the skeleton key. "Do you have any idea what this key might fit? I found it in Mama's jewelry safe."

Bebe squints as she looks across the room at the key. "Nah. I've never seen it before."

Amelia closes her hand over the key. "Okay. Thanks."

She retreats down the hall to her father's study where she places the call to the security company. When she explains the situation, the representative says, "Let me see what I can find out."

Amelia hears the woman typing away on the keyboard. "At eight forty-seven this morning, someone disarmed the alarm using the code 0913."

Amelia jots down the code on her notepad. "Wait, a minute. The only code I'm aware of is 2090. Who authorized this code?"

"I don't have that information, ma'am. You must speak with my supervisor who is at lunch at the moment. Would you like her voice mail?"

"Yes, in a minute. But before you transfer me, can you tell me if any windows were breached this morning?"

Amelia hears more typing, and the representative says, "No, ma'am. Everything appears in order."

"Thank you for checking. Please put me through to your

supervisor's voice mail." Amelia leaves a detail message and ends the call.

She stares down at the notepad. 0913. September thirteen. Robin's birthday. How did she get her own code? If no windows were breached, Robin entered the house through a door. Which means she somehow got her hands on a key. Anger surges through Amelia's body. The last thing she needs is a psychotic sister snooping around.

Amelia searches the internet for local locksmiths, going down the list until she finds one who can come right away. After meeting with the locksmith, she spends the rest of the afternoon in the study searching the internet for information on Robin's biological father. There are many Joseph Boones, but none with an obvious connection to Dottie.

At four thirty, the supervisor at the alarm company returns her call. According to Jose Curtis, Dottie Fairchild made the request to add the additional code on Thursday, August fifth.

"But Dottie Fairchild died on August third," Amelia argues.

"I'm sorry for your loss, ma'am. I can only tell you what our records show."

"I called last Sunday to change the primary code. Why didn't your representative notify me of the additional code at the time?"

"I can't say for sure, ma'am. But I promise I'll look into it."

Thanks for your help," Amelia says and hangs up.

She walks over to the window and looks out at the calm ocean. Her sister was at Point Pleasant on August fifth. But was she here earlier than that? Did Robin spend time with her mother? Did the two of them reconcile? Or did they fight? Did Robin upset her mother, causing her to have a stroke in her sleep?

When Amelia hears the doorbell, she leaves the study and goes to the front door to let Jonathan in. "Did you find out anything from the files?"

With a grim expression, he shakes his head. "I'm sorry."

"No worries. I expected as much." She ushers him through

the living room. "I thought we'd meet on the porch. I don't want that woman inside my house."

They've no sooner passed through the french doors onto the porch when Robin comes strolling across the lawn in yet another one of Dottie's sundresses. As Robin draws closer, Amelia can see she's wearing makeup, and her hair is brushed back into a tidy bun. Her sister has dressed to impress Jonathan.

Robin gestures at the locksmith's van parked in the driveway. "What's with the locksmith?"

"I'm getting rid of an intruder," Amelia says.

"That intruder won't be an intruder for long," Robin says and turns her attention to Jonathan.

Once the introductions have been made, they sit down at the table, which Bebe has set with a pitcher of sweet tea and three glasses. While Robin appears somewhat calmer today, her hazel eyes dart about from Amelia to Jonathan to the ocean and back to the porch, never landing on any one subject longer than a few seconds. She's watching a sailboat enter the mouth of the inlet when she asks Jonathan, "Did you bring a copy of my mother's will?"

Jonathan unzips his leather portfolio and hands out stapled sheafs of paper. "As you can see, your mother made no provisions for you in her will."

Robin thumbs through the pages. "I'm not surprised. Mama and I haven't spoken in forty-five years."

Amelia glares at her. "Are you sure about that?"

Robin's scowl lines deepen. "What's that supposed to mean?"

"I have proof you came to Palmetto Island earlier than you claim. You saw Mama before she died, didn't you?"

Robin lets out a snort. "What proof?"

Amelia holds her sister's gaze. "I'd rather not say."

"Because you're lying." She turns her attention back to Jonathan. "Mama thought I was dead. That's why she didn't leave me anything. As you can see, I'm very much alive. I'm as much her daughter as Amelia, and she would want to take care of me. I'm within my rights to contest the will, am I not?"

Jonathan gives his head a solemn nod. "You are."

"Can you or someone in your firm handle the lawsuit?" she asks.

"I'm sorry, but that would be a conflict of interest." Jonathan steeples his fingers under his chin. "Lawsuits can be costly and messy. Perhaps we can settle this out of court. What, exactly, do you feel you're entitled to?"

Robin smiles smugly. "Point Pleasant and half of everything else."

"You're outta your damn mind," Amelia says. "No way in hell I'm giving you Point Pleasant."

Jonathan shoots Amelia a warning look. "No one can stop you from suing for the property, Robin, but I doubt any judge would give it to you. Not when you've been absent from your mother's life for forty-five years."

Amelia's chest tightens. Thanks to Nelson, the bastard, she hasn't played a major role in her mother's life either. At the thought of her husband, her blue eyes dart about the grounds, from the ocean to the inlet to the driveway.

Robin fumbles in her pocket for a pack of cigarettes. "What difference does it make whether I've seen Mama or not? I'm still her daughter," she says, lighting the cigarette.

"We'll let the judge decide that. I assume I will represent Amelia in this lawsuit." When he looks to Amelia for confirmation, she nods. "I'll be digging into your past in order to prove your mother had good reason not to provide for you in her will. Is that what you want, Robin? Are you ready to tell the world why you ran away?"

Robin sucks hard on her cigarette. "I have nothing to hide."

"Are you sure about that?" he asks.

Robin looks away without answering.

Amelia observes the exchange as one might watch a tennis

match. She's impressed with Jonathan's ability to manipulate the conversation.

He sits back in his chair, resting his clasped hands in his lap. "Perhaps we can work something out to avoid going to court."

Robin stomps the cigarette out on the porch and lights another. "What'd you mean? Like a settlement?"

"That would be one course of action. Amelia could give you an agreed-upon amount of money. A onetime payment."

Robin stabs her cigarette at him. "You're trying to settle because you know I'll win in court."

He raises an eyebrow. "Are you willing to take that chance?" When she doesn't respond, he says, "Why don't you take the weekend to think about it?"

"I'll do that." Robin pushes back from the table and storms off the porch.

They watch Robin as she crosses the lawn and climbs the steps to the garage apartment. "Is she always so jittery?" Jonathan asks.

"She's usually worse." Amelia returns her gaze to Jonathan. "You handled that brilliantly. But what if I decide not to settle with her?"

"Then you'll go to court. Which will prolong her presence in your life." Jonathan pats Amelia's hand. "Look at the bright side. Robin appeared to have gotten the message. The big prize, Point Pleasant, is off the table."

"I wouldn't be so sure about that. I'm getting a clearer picture of my sister. And she's definitely not playing with a full deck."

TWENTY-THREE

Max spends Friday morning at Ron's bedside, carrying on a one-sided conversation with him, encouraging him to wake up and tell his version of the events relating to the fire. She's grasping at straws. She has no better plan. There's a good chance he won't remember what happened. And even if he does, she doubts he'll tell the truth. Ron remains perfectly still. He doesn't flutter his eyelids, wiggle his fingers, or move his lips.

Finally, frustrated, she returns to Birdie's. She promised Birdie she'd help out behind the coffee bar, but the impending tropical depression has driven vacationers away, and the cafe is deserted. With nothing to occupy her time, she goes for a long walk on Ocean Avenue and the neighboring streets.

She's waiting in the park for Davis when he arrives a few minutes before four. He's dressed in jeans and a polo shirt and he smells like sawdust.

"Did you come from working on a project?" she asks on the way to tour Pauline's guest house.

He nods. "A small one. An older couple is adding a first-floor master bedroom and bath. They own a beautiful home on the inlet a few miles outside of town."

She stares out the window as they cross the causeway. "If I don't find a way to occupy my time, I may take you up on the offer to work on your demolition crew."

He snickers. "Are you going stir-crazy already?"

"I have an inherent need to keep busy. Maybe I'll get a part-time job somewhere."

"You'll be plenty busy making construction decisions once we get started."

"I hope you're right," she says, more to the window than him.

Davis turns off the main road and parks in front of a sprawling oceanfront home with yellow siding. Killing the engine, he turns toward Max. "Coincidentally, I spoke with the fire marshal this morning. I told him about discovering faulty wiring and finding Ron lurking in the hallway outside your office while we were discussing the renovations. He promised to look into it."

"Let's hope he does. I left a message for Reynolds about the key cards, but he never called me back."

They get out of the truck and walk together to the front door. Pauline Hicks is a grim-faced woman with stooped shoulders and bags under her eyes. She looks Max up and down and then nods her head as though she approves.

"Let me show you the guest house." Pauline leads them across the lawn to a charming one-story cottage with flower boxes and a small front porch. "I don't allow smoking or pets."

"I don't smoke, and I don't have any pets," Max says.

"No wild parties and no live-in boyfriends." Pauline cuts her eyes at Davis.

"Yes, ma'am. I don't have a boyfriend."

Pauline unlocks the door, and they enter a large room that serves as living room, dining room, and kitchen. The bedroom is small, and the bathroom outdated with pink tile, but being on the ocean makes up for what the guest cottage lacks. And it's only for a few months.

"Will you consider a short-term lease?" Max asks. "I'm renovating my hotel. If all goes as planned, we should be finished by Christmas."

"Your hotel?" Lines deepen on Pauline's face as she looks intently at Max. "Wait a minute. I've heard about you. You're that woman who tried to burn down the Palmetto Hotel for the insurance money."

Davis starts, "Hold on a—"

Pauline wags an arthritic finger at him. "You have some nerve suggesting I rent my guest house to an arsonist."

Anger surges through Max, and she gets in the woman's face. "This is America, Mrs. Hicks, where people are innocent until proven guilty. In my case, I *will* be proven innocent, because I *am* innocent."

Max flees the guest cottage with Davis on her heels. She makes it to his truck before breaking down into uncontrollable sobs. He pulls her to him, comforting her as best he can with the center console between them. "I'm so sorry, Max. I can't believe she said those things to you."

Pushing away from him, Max says, "Please, just drive. Get me away from that woman."

Davis reverses out of the driveway, but instead of going back toward town, he heads in the opposite direction. He drives a quarter of a mile and parks at a beach access. Opening the compartment in his center console, he hands her a travel-size package of tissues. "Wanna go for a walk? The fresh air might do you some good."

"Okay." Removing a tissue from the packet, she wipes her eyes and blows her nose.

They stroll down the boardwalk to the beach in silence. Dark clouds loom overhead, and there's not a soul in sight in either direction. Kicking off their shoes, they walk side by side toward the mouth of the inlet.

"I'm sorry for losing it on you," Max says. "I don't know what got into me. I rarely cry."

"Really?" he says in a surprised tone. "I cry all the time."

She bumps him with her elbow. "You do not."

"I do. I promise." He places his hand over his heart. "I'm a basket case when I watch sappy movies and a blubbering fool at weddings. I even tear up sometimes when I see a sentimental commercial. Keeping anger and hurt trapped inside will wear you down over time. You're better off having a good cry and letting it all out."

Max inhales a deep breath. "I admit, I do feel better."

"Pauline is difficult to work with. I should've known she would be persnickety about who rents her guest house."

"I'm in the hotel business, Davis. I deal with people like Pauline Hicks every day. Normally, I don't let them get to me. But she rubbed me the wrong way at the wrong moment. I'm just so frustrated. I feel like I'm swimming against the tide. When Ron wakes up from his coma, I have a sick feeling he's going to lie about the fire, and I'll have to go to jail for something I didn't do."

"Then you need to be one step ahead of him. You didn't start the fire. There must be some evidence somewhere that proves he did."

Max shakes her head. "I don't think so. The fire marshal has combed through the entire fourth floor."

They walk on for a minute in silence. "About your housing dilemma," Davis says. "I have another idea. I recently converted the second floor of the Island Realty building on Ocean Avenue into loft apartments."

"I heard about those. The location is ideal."

Davis stuffs his hands in his pockets. "But there's a catch. I didn't mention the lofts sooner, because they require at least a six-month lease. I'm gonna be honest with you, Max. I poked around the fourth floor this morning. The smoke and fire damage are more extensive than I'd originally thought. The pending investigation may delay us from starting the renovations right away. We are looking at six months, minimum."

"I'm not surprised," Max says. "I'll look into the loft. Thanks for the tip."

"You're welcome." Placing a hand on her hip, he pulls her in for a half hug. "You need a friend right now, Max, and I'm here for you. Lean on me anytime."

She rests her head on his shoulder. "I will take you up on that offer."

Vacationers watching Max and Davis from their porches might mistake them as lovers out for an afternoon stroll. But Max neither wants nor needs a relationship. Her desire for romance got her into this mess in the first place. But she won't turn down Davis's offer of friendship. She hasn't had a strong shoulder to cry on since Daniel died. Her thoughts drift to her late husband. She often cried on Daniel's shoulder when guests made her angry or hurt her feelings. Since his death, she's had to be strong, to suck it up when the going got tough. She's had no one to lean on except Birdie. And Birdie, with her addiction problem, has done most of the leaning.

More tears spill from her eyes, and this time she doesn't wipe them away.

They walk for a while in silence. When they reach Point Pleasant, Davis says, "Wow! What a stunning home. The views from inside that house must be incredible. Do you know who owns it?"

"That's Point Pleasant. My friend, Amelia, grew up there. I told you about her. She's the one whose mother just passed away." They stop to admire the house. "And now the property belongs to Amelia. She claims she's staying in town for a while. And I hope she does. I've missed our friendship. If so, I'll take you there sometime. You'd enjoy the views. They're spectacular."

Max arrives at the cafe to find Birdie twirling a strand of her shoulder-length blonde hair as she paces the floor in the kitchen. "What's wrong, Birdie?"

"I just fired one of my servers. I've never had to fire anyone before, and I feel awful about it. But I had no choice. Celeste showed up for work, high on something. Probably marijuana. Now I'm short-staffed and we're booked solid."

"Seriously? Even with the tropical storm coming? The cafe has been dead all day."

Birdie stops twirling her hair. "I know. It's the strangest thing. We had a mass of cancelations early this morning. But the online reservations schedule booked back up before noon. I assume these folks are all locals."

Max gives her a high five. "That's outstanding. Your cafe is a success."

Birdie falls back against the counter. "At least for now. Restaurants usually do well in the beginning. People are always looking for something new. Let's hope we can survive the test of time."

"You will. Remember, the power of positive thinking."

"If only life were that simple." Birdie tilts her head to the side as she studies Max. "Have you been crying?"

Max's face warms. "I had a mini meltdown. But I'm better now."

"You're overdue a meltdown with all you have going on. Can I help in any way?"

An idea strikes Max. "Actually, you can. Let me work in Celeste's place tonight."

"Ha. What do you know about waiting tables?"

"Duh. I worked at Shaggy's during summers back in high school."

"I'd forgotten that. Only it wasn't Shaggy's back then. It was The Back Porch. And that was a long time ago. A lot has changed in the restaurant business since then."

"I'm sure it has. But I run a hotel. I'm used to sucking up to customers. Besides, I really need to make myself useful. All this free time is wearing on me. Let me run upstairs and change. I'll be right back." Before Birdie can object, Max spins on her heels and dashes up to the apartment.

Dressing in black jeans and a white cotton blouse, Max takes a few minutes to repair her makeup before returning to the kitchen where Sydney briefs her on the night's specials and Kathleen shows her which tables belong to her section.

The evening hours fly by. Max enjoys being on her feet, racing back and forth between her tables while balancing the many requests from her patrons. At the end of the night, she's counting her tips at an inside table when Birdie takes a seat opposite her.

"You did a superb job tonight, Maxie. The customers loved you. I know you've been feeling unsettled without the responsibilities of the hotel to occupy your time. If you're interested in a temporary position, until the renovations are finished, I'd love to hire you."

Max doesn't hesitate. "That would be great. At least for a while, until the demands of the renovations take up more of my time. But I'll give you plenty of notice to find someone else."

"Wonderful. You'll be an awesome addition to my staff."

They talk for a minute more before Birdie heads up to bed. Max remains at the table long after the lights on the boats in the marina have gone out. Davis's words play over and over in her mind. *Then you need to be one step ahead of him. You didn't start the fire. There must be some evidence somewhere that proves he did.*

Max arrives at the hospital as the nurses are changing shifts at seven o'clock on Saturday morning. In the midst of all the chaos, no one notices her slip into Ron's room. She pauses beside his bed, looking down at him. He appears unchanged since she was last here. His face is pale and his body still as monitors beep his vitals at the head of his bed.

Max removes two surgical gloves from the box on the counter and tugs them on her hands. She opens the door to the wooden locker where patient's personal items are stored. The clothes Ron was wearing the night of the fire are folded neatly on the shelf with his wallet still tucked in the back pocket of his shorts. Using the locker door to shield her, she fingers through the cards. Behind his Mastercard, she finds a Florida driver's license for Ronald James Morton, listing his address as Miami. *Florida? Not Philadelphia?* Flipping through more cards, she discovers a master key card that fits all interior doors in her hotel. Which would've allowed him access to the unoccupied room where the fire broke out.

Taking photographs of the key card and driver's license with her phone, she returns both to the wallet and sets the wallet aside. She holds his shorts upside down, giving them a gentle shake. A square plastic object falls to the floor and scatters across the tile, disappearing under the locker. On all fours with face pressed to the floor, she slides her hand beneath the locker and retrieves the square object. A pencil sharpener. *Bingo!* Sitting back on her haunches, she turns the pockets of his shorts inside out. Pencil shavings rain down to the floor. She snaps images of the pencil sharpener and shavings, and then scrapes up the pencil shavings and returns them to the pocket along with the sharpener. After placing the wallet in the back pocket of his shorts, she puts the shorts back in the locker.

Racing back to Birdie's, Max locks herself in her room with

her laptop. A quick search of Facebook reveals a profile for Jimmy Morton. The profile picture is of a much younger Ron. His occupation is listed as pyrotechnics expert. Max does a double take. *A pyrotechnics expert?*

Grabbing her phone, Max clicks on Toby's number. When he answers, she doesn't bother with pleasantries. "I found evidence that proves Ron is a liar, a thief, and an arsonist." She gives him the details of her discoveries.

"You didn't touch anything, did you?" Toby asks.

"I'm not that stupid, Toby. I was wearing surgical gloves. Send Jared over to the hospital to collect Ron's belongings as evidence."

"I can't send Jared anywhere, Maxie. Remember, I recused myself from the case. But I can pass along this information."

Max tightens her grip on the phone. "So, you were lying when you said you had my back?"

"I'm sorry, Maxie. My hands are tied."

"I'm an island here, Toby. No one is helping me. Including you. Thanks for nothing," Max says and hangs up on him.

She clicks on her attorney's number. Despite the early hour, Charles Sullivan answers right away. She explains the situation to him. "I don't understand what's going on. Why won't the police do their jobs?"

"Send me the pics, and I'll pressure Jared and Reynolds to look into the matter. Coincidentally, I've put our best private investigator on the case. He's digging into Morton's past. Knowing he goes by Jimmy and having a copy of his driver's license will help. I'll call you when I find out more."

A wave of relief washes over Max as she texts the photographs to her attorney. Finally, someone in a position of authority is on her side.

TWENTY-FOUR

Amelia wakes on Saturday morning with a stiff neck from sleeping all night in her father's leather recliner. Her handgun is loaded and cocked on the table beside the chair. Nelson is coming for her soon. She feels it in her bones. Beside the handgun is the skeleton key. She's tried every drawer and door in the house. The key fits none of them. Raising the chair to an upright position, she stands and stretches her arms, neck, and lower back. She uncocks the gun, stuffs it in the waistband of her jeans, and slips the skeleton key into her pocket.

In the kitchen, she brews a pot of coffee and takes it to the breakfast-room window, looking out on the dreary landscape. The rain has set in, and the forecast is calling for an increase in wind speed and a chance for strong storms later in the day. Amelia can't see her sister through the garage apartment window, but the red tip of a burning cigarette is evidence she's there. She wonders how her sister, aside from chain-smoking cigarettes, will spend this stormy day. How might their lives have turned out differently if Robin hadn't run away? Would they ever have grown close? Would they have had anything in common? Would Amelia have confided in her about the problems in her marriage?

Amelia moves from window to window as she surveys the property. But she notices nothing out of the ordinary. Returning her empty coffee mug to the kitchen sink, she heads upstairs to shower. When she reaches the second floor, she pauses in front of the attic door, the one place she hasn't searched for a lock the skeleton key might fit. Opening the door, she flips the light switch and climbs the stairs. She catches sight of the steamer trunk in front of the window at the south end of the house. Kneeling down in front of the trunk, she inserts the key in the lock and turns. She lifts the trunk lid to reveal carefully folded garments, old-fashioned hats and opera-length gloves, a family Bible, and a leather-bound journal.

Sitting cross-legged on the floor, she opens the journal and recognizes her mother's neat cursive handwriting. The first entry is dated Valentine's Day, 1958. It reads: *Sixteen years old and pregnant. My life is over. No decent boy will ever marry me now.* The entry is signed—*Dottie Christensen*

Her mother's journal. Proof of Robin's illegitimacy. Sixteen and pregnant. Amelia has never given any thought to how young her mother had been when Robin was born.

Amelia locks the trunk and takes the journal downstairs to her mother's room. Turning on a table lamp, she crawls into bed and flips through the pages. The journal entries are inconsistent. Most are only a few lines, but a few are longer. Some are spaced days apart while others are separated by months and years. Anxious to learn the answers to her many questions, she settles deeper beneath the covers and begins to read.

February 15, 1958

Daddy is furious when I confessed that his best friend, a man I've known all my life, raped me during their annual Christmas party. Uncle Joe lured me into Daddy's study with the promise of a glass of champagne. When we entered the study, he locked the door behind us. He said he had a special Christmas surprise for me. This was not unusual. Uncle Joe always brought me presents. Everything happened so fast. I tried fighting him off, but he was too strong.

I should've told Mama and Daddy about the rape the night it happened. But Uncle Joe threatened me. He said he'd destroy my life if I told anyone. And I believed him. He's a powerful man in Texas. Mama begged Daddy to go to the police, but Daddy said he'd handled Joe his own way. And he did. He handled Joe into giving me a million dollars to make this baby disappear. Daddy should've asked for more. A million dollars is a day's pay for an oil tycoon like Joe.

March 3, 1958

Mama is shipping me off to live with my aunt and uncle in Charleston until the baby comes. At which time I'm to give it up for adoption. After that, I will attend a girl's college of my choice in the Carolinas or Virginia.

March 30, 1958

Aunt Gertrude and Uncle Henry are a dear couple, even if they are eccentric. They adhere to strict schedules. Up every morning at five to walk their corgis, Queen Elizabeth and Prince Philip. Henry leaves for his job at the bank at nine, and Gertrude spends her afternoons playing bridge and having tea with friends. Their home is two streets off the Battery with double-decker porches, which the Charlestonians call piazzas. I read a lot. There's not much else to do.

May 15, 1958

Gertrude and Henry are showing me the Lowcountry. On weekends, they take me to visit neighboring towns and islands like Beaufort and Savannah and Edisto. Palmetto Island is my favorite. I will

*one day make it my home. I can envision it now. A small oceanfront
cottage for my baby and me.*

June 5, 1958

*Gertrude and I are spending the summer at their second home on
Sullivan's Island. I go for long walks on the beach and take naps in
the hammock on the porch. Gertrude is an excellent cook, and I've
gotten big as a whale.*

August 13, 1958

*Mama and Daddy came for a visit. They insist I put the baby up
for adoption. They said I can't come home if I keep the baby. That's a
sacrifice I will make in order to keep my baby. I bid them a tearful
goodbye, knowing I will likely never see them again.*

October 15, 1958

*The baby arrived on September thirteenth. Robin Lucille Chris-
tensen. They let me give her my name, but they made me list Joseph
Boone as the father. Poor little darling has colic. Whenever she isn't
sleeping, she's crying. Gertrude politely asked me to leave. And I don't
blame her. They've been kind to me, and I've overstayed my welcome.
Thanks to good old Uncle Joe, I don't have to worry about money. I
bought a bright red '53 convertible, drove my screaming child to
Palmetto Island, and rented a house on the beach. We mostly keep to
ourselves. For those who ask, I tell them a sad story about my late
husband, Robin's father, who died in a tragic car accident in upstate
South Carolina three months before she was born. Palmetto Island
has special healing powers. I've forgiven my parents for disowning
me. They did what they thought right. Now I'm on my own. I have
no one to answer to except my child.*

· · ·

April 8, 1959

Robin is growing up so fast. She's crawling around and pulling up and developing a feisty little personality. She's prone to ear infections, but I don't mind the frequent visits to the doctor's office. Our pediatrician, Clay Fairchild, is dreamy—tall with dark hair and strong facial features. He's adorable when he tries to flirt with me. His face goes red, and he stumbles on his words.

October 25, 1961

My, how time flies. I can hardly believe it's been over two years since I last wrote. Clay and I are married. We've just returned from a glorious honeymoon in Carmel. I left Robin with Marcella, a sitter who came highly recommended by friends. She called Robin a little devil. And she didn't mean it in a good way. I've noticed some things about Robin myself. She doesn't play well with others, and Clay says her violent temper tantrums are not normal. He's the expert. He would know. I pray every night she outgrows them. I've decided not to tell Clay about Robin's father. He wants to adopt her. I worry he'll change his mind if he found out her father is a rapist.

November 22, 1961

I'm cooking my first Thanksgiving dinner for my new husband in our new home. Point Pleasant has been in Clay's family for generations. With water views on three sides, I feel as though I'm living on my own private island. I'm incredibly happy. But I have a sinking feeling in the pit of my gut that the happiness won't last.

February 17, 1963

Robin's kindergarten teacher gave the most dreadful report about my child. She says Robin bites and kicks the other children. Clay has warned me about her mean streak. Robin isn't his biological child. I don't expect him to love her like I do. But lately he's been keeping his distance from both of us. Except in the bedroom. He's desperate for his own child.

December 24, 1966

Clay and I had the most dreadful fight. I'm not sure our marriage can survive Robin. It would certainly help if I could conceive a baby of our own.

January 21, 1968

At long last, I'm pregnant. Clay is beside himself. The past few years have been difficult as problems with Robin have grown more serious. She lies, tests us at every turn, and bullies the other children at school. I'm terrified she'll try to hurt her baby brother or sister. Clay hasn't expressed his concerns, but I know he's worried as well. Robin is my child. I love her despite her flaws. Clay thinks she needs psychiatric help. But she's still so young. Not even ten years old.

May 31, 1968

Amelia Katherine Fairchild was born 7 lbs and 7 ounces on May 18. She's an angel of a baby. Her father and I both have fallen head over heels in love with her. But I worry Robin isn't adjusting well to the change in our family. This morning, I caught her standing over the crib, staring down at the baby with an expression I couldn't interpret. For now, I won't leave Amelia alone with her older sister.

January 15, 1973

Robin is slipping further and further away from me into a dark place that seems to suck the life out of her. I've tried to get her involved in school activities. She's not an athlete. We all agree on that. I've suggested acting and learning to play an instrument and the debate team. But my intrusion into her life only angers her. She performs well in school, even though she puts little effort into her work. She cares less and less about her appearance, choosing torn jeans over the pretty dresses I buy for her. She rarely brushes her hair anymore, and she listens to heavy metal music by bands like Black Sabbath. She has complete disregard for Amelia. She's neither protective nor loving nor mean. She acts as though Amelia doesn't exist. And her volatile relationship with Clay continues to deteriorate. He wants me to send her to boarding school in Virginia. I'm considering the idea. I relish the idea of restoring peace to my home.

August 8, 1974

Will this summer ever end? I finally agreed to send Robin to boarding school this fall, but she intentionally botched her interviews. She refuses to leave her friends. Two more years until she goes off to college. I'm not sure we can make it. She disobeys our rules and refuses to go to church with us. She breaks curfew every night, and when we ground her, she finds ways to sneak out. She's a regular Houdini. She's distanced herself from her old friends and is associating with a small group of . . . I hate to say it, but her new friends are freaks. I don't know how much more I can take. I don't know how much more my marriage can take. I'm furious at her for what she's doing to my family. I'm certain I'll burn in hell for feeling such negative thoughts about my own child. But I can't help how I feel.

January 20, 1976

I don't understand Robin's desire to go to college in California. Academically, I believe she'd have better choices of schools on the east coast. But Robin wants to be with her friends who are all headed to California. And frankly, the thought of having all those miles between us offers some relief.

. . .

April 15, 1976

I've noticed splatters of blood on Robin's clothing before, but yesterday morning, at the bottom of her laundry basket, I found a pair of blue jeans covered in blood. The same jeans she was wearing when she went out with her creepy friends on Saturday night.

I waited until she left for school this morning to search her room. I'm still shaken by what I discovered in her drawers. A small sharp knife with an elaborate silver handle. A silver necklace with an inverted cross charm. And a notebook with bizarre drawings of beast heads with human bodies. My suspicions are confirmed. My daughter belongs to a satanic cult.

July 4, 1976

Our nation's bicentennial. We hosted a picnic for a large group of friends to celebrate. The evening was lovely, complete with a professional fireworks display. Robin and her drunk friends crashed the party. Fortunately, they didn't arrive until close to midnight and most of our guests had left.

July 10, 1976

Robin discovered her birth certificate. I should've thought to hide it in a safe deposit box. I should've told her the truth about her real father long ago. But I worried that knowing she's the product of a rape would've only complicated an already vulnerable situation. She confronted me in the kitchen after Clay left for work. For the first time, I feared she might hurt me. She was as furious as I've ever seen her. Her eyes were wide and wild. The leader of her cult has worked his voodoo on her. My daughter is possessed by the devil. Only thirty-three more days until she leaves for college.

TWENTY-FIVE

Lightning flashes in the night sky and thunder booms off in the distance. Eight-year-old Amelia hides in the shadows on the porch. Through the french doors, she sees her parents standing with her sister near the fireplace.

Mama places a hand on Robin's cheek, but Robin brushes it away. Mama says, "Please, Robin, I beg you to let us help you. This cult leader has a hold on you. You must free yourself from them before it's too late."

The sound of Robin's maniacal laugh makes Amelia shiver. "Why would I want to free myself from my friends? They're my family, more than you ever were." She glares at Daddy. "And you're not my real father. Now I understand why you worship your precious little Amelia. You can't stand the sight of me, because I'm your wife's bastard."

Mama covers her ears. "Don't say that," she cries. "You are not a bastard. I was married to your biological father. He died in an accident."

"I don't believe you." Robin balls her fists at her sides. "I hate you! Both of you!"

Daddy jabs a finger at Robin. "Don't you dare talk to your mother like that."

"Who's gonna stop me?" Robin reaches into the back pocket of her jeans and removes a black object. She presses a button on the object and a sharp blade appears. Mama and Daddy don't see the knife. Amelia wants to warn them, but everything happens too fast.

"I'll stop you," Daddy says, stepping closer to Robin. "It's high time someone stands up to you."

"Like hell you will." Robin plunges the knife into the center of his chest. When she yanks the knife out, blood spews from the wound, and Daddy crumples to the floor like a rag doll. Robin stares down at their father. Are those tears on her cheeks? Amelia has never seen her sister cry.

Dropping to her knees, Mama screams, "What have you done?"

"I killed him," Robin mumbles in a tone so low Amelia can barely hear her. "Serves him right. He deserved to die."

Mama's head jerks up. "You're the devil." Tugging Daddy's wallet free of his back pocket, she removes a wad of bills and stands to face Robin. Shoving the money at her, she orders Robin to leave their house and never come back."

Robin takes the money, runs out of the living room, and disappears into the sand dunes.

Amelia eases into the living room, staying hidden behind the curtains near the french doors while Mama places a call for help. "I have an emergency," she screams. "My husband's been stabbed, and my daughter kidnapped."

Kidnapped? Isn't that when bad men take children away from their parents? Why did she lie to the person on the phone? Mama has always taught Amelia that lying is a sin.

Amelia can't take her eyes off her father. She's shaking all over, her chin quivering and teeth chattering. Mama sees her, and when she hangs up the phone, she hurries over to her. Patting her body all over, she says, "Amelia! Are you okay, sweetheart? Are you hurt?"

Amelia shakes her head.

"Did you witness what just happened?"

Amelia bites down on her lower lip. She doesn't say the words. Her mama knows the answer.

Mama points at the stairs. "Go to your room and don't come out. If anyone asks, you were in your room the whole time and didn't see a thing." Cupping Amelia's face in her hands, Mama says in a stern voice, "Do you understand me, Amelia?"

Amelia sobs, "But you told me never to lie."

Mama takes Amelia in her arms. "I know, sweetheart. Sometimes we have to do things we know are wrong to protect the ones we love. This is one of those times. Do you understand?"

"Yes, ma'am." Pushing away from her mama, Amelia walks over to her father and kneels down beside him. "Please don't die, Daddy." She kisses his forehead, but his skin is cold against her lips. Despite her young age, she understands she'll never again see her father.

A loud clap of thunder wakes Amelia from her nightmare. Beyond the window, flashes of lightning light up the darkened room. Sitting up in bed, she reaches for the lamp, but when she turns the switch, nothing happens. The power is out. How long has she been asleep? She reaches for her phone and turns on the flashlight. The journal is lying open and face down on the bed beside her. Her mother recorded the next entry two days after her father's death.

July 12, 1976

I share responsibility in the death of my husband. I knew Robin was violent, yet I did nothing to stop her. If only I'd sent her away sooner. I will have to live with the gruesome memory of Robin stabbing Clay for the rest of my life. This is my punishment. I will take it to my grave.

The cell phone vibrates in Amelia's hand with a call from Jonathan. When she answers, he asks, "Are you okay?"

"I've just woken from a nap. The power appears to be out."

"A terrible storm just blew through," he says. "You must have slept through it. There are widespread power outages all over the island. You shouldn't be alone on the Point with no lights."

Her gaze shifts to the security control panel. The screen is black. She swings her feet over the side of the bed and waits for a wave of dizziness to pass. When was the last time she ate anything?

"Amelia, are you still there?"

"Yes. Sorry. I'm still a little groggy from my nap. My alarm is out. We have a battery backup. I'm not sure what happened." Amelia hears a loud crash coming from downstairs. She gasps. *Nelson.*

"Amelia? What is it?"

Amelia doesn't want to alarm him. She's been preparing for this moment for years. She doesn't want anyone to interfere with her plan. And she doesn't want Jonathan to get hurt. "I heard something. I'm sure it's nothing, probably a tree branch falling on the house."

"I'm on my way."

"That's not necessary, Jonathan. I'm fine. I'll call you back after I figure out the source of the noise." She hangs up before he can argue.

Slipping her phone into her pocket, she cocks her gun and

tiptoes out of the bedroom. She grew up in the house and knows every inch of it by heart. Under the cloak of darkness, she makes her way down the hall. When she reaches the top of the stairs, a flash of lightning illuminates the foyer downstairs where the shattered remains of Dottie's priceless antique Chinese vase litter the floor.

With back against the wall, training the handgun in a sweeping motion from left to right, she glides down the stairs. She's been expecting him, but the sight of Nelson standing with a lit candle by the fireplace in the living room gives her a jolt.

"Amelia, darling. I've missed you."

When he moves toward her, she extends her arms in front of her, her pointer finger on the trigger. "Stay back, Nelson. Don't you dare come any closer."

His dark eyes grow wide. "Where'd you get a gun?"

"I bought it years ago. I have a concealed carry permit, and I'm an excellent marksman."

He scoffs. "You don't have the guts to shoot me."

"Wanna bet?" She aims the gun to the right of his head a few inches and fires. The shot rings out throughout the house, nearly deafening her.

His free hand shoots up. "Are you crazy? That bullet just whizzed by my head."

"Next one pierces your skull. What're you doing here, Nelson? What is it that you want from me?"

"I know you're upset about your mother. It takes time to recover from such a significant loss. Come home with me and let me help you heal."

"Are you kidding me? You'll break every bone in my body. I don't need your kind of *healing*. And I'm not going anywhere with you ever again." She notices a broken pane in the french door behind him, his obvious point of entry. She didn't hear the glass shatter. She must have been sleeping hard.

"Come on, Amelia. Don't be like this."

"Don't be like what, Nelson? Strong? Courageous? For years, you've physically abused me and controlled every aspect of my life by threatening to hurt my mama. But now that she's gone, you have nothing to hold over my head."

He inches toward her, and she shoots the floor at his feet. "I told you not to come any closer."

He jumps back. "Okay. Take it easy. We've had some problems in our marriage in the past. But we can work on those. We can see a marriage counselor if necessary. We have a bright future together. Did you know I'm running for Congress?"

"I saw. Congratulations," she says with a straight face, in a deadpan tone.

"I need my wife by my side."

"As what? Your showpiece? No thanks. Besides, there are plenty of single politicians."

"But I'm running on a platform that highlights traditional values." He takes the candle over to the fireplace and lights others on the mantel. He turns toward her. "There now. That's better. I can see my beautiful wife. You look healthy. The South Carolina sunshine agrees with you. The press loves you, sweetheart. You'll be on the cover of every major fashion magazine in the country."

"I want a divorce, Nelson. I'd rather die than go home with you."

His lips part in a soft smile, one she hasn't seen in years. "Is being married to me really that bad? Most women would do anything to be in your shoes, to live your lifestyle. Designer clothes. Beautiful homes. A staff to serve your every need."

"I'd rather be a homeless beggar than be with you. Either agree to the divorce, or I'll put a bullet in you right now." Amelia shoots at the ceiling, and bits of plaster rain down around her.

Robin's face appears in the windowed door behind Nelson. Her eyes are red, her hair standing on end. Before Amelia can warn her husband, Robin flings the door open and comes after him with a butcher knife, repeatedly driving it into his back while screaming, "I hate you, Daddy. You love Amelia more than me."

Amelia aims her gun, but Nelson is in the way, preventing her from getting a clear shot at her sister. When Nelson drops to the floor, Robin spins on bare feet and flees the house, her sheer white nightgown billowing out behind her.

Seconds later, Amelia is standing in the same spot, paralyzed by fear, when two police officers appear in the doorway on the porch. "My sister did this! Go after her! She's wearing a white nightgown and no shoes. She couldn't have gone far."

As the officers take off after Robin, two different cops, followed closely by Jonathan and Chief Summers, bust through the front door into the foyer. While Summers is rushing to Nelson's aid, Jonathan takes the gun from Amelia, and she falls into his arms. With her face partially buried in Jonathan's chest, she watches a policewoman check Nelson's pulse and shakes her head.

"Everyone out!" Summers shouts. "This is officially a homicide investigation."

Jonathan leads Amelia to the study and pours her a shot of brandy. With a trembling hand, she takes it from him, downs it, and hands the glass back to him. "More, please."

He refills her glass and pours one for himself. Pulling her down on the love seat beside him, he asks, "Do you want to talk about what happened?"

She tells him everything. About her discovery of the journal, what she learned from the entries, and the revelations from her dream. And she walks him through the events of the evening, from discovering Nelson in her living room to Robin's attack.

"Robin went berserk, like a wild animal. She was confused. She called him Daddy. I can see why." Amelia lifts the framed photograph of her parents from the desk and hands it to him. "Nelson looks . . . *looked* an awful lot like my father."

Jonathan studies the photograph and hands it back to her. "I can definitely see the resemblance." He places an arm around her, and she nestles close. "It's over now. The police will handle it from here. They'll find her."

"I wouldn't be so sure about that. Robin disappeared once. For forty-five years. If the police don't find her, I'll be spending the rest of my life looking over my shoulder."

One threat has replaced another. Amelia has been released from one prison only to be confined to another. She feels no remorse or guilt over the death of her husband, only relief not to have his blood on her hands.

TWENTY-SIX

Max spends much of Saturday afternoon helping Birdie drag tables and chairs into the cafe from the outdoors seating area. In the kitchen afterward, Max is rummaging in the refrigerator for a snack when Birdie says, "I'm going to ride out the storm at Stan's. Why don't you come with me?"

"I'm not very good company right now. I'll stay here and wallow in my misery alone," Max says, sinking her teeth into a ripe peach.

"I refuse to take *no* for an answer. You're coming with me." Birdie slings her duffel bag over her shoulder. "Get your things. We're spending the night. But hurry before the storm gets worse."

Max takes another bite of peach, the juices running down her arm. "No thanks. I don't wanna be a third wheel."

"You won't be. It's not like that between Stan and me. Not yet, anyway. I'm planning to sleep in Stan's guest room."

"What is wrong with you, Birdie? This is the perfect opportunity for you to have a cozy, romantic hurricane party. You care about him. That much is obvious. What's holding you back? We're not getting any younger. You never know what tomorrow will bring." Max has never been more aware of the fragility of life as she is right now with the possibility of a prison sentence hanging over her head.

"But you're my best friend, Max. And I'm worried about you. Please come with me. Stan has a generator."

"Good for Stan."

"We're going to make homemade pizzas and work jigsaw puzzles."

Max rolls her eyes. "Sounds riveting."

Birdie laughs. "Okay. Forget the puzzle. We'll play poker."

"Since when do you play poker?"

"Stan's teaching me."

"I'm not going with you, Birdie. And that's final." Taking hold of Birdie's duffel bag, Max drags her to the back door. "Run along now. And tell Stan hello." She opens the door and slams it shut against the driving wind and rain. "You can't go out in that."

Birdie pulls the hood of her raincoat over her head. "I'll be fine. I promise. I'll text you when I get there."

"Please do." Max opens the door again, and with head ducked against the wind, Birdie makes a dash for her car.

Max brews a cup of coffee and makes her way through the maze of furniture in the cafe to the front door. She stares across the park at her hotel. The yellow crime scene tape is like a scarlet letter, warning locals and vacationers to stay away, that something bad has happened within. She looks up at the windows of her fourth-floor apartment. She's weathered many storms in that apartment over the years. She longs to be there now, camped out on the sofa in her living room, reading a novel and watching the weather channel.

Loud banging on the back door jerks Max out of her reverie. Hurrying back through the kitchen, she's surprised to find Davis at the door, rain bouncing off his yellow slicker. "You're soaked. Come in." Taking him by the arm, she jerks him inside and closes the door. "What're you doing out in this mess?"

Water streams off his coat, pooling on the floor. "I was on my way home from boarding up Pauline's windows, and I wanted to check on you, to make sure you're safe."

"Boarding up her windows? This is a tropical depression, not a hurricane."

"I tried to tell her, but she wouldn't listen. Are you here alone?"

Max nods. "Birdie left for Stan's a while ago. I was getting ready to raid the refrigerator. Wanna stay for dinner?"

The lines around his brown eyes crinkle. "Seriously? The refrigerator in the kitchen of the hottest new restaurant in the Lowcountry. How could I say no to that?"

"Right?" Max removes a set of keys from her pocket. "I even have the key to the wine closet. I'm sure we can find a nice bottle of red."

"I'm sold. But I'm soaking wet. Can I throw my clothes in your dryer?"

"Of course. Come upstairs." Taking his coat, Max drapes it over the back of a bench and shows him upstairs to her bedroom. Retrieving her pink fluffy robe from the bathroom doors, she says, "You can wear this while your clothes are drying."

He eyes the pink robe with one brow raised. "You're joking, right? I'm not wearing that."

"Men!" she says in an exasperated tone. "You have such egos." She snatches the robe from him and digs through her drawers for her largest gym shorts and T-shirt. "This is the best I can do."

Davis takes the clothes. "Thank you."

"I'll give you some privacy." She waits for him in the living room, and when he emerges from the bedroom, she bursts out laughing at the sight of him in the too-tight shirt and butt-hugging shorts.

"Go ahead. Have your fun." He dances in a circle, modeling the outfit for her.

She laughs harder. "You look precious. Now, give me those

clothes." She takes the wet garments from him and places them in the dryer. "Let's eat before the power goes out."

Downstairs in the kitchen, they survey the contents of the refrigerator, deciding on lamb chops, scalloped potatoes, and an arugula salad. While Davis makes the salad, Max puts the potatoes in the oven to reheat and pours olive oil in a pan to sauté the lamb chops. When dinner is ready, she unlocks the wine closet, and they study the large assortment of wines.

"Why do *you* have the key to the wine closet?" Davis asks, picking an inexpensive but reliable pinot noir from Oregon.

"Because Birdie is a recovering alcoholic. She doesn't like having the key in her possession."

"That makes sense." Davis ponders the situation for a minute. "I imagine the temptation for her to drink is great. People go out to dinner to have a good time, which includes having alcoholic beverages."

Max locks the wine closet behind them. "It's hard for her at times. But she's handling it. She's overcome so much. She's a strong woman."

Davis uncorks the wine and pours two glasses while Max sets a table for two by the window in the cafe. Once they are seated and eating, Max says, "I took your advice. I found evidence that Ron started the fire."

Davis freezes with a forkful of potatoes in midair. "You're kidding?"

She tells him about finding the master key card, pencil sharpener, and shavings. "I told Toby, who promised to pass the information along to his detective and the fire marshal. But I doubt they'll do anything about it. They're content to let me take the fall. But I'm not giving up. I have an idea of a way to trap Ron."

"What's that?"

"No risk, no reward. I've downloaded a voice recording app to my phone. When Ron wakes up, I'm going to pay him a visit and get him to confess." Max bites into a lamb chop. "It's not very original. But it's the only plan I've got."

"That sounds dangerous, Max."

She shrugs. "What choice do I have? The police aren't helping me. My attorney has hired a private investigator to look into Ron's past, but I'm not holding my breath he'll turn up anything."

Davis wipes his mouth with his napkin. "And just how are you going to get him to confess?"

"I'm going to make nice, like I'm interested in a reconciliation. I'm still working on the narrative."

Davis sips his wine. "Again, Max, this sounds dangerous."

"I'll be careful. This is the best shot I've got at proving my innocence."

They polish off the bottle of wine with dinner, and after cleaning up the dishes, they open a dessert wine, which they take up to the apartment. "Do you mind if I crash here tonight?" he asks, punching the sofa cushion beside him. "I've had too much to drink to drive, and I'm sure no Uber drivers are out in the storm."

"Not at all. I'm grateful for the company."

He smiles. "I was dreading going home to an empty house. One should never weather a storm alone."

"We're lucky we haven't lost power." As the words leave Max's mouth, the lights flicker for the first time.

He wags a finger at her. "You jinxed us."

The lights flicker again and go out. "That's it. We're doomed. With no air conditioner, we'll be sweating in thirty minutes."

Davis accesses the radar app on his phone. "Looks like the worst of the storm is almost over. Give it a few more minutes, and we should be able to open the windows." Settling back against the sofa, he inches a little closer to her. "I have a secret. Wanna hear it?"

She tilts her head back, looking up at him. "Sure. I'm good at keeping secrets."

"I have a ginormous crush on you. I realize the timing is all wrong for you. And I'm willing to wait as long as it takes. I just felt the need to confess my feelings."

Suddenly claustrophobic, Max gets up and goes to the window. With her back to him, she says, "I'm carrying a lot of baggage right now, Davis. I may very well be facing jail time."

He joins her at the window. "I won't let that happen, Max. We *will* prove your innocence."

"I appreciate your vote of confidence. But it's more than just the arson charges. I jumped into a relationship with Ron, and now I'm paying for it. I won't make that mistake again. You and I also have our business relationship to think about. I'd hate to ruin it with a romance gone wrong."

"I agree, that's an important factor. I propose we take our time in getting to know each other during the renovations. I'm not looking for a one-night stand, Max. I'm hoping to find a meaningful and lasting relationship, someone to share my life with."

With racing heart, she smiles over at him. "Sounds like we're on the same page."

A commotion on the boardwalk below gets their attention, and they watch as hordes of police officers swarm the marina dock. "Wonder what's going on." Max raises the lower sash of the window, but they are too far away to make out what the police are saying.

"Maybe I can find out something from my police scanner app." Davis taps his phone screen and staticky voices fill the room. He brings the phone to his ear. "They're searching for a missing person. A woman in a white nightgown. They're calling her a fugitive. I think maybe she killed someone. At Point Pleasant. Isn't that where your friend lives?"

"Yes! Amelia! What are they saying?"

"She stabbed a man and fled the scene. They're saying she took off on foot down the beach."

Max presses a trembling hand to her mouth. "That's awful."

"Here." Max hands her the phone. "You listen."

Max's eyes pop as she follows the conversation between police officers and dispatch. "This is bad, Davis," Max says as she gives him his phone. "The victim was Amelia's husband, Nelson Archer. Amelia never mentioned her husband was coming to town. Did he show up out of the blue? She hinted he was abusive. Did he try to hurt her in some way and she killed him in self-defense? Poor Amelia. She must be terrified."

Max's throat swells and tears fill her eyes. *Damn these tears.*

Davis takes the phone from her and turns her toward him. "You look like you could use a hug. Despite what I said about having a crush on you, I'm not trying to make a move on you, merely comforting a friend." He tilts her chin toward him. "Can I hug you?"

She nods as tears spill from her lids. In spite of her concern for Amelia and whatever is happening at Point Pleasant, Max can't help but notice how perfect she fits in his arms. Is it possible they are meant to be together? *Chill, Max. Don't even consider getting involved in another relationship until you've cleared yourself of the arson charges.*

TWENTY-SEVEN

With no electricity to power a hair dryer, Amelia combs her shoulder-length locks into a low ponytail at the nape of her neck. She spreads more than the usual amount of makeup onto her face, the extra layer of concealer goes a long way toward hiding the dark circles under her eyes. Inspecting her appearance one final time in the mirror, she tucks her mother's journal under her arm and heads for the stairs. She pauses in the foyer, bile burning her throat at the sight of the bloodstain on the seagrass rug where her husband died only hours ago. The coroner removed the body during the night while she dozed in her father's recliner in the study with Jonathan sleeping on the love seat next to her.

Jonathan is waiting for her in the kitchen, leaning against the counter sipping coffee and eating a donut. In the adjacent breakfast room, Chief Summers is seated at the table, talking on his cell phone.

"Where did all this come from?" Amelia asks about the cardboard craft container of coffee and pastry boxes of donuts, muffins, and croissants on the counter.

"Max brought it." Jonathan pours Amelia a cup of coffee.

"She's on the porch. She offered to stay with you while I go home and shower. I hope you don't mind."

"I don't mind." She looks up at him as she sips her coffee. "I'm grateful, in fact. I prefer not to be left alone without an alarm. I wonder when the power will come back."

"I called the power company. They couldn't give me an exact time, but they promised they would get the power restored today."

"Good." Amelia opens the pastry box, surveys the contents, and closes it again. Her stomach is tied in too many knots to think about eating.

Jonathan inclines his head at Summers. "Are you ready for this?"

"As ready as I'll ever be." She closes her eyes and steadies her breath.

"Just tell the truth." Placing a hand at the small of her back, Jonathan walks her to the breakfast room, and they sit side by side opposite Summers.

Summers sets his gaze on Jonathan. "I assume you're here in a professional capacity."

"That's correct," Jonathan says. "I'm her attorney."

Summers looks to Amelia for confirmation, and she nods.

"All right, then. Let's get started." There's a legal pad on the table in front of the police chief, but his eyes are on her. "Why don't you walk me through what happened last night."

Amelia tells him about finding Nelson in the living room and her sister appearing in the window. "Something was off about Robin. She has an agitated demeanor by nature. But last night, she was not in her right mind. Before I could register what was happening, she'd entered the living room and was stabbing my husband."

"We found three nine-millimeter bullet casings and holes in the ceiling, floor, and wall. The shots obviously came from your weapon. Did you shoot at your sister?"

Amelia stares down at her mother's journal in her lap. "As I said, everything happened so quickly. By the time I got a clear aim at her, she was running toward the door. My gun safety instructor taught me never to shoot an intruder in the back as they are fleeing a scene."

Summers massages his double chin. "You witnessed her murder your husband. This would've been the exception to that rule. Who did you shoot at if not Robin?"

"I was trying to get my husband's attention." Amelia folds her hands over her mother's journal to prevent them from shaking. "I asked Nelson for a divorce. I wanted him to know he couldn't hurt me anymore. Nelson has been abusing me for years, both mentally and physically." She tells Summers about her troubled marriage, and Nelson threatening her mother's life.

"Do you have proof of this abuse? Hospital records, eyewitnesses, that kind of thing?"

"Nelson always knew when to stop. He was careful not to go too far." A thought occurs to Amelia. "Our staff—our cook and housekeeper and Nelson's personal assistant—witnessed plenty over the years. But they were too terrified of Nelson to do anything about it. Now that he's dead, they may be willing to tell the truth about what they know."

Summers sits back in his chair with folded arms resting on his gut. "You know what Amelia? I think you conspired with your sister to kill your husband. Your plan was to make it look like a home invasion, but then you betrayed your sister."

Amelia sits up straight in her chair. "What? Are you crazy? That's preposterous."

Summers drums his fingers on the table. "I have to ask myself why you would turn on Robin. Was she threatening to contest your mother's will?" When Amelia doesn't respond, Summers looks to Jonathan for an answer. "You're Miss Dottie's estate attorney. You should know."

Jonathan keeps a straight face. "I'm not at liberty to discuss that with you."

Amelia's stomach churns, and she fears she might vomit. While his scenario is far from the truth, the chief could easily build a case based on this theory.

Amelia places the journal on the table and slides it over to the chief. "I found this in a trunk in the attic yesterday. It's my mama's journal. My sister was a rebellious teenager. She even belonged to a cult. Robin killed my father, stabbed him with a knife just like she stabbed Nelson."

The chief picks up the journal and studies the cover. "All that is in here?"

"Most of it. She doesn't spell out the crime. But I remember it now. It all came back to me in a dream yesterday."

He fans the pages of the journal. "Dreams are funny things, Amelia. How can you be sure you're remembering the actual events?"

Amelia shakes her head. "I can't be positive. Bits and pieces have been coming back to me for a while. It makes sense. Mama fabricated the kidnapping story to protect Robin. And she convinced Chief Swanson to destroy the records."

"I'll be interested to hear your sister's version of events." Summers closes the journal and sets it down on the table.

"Has there been any sign of my sister?"

"Not yet," Summers says. "From what we know of her past, she's liable to be long gone by now."

"Maybe, but I don't think so. I have an eerie feeling she's nearby, watching me." Amelia shivers and Jonathan drapes an arm across her shoulders.

"I need to get to the station," Summers says, and the three of them rise from the table in unison. "I'm sorry to say this story has leaked to the press. Considering your husband was a public figure, it's only a matter of time before reporters swarm the house. I'll have my officers on guard 24/7 until things settle down."

"I didn't kill my husband, Chief Summers. Although he deserved to die after the pain he's caused me over the years. My sister went psycho last night. She did this." Amelia's voice tightens as tears threaten. "I saw her stab him with my own two eyes."

Jonathan pats her arm. "Amelia, you should show the chief the photograph of your father."

"Excellent idea. I'll be right back." Hurrying down the hall to the study, she returns with the photograph of her parents on their honeymoon. She hands the photograph to Summers. "As you can see, my husband bore an uncanny resemblance to my father. I think Nelson's presence in our living room triggered my sister's memories from the night my father died—the night she killed him—and these memories sent Robin off the deep end."

Summers lets out a grunt. "That's pretty farfetched," he says, handing her back the photograph.

"My sister is an unstable woman, Chief. I think she's always had mental problems. Mama alludes to it in the journal. I'm telling you, Robin was not in her right mind last night. Her eyes were wild and the whole time she was stabbing Nelson, she was screaming, 'I hate you, Daddy. You love Amelia more than me.'" Moving to the window, Amelia stares out across the lawn at the garage apartment. "Why didn't you order an autopsy on Mama's body?"

"Because we had no reason to suspect foul play."

"I think Robin was responsible for her death. Mama was perfectly healthy. I don't believe she just died in her sleep."

Summers comes to stand beside her. "Was your sister even in town at the time?"

"Robin told me she arrived in town last Saturday. But, according to the supervisor at the security alarm company, a woman claiming to be my mother made a request to add an additional code on Thursday. As you know, Mama died on Tuesday."

"I need to look into that." Summers retrieves his legal pad from the table. "Do you remember the name of the person you spoke with at the alarm company?"

"Jose Curtis. He's a supervisor."

Summers scribbles a note on his pad. "I'll look into it." He wipes the perspiration off his face with a blue bandana. "What a scorcher. I hope you get your power back soon." He turns away from the window. "I'm headed to the station. You have my number if something comes up." He disappears through the kitchen and out the back door.

From the window, Amelia watches the chief get in his patrol car. Gravel spits out from his rear tires as he speeds off. "Should I be worried, Jonathan? You know the chief better than I do. Does he really think I *conspired* with my sister to kill my husband?"

"Don't worry. Summers likes to throw his weight around sometimes. Once they find your sister, they'll have the answers they need."

"I hope you're right." She turns to him. Beard stubble covers his face, and his hair is sticking up in the back. "You need to go home and rest, Jonathan. I've taken up enough of your weekend."

"I'll go home and shower. But I'm coming right back. I'll pick up sandwiches for lunch."

"Are you sure?"

He kisses her forehead. "I'm positive. And you have a nice visit with Max. Try to take your mind off of things for a while."

Amelia's hand flies to her mouth. "Poor Max! I forgot she was here. I'd better go see about her."

Amelia finds her old friend in a rocker on the porch thumbing through this month's issue of *Veranda* magazine. When Max looks up, Amelia says. "I'm sorry that took so long."

"No worries." Tossing the magazine aside, Max gets to her feet. "How'd it go? Any word on Robin's whereabouts?"

"Not yet," Amelia says as more tears blur her vision.

"Oh, honey. You've been through so much," Max says, embracing her.

Amelia collapses against Max's thin frame. "I'm so sorry. I can't hold back any longer."

"And you don't have to. Let it all out. You'll feel so much better." Max rubs circles on her back while she cries. "A wise man recently told me that keeping anger and hurt trapped inside wears us down over time. And it's true."

Amelia cries like she hasn't cried in years. Letting her emotions out leaves her feeling spent but oddly rejuvenated. She withdraws from Max's arms and lowers herself to a rocker.

Sitting down beside her, Max asks, "Do you wanna talk about what happened?"

Amelia recounts the events of the previous evening. "Summers thinks I conspired with Robin to kill my husband. While it didn't happen the way he thinks, I am guilty of plotting to murder him. I've been waiting for Nelson to show up. I knew he'd want me to go back to Boston with him. But I've had enough of his abuse. I was going to kill him, Max."

"But you didn't. And even if you did, it would've been self-defense." Max gives her elbow a bump. "Look on the bright side. We could end up sharing a jail cell."

Amelia frowns. "The police still think you started the fire?"

"Yep. Even after I found undeniable evidence against Ron." She tells Amelia about finding a master key card along with a pencil sharpener and shavings in the pockets of the shorts he was wearing the night of the fire.

"Did you tell all this to the police?" Amelia asks.

"I told Toby about it. I haven't heard whether Jared or Reynolds has investigated it yet."

"Your nephew is out to get us both. To save the honest citizens of his community from the big bad villains," Amelia says, and they burst into laughter.

Max rests her head against the back of the chair. "Let's talk about something more pleasant. One of Birdie's waitstaff quit. She hired me to replace her. At least until the renovations are complete."

"So, you and Birdie are now living *and* working together? That's a lot of togetherness."

Max snickers. "Tell me about it. I love Birdie dearly, but I don't plan to live with her much longer. I'm looking for an apartment to rent."

"Once I straighten out this mess with Robin, if you can get past the stench of cigarette smoke, you're welcome to stay in my garage apartment. After everything I've been through lately, I would appreciate having someone I trust nearby."

Max's face lights up, but she says, "Let's wait and see what happens with Robin first. You may change your mind."

Amelia stares out at the ocean. "I don't know what the future holds for me. At some point, I'll need to clean out and sell the house in Boston. But that can wait. For the moment, all I can think about is a long, relaxing vacation. A month of sitting on the beach reading romance novels."

"Hmm," Max says with a dreamy expression. "Maybe I'll join you, once I nail Ron with this arson charge."

A comfortable silence settles over them as Amelia comes to terms with her new reality. Nelson is dead. The abuse is over. Soon, she'll be free to live her life as she chooses.

Jonathan returns around noon with a bag of BLTs from the Sandwich Shack. "The news people are gathering in front of the house," he reports. "The police are doing their best to keep them at bay, but you may need to make a statement at some point."

Amelia gives him a mischievous smile. "Isn't that the attorney's job?"

"I'm happy to do it. We'll craft the statement together after we eat."

They are spreading their picnic out on the porch table when Max's phone rings. "It's the hospital." She accepts the call and listens for a minute. "Tell him I'm on my way." She drops her phone in her purse. "I'm sorry. I've gotta run. Ron's awake and asking for me. I need to get to him before the police do." She wraps her sandwich up and kisses Amelia on the cheek. "Wish me luck."

"Good luck! Let me know how it goes," Amelia calls after Max as she disappears around the front of the house.

She turns back to Jonathan. "I'm not sure which one of us is in more trouble."

"Both of you are unjustly accused. My firm is representing both of you. We will do whatever it takes to prove your innocence."

Amelia smiles at him. While it's way too soon for her to be contemplating a new relationship, she can't ignore the sneaking suspicion that Jonathan will play an important role in her future.

TWENTY-EIGHT

Max races to the hospital. Ron is asking to see her. This could play right into her plan.

She pauses outside of his hospital room to catch her breath. She clicks record on her voice recording app, slips it into her back pocket, and enters the room. Ron tears up when he sees her. "You're here."

"Of course." Dropping her bag in a chair, she moves over to the bed, taking his hand in hers. "I've been here a lot, actually. I slipped out today to visit a friend who lost her husband. How do you feel?"

"Like I have the worst hangover of my life," he grumbles.

She smiles. "You really scared me, Ron. I thought I'd lost you."

He squeezes her hand. "You can't get rid of me that easily."

When a nurse enters the room, Max drops Ron's hand and steps away from the bed.

The nurse is a pretty blonde with a bubbly personality. "Look who's awake," she says, fussing over Ron's bandaged head. "You had a nice long nap. How're you feeling?"

"Like an elephant stomped on my head. Can you give me something for the pain?"

Ron can't take his eyes off the nurse, and Max uses the opportunity to inspect the storage locker. Much to her dismay, his belongings are just as she left them. *Damn Toby.* She glances back at Ron, who is smiling up at the nurse as she listens to his chest with her stethoscope. Slipping his wallet out of the back pocket, Max flips it open and confirms that the driver's license and master key card are still there. *And they call themselves detectives.*

Closing the locker door, she strolls back over toward the bed. She asks the nurse, "Now that he's out of a coma, will the doctor move him from the ICU to a normal room?"

"Yes, ma'am. The transfer is in the works. Although I doubt he'll be moved until tomorrow morning." The nurse finishes her duties and leaves the room.

Removing her phone from her back pocket, Max lowers herself to the edge of the bed. She casually places the phone, screen down, on the mattress. "Do you remember anything about the night of the fire?"

He winces as though in pain. "I had too much to drink. Some parts are clearer than others. Have you settled with the insurance company yet?"

Max's heart pounds against her rib cage. This is it. "There won't be any insurance money."

"Why not? Aren't electrical fires covered under your policy?"

Despite an overwhelming urge to strangle him, Max forces herself to remain calm. "How did you know the fire was electrical?"

"I just assumed. I heard your contractor tell you your wiring is bad."

"While that may be true, the police and fire marshal have reason to believe I started the fire to get the insurance money."

The rest of color drains from Ron's pale face. "What'd you mean? What reason?"

"Someone used a crude device to make the fire look electrical."

"Are you talking about arson?"

"Yes. Arson. Which means no insurance money for me to rebuild. The damages from the fire amount to way more than I planned to spend on the renovations. I'm ruined. Doesn't matter anyway, since it looks like I'll be going to jail."

"I'm sorry, Maxie. I was only trying to help. I didn't mean to get you in trouble. I wanted you to have the insurance money so you could do your renovations."

Max frowns, and deep lines in her forehead appear. "What are you saying, Ron? Did you start the fire?"

He looks away without answering.

She gets to her feet, careful to keep her phone's screen hidden from him. "I didn't need the insurance money, Ron. The bank approved my loan request."

"Oh. I didn't know that."

She stares down at him. "You'll tell the police the truth, won't you? To clear my name?"

He shakes his bandaged head. "I'm sorry, Max. I can't do that."

"Wait a minute. Let me get this straight. You're going to let me pay for something you did?"

"Well, I'm sure as hell not going to jail."

She gapes. "But you're the one who's guilty."

"The police don't know that. They'll believe me over you. I had no motive. But you did."

Max is tempted to show him the voice recording app. She wants so badly to say, "Gotcha." But she needs the police to confiscate his belongings first.

"You're a bigger jerk than I thought." Grabbing her purse, Max storms out of the hospital room. At the end of the hall, she bursts through the swinging doors into the ICU waiting room. Leaning against the wall, she takes in deep breaths to steady her nerves. She clicks pause on the app and then saves the voice recording. She did it. She got his admission of guilt on tape.

She's still staring at the phone when she hears a familiar voice. "I hear Ron is out of the coma. That's wonderful news."

She looks up at Detective Jared Carlson. "Even better news that he just confessed to starting the fire." She pushes play on the recording and Ron's voice spills out from her phone.

"Did you tape that without Ron's knowledge? If so, it's inadmissible as evidence."

She clicks pause. "His confession clears my name. Now listen, damn it!" She taps on play again and holds the phone in front of him.

Carlson massages the back of his neck as he listens. When the recording ends, the detective lets out a long sigh. "Can you text that to me?"

"I'll send it in a group text to you, Toby, and Reynolds. Did Toby mention the evidence I found in Ron's belongings?"

A flush creeps up Carlson's neck. "He may have mentioned something."

"But you didn't follow up on it, did you?"

"I haven't had a chance."

"Well, do it now. I just checked the locker in his room, and the evidence is still there. In the back pocket of the shorts he was wearing the night of the fire, you'll find his wallet. In his wallet behind his driver's license is a master key card for the hotel. In the front pockets of his shorts are a pencil sharpener and shavings. I don't know how much more evidence you need. Do your job, Detective, or I'll bring charges against you."

Pushing off the wall, she leaves the waiting room. As she waits for the elevator, she places a call to Toby. When he answers, she blurts, "Ron just admitted to starting the fire. I have his confession on tape. I'll send it to you as soon as we hang up. Do something about this, Toby. I'm not taking the fall for a crime I didn't commit." She hangs up and forwards the recording.

Tears burn the back of her throat as she rides the elevator to the ground floor. But these are happy tears. For the first time in days, she allows herself to contemplate a future that doesn't include a jail sentence.

TWENTY-NINE

Amelia and Jonathan spend two hours drafting a thirty-second press release, which he delivers to the reporters barricaded behind police lines at the edge of the property near the driveway.

"Nelson Archer was murdered by an intruder during a home invasion yesterday evening. The suspect is still at large. Please respect Mrs. Archer's privacy while she mourns the loss of her husband."

The reporters pepper him with questions, but he walks away without answering them.

Changing into her bathing suit and a cover-up, Amelia rides with Jonathan to his house. They spend the rest of the afternoon on the ocean in his thirty-foot center console boat.

They return to the dock around five o'clock. They are tying up the boat when Jonathan says, "I'm going to stay with you tonight. You shouldn't be alone, whether or not the power comes back on." When she protests, he holds up his hand to silence her. "No arguing."

She smiles. "Yes, sir. I'm grateful for your company. But I'm not sure I can afford all this time you've been spending with me. What is your hourly rate?" she asks in a teasing tone.

He laughs. "You don't want to know. Lucky for you, I'm not here in a professional capacity."

Amelia waits on his porch while Jonathan packs an overnight bag. They return to Point Pleasant to find Bebe on hands and knees scrubbing the bloodstained carpet.

When she sees them in the doorway, Bebe jumps to her feet and rushes over to them, throwing her arms around Amelia. "Oh, sweetheart. Why didn't you call me?"

"I didn't want to ruin your weekend."

"You're like family to me. And family should be together at a time like this." Bebe tightens her grip on Amelia. "I'm so sorry, baby girl. First your mama and now your husband."

Amelia locks eyes with Jonathan over Bebe's shoulder. He points at the door and slips outside to the porch to give them some privacy.

"Let's sit down, Bebe. I have some things I need to tell you."

Seated side by side on the sofa, Amelia shares the events of the weekend. Beginning with Robin claiming she's entitled to Point Pleasant to finding her mother's journal in the attic to Robin stabbing Nelson to death.

"I tried to warn you," Bebe says. "Your sister is rotten."

"Rotten and dangerous, and now she's on the loose." Amelia looks over at the damp spot on the carpet. "You almost got the bloodstain out."

Bebe follows her gaze. "That's almost the exact spot where your father died." She shakes her head. "The years leading up to his death were difficult times. Your mama was a nervous wreck. She lost so much weight I thought she was gonna waste away." She cuts her eyes at Amelia. "Much like you. Which is why I made fried chicken and macaroni and cheese for your dinner."

"You shouldn't have done that, Bebe. Today is Sunday. You should be home with Claude." When Bebe appears wounded,

Amelia strokes her arm. "But I appreciate your efforts. Comfort food is just what I need." Standing, she pulls Bebe to her feet. "But I want you to go home now. And enjoy the rest of the weekend with your husband. I'll see you tomorrow morning."

Bebe thumbs Amelia's cheek. "Will you promise to call me if you need me?"

"I promise," Amelia says and gives Bebe a hug.

Amelia dozes in the hammock on the porch while Jonathan reviews a case he's arguing in court in Columbia on Tuesday. The power is still out, and darkness is settling in by the time they think about dinner. With no means of heating the food, they eat cold fried chicken and macaroni and cheese by candlelight on the porch.

Amelia, having little appetite, merely picks at her food. When her phone vibrates at the table with a text from Chief Summers, she snatches it up and reads the text aloud. "The police have an APB out on Robin. So far, there's been no sign of her." She shivers, despite the warm evening. "I have this creepy feeling she's watching us. It doesn't look like the power's coming back on tonight. Despite the police presence, I'm not thrilled about sleeping in this house with no alarm."

"We could go to my house, but I just checked the power company's website, and my electricity is still out too." Jonathan forks a chunk of congealed mac and cheese into his mouth. "I'm spending tomorrow night in Columbia, and depending on how the trial goes, I may have to stay through Tuesday as well. Even if your power is restored, I think someone should stay with you until Robin is apprehended."

"I agree. I'll ask Max. If she has to work, I'll get Bebe and Claude to stay with me." Tears blur Amelia's vision as she stares down at her plate. "What if the police never find Robin? What if she's gone back to California? I'll be looking over my shoulder for the rest of my life. I don't think I can take that."

Jonathan pushes his empty plate away. "Don't get the cart before the horse. I doubt Robin has gone far. You have what she wants. She's not going to leave until she gets her share of the inheritance."

"I'm not so sure about that." Sitting back in her chair, Amelia sips her sweet tea. "The rules of the game have changed now that she's wanted for murder. Her inheritance won't do her any good in jail."

Clasping his hands on the table, Jonathan twiddles his thumbs. "Let's assume for a minute she did decide to run. Does she have any money to travel?"

"I gave her two hundred dollars."

"She won't get far on that."

Amelia stares out into the black night. "You don't know my sister. She's resourceful. She could be anywhere."

"We're exposed out here. Like sitting ducks." Jonathan gathers their plates. "Let's go inside."

Locking the french doors behind them, they take the dishes to the kitchen. They are placing the last one in the dishwasher when the lights blink on. Amelia lets out a squeal. Grabbing Jonathan's arm, she says, "Listen to those air conditioners hum. Isn't it the most wonderful sound ever?"

"Yes!" He punches the air. "We will both sleep well tonight."

However, despite being exhausted, sleep does not come easily for Amelia. Opening the top drawer of the bedside table, she pulls out her bottle of sleeping pills. But the bottle is empty, and she remembers taking the last one on Friday night.

Throwing back the covers, she gets out of bed and goes into the bathroom. She opens the medicine cabinet and examines the bottles of over-the-counter and prescription medicines. She finds one labeled Zolpidem, the generic term for Ambien, but this bottle is empty as well. Why would her mother put an empty bottle back in the medicine cabinet? She studies the label. The prescription was filled on Monday, August 2, the day before her mother died. Carefully setting the bottle on the bathroom counter, she slips on her robe and goes down the hall to the guest room.

She taps on the door, and in a soft voice, she says, "Jonathan, sorry to disturb you, but I need to show you something."

When he opens the door, he's still fully dressed and wearing his black-framed reading glasses. Behind him, files and papers are scattered on top of the bed alongside his laptop.

"I thought you'd be asleep by now," she says.

"I'm still reviewing this case. What's up?"

"I may have found evidence that Robin killed Mama. Let me show you." She motions for him to follow her back to the master bedroom. In the bathroom, she points to the pill bottle on the counter. "Don't touch it. Unfortunately, my fingerprints are already on there. The prescription was filled the day before she died, but the bottle is empty."

"Strange," Jonathan says, bending over to read the label.

"Robin was coming in and out of this house undetected. She could've crushed all those sleeping pills into a glass of water and forced Mama to drink it."

"We need to tell Summers. Do you want to call him or should I?"

"I will." She retrieves her phone from the bedside table and taps on the chief's number.

He answers on the second ring. "Summers."

Amelia quickly explains about her discovery of the empty pill bottle.

"Maybe your sister emptied the bottle and is taking the pills herself," he suggests.

"Maybe. But I doubt it. My sister just murdered my husband with a butcher's knife. I told you earlier today that I don't believe my perfectly healthy, eighty-year-old mother died in her sleep. We need to exhume her body and perform an autopsy."

"If your sister is guilty of such a crime, why would she leave the pill bottle behind as evidence?"

"To make it look like suicide, of course. Why am I answering the questions when you're the chief of police?"

Jonathan takes the phone from Amelia. "Chief, this is Jonathan. Considering the circumstances, an autopsy is warranted." He listens for a minute before hanging up. "Summers is going to speak to the coroner first thing in the morning."

"Great! Now I'll never sleep." Amelia's dam of emotions breaks and tears stream down her face. "I can't take it anymore."

Jonathan opens his arms, and she walks into them. "You've had more than your fair share to cope with lately. You don't always have to be strong, Amelia. Let someone else look out for you for a change."

With his muscular arms supporting her, she cries until her well is empty, releasing years of pent-up anguish. Finally, when his polo shirt is soaked with tears and snot, she lifts her head to look at him. "Do you have any sleep aids?"

He chuckles. "No, but I can recommend something better."

"What's that?" she says, reaching for a tissue and blowing her nose.

"Miss Dottie's smooth, aged bourbon." Taking her by the hand, he leads her downstairs to the study. He pours two fingers into a crystal lowball glass and hands it to her. "Drink up."

She downs the bourbon and holds the glass up for more. He gives her another healthy splash and pours some into a glass for himself.

This time she sips the bourbon. "I'm sorry for disrupting your life, Jonathan. You have work to finish, and I can look out for myself. Maybe I'll watch a movie." She lowers herself to the love seat.

"I'm ready for court. I was just looking over my notes one

final time." Sitting down beside her, he aims the remote at the television. "Comedy or drama?"

"Your choice." Amelia rests her head against the back of the sofa. The bourbon relaxes her, and within minutes, she's dozing off.

She wakes the following morning in her mother's bed with a vague recollection of Jonathan helping her up the stairs. A knock on the door startles her, and she glances over at the alarm clock. Six thirty. Jonathan is up early. Then she remembers he's going to Columbia today.

"Come in," she calls, pulling the covers up over her body.

Jonathan enters the room, dressed in a dark suit and carrying two mugs of coffee. "Good morning. I trust you slept well." He hands her a coffee. "I hated to wake you, but I just got a call from Summers. They are exhuming your mother's body at eight. You have a right to be there if you wish. But you'll need to hurry."

Amelia shakes her head. "I can't go through that again. I hate the thought of what they'll do to her poor body. How long will it take to get the results of the autopsy?"

"Since they know what they're looking for, the process will be minimally invasive, and we should hear something back in a day or two at the latest. Summers wants to check the pill bottle for fingerprints. Whenever you're ready, he'll send an officer to collect it."

"Okay. I'll get dressed and call him in a minute."

"What time does Bebe come to work? I need to get on the road to Columbia soon, and I don't want to leave you alone."

"Bebe is usually here by nine." Amelia motions him to the door. "But you go on."

"Are you sure?" he asks in an uncertain tone.

"Positive. You have to stop worrying about me, Jonathan. I appreciate your concern, but I survived an abusive marriage for thirty years. I can take care of myself."

"Alright then, I'll go. But only because I'm due in court in

Columbia at nine. No matter what you say, I won't stop worrying about you until the police catch your sister."

She waits until he leaves the room before putting on her robe and hurrying after him down the stairs. She catches up with him in the kitchen. "Jonathan, thanks for everything. I don't know what I would've done if not for you these past days."

He kisses her cheek. "You're more than welcome. I'll be back from Columbia as soon as I win this case. Hopefully, no later than tomorrow evening."

From the window, she watches his car leave the driveway. With a heavy heart, she takes her coffee to the breakfast room. She already misses him. He's a wonderful man, and having someone she trusts to lean on has given her a sense of peace she hasn't felt in a very long time.

THIRTY

Amelia is seated at the breakfast room table, staring blankly out the window with a cup of lukewarm coffee in front of her, when Bebe arrives for work around nine.

"What's wrong?" Bebe asks when she sees Amelia's despondent expression. "Did the police find Robin?"

"Not yet." Amelia pats the banquette next to her. "Sit with me for a minute."

"Let me get some coffee first. Looks like I'm gonna need it."

Amelia slides her cup across the table. "May I have a refresher too, please?"

Bebe takes Amelia's cup and returns a minute later with two steaming mugs. "Talk to me," she says, sliding onto the banquette.

"They're exhuming Mama's body this morning," Amelia says and explains about finding the empty bottle of sleeping pills.

Bebe's eyes are moist. "That poor woman. Miss Dottie was one of the finest people I ever met. She deserved better than what Robin gave her."

Amelia hangs her head. "She deserved better than what I gave her."

"Don't beat yourself up, baby girl. Your circumstances were unique."

Amelia sets down her mug and leans across the table. "When I first got home, you mentioned that Mama hadn't been herself lately. Can you be more specific?"

A faraway expression settles on Bebe's face. "I can't put my finger on anything concrete. During the two weeks leading up to her death, she seemed angry. And preoccupied. She even snapped at me once, when I forgot to put away the vacuum cleaner."

"Hmm. That doesn't sound like Mama. Did she confide in you a lot? Would she have told you if Robin was back in her life?"

Bebe hesitates before answering. "She confided in me about some things. But she had a secret side to her as well. She knew how I felt about Robin. I never cared for your sister, even as a child. And I certainly didn't trust Robin. Do you think Robin was trying to extort money from her?"

"Definitely. But after reading her journal, I don't think Mama would've given Robin a dime. Which is why I think Robin killed her."

Bebe collapses against the banquette. "And now she's gonna come after you."

"But she won't get to me. The police are outside. You're here today. And I'm hoping Max will spend the night tonight."

"If she can't, Claude and I will. I don't want you in this house alone until Robin is in jail."

"Thank you, Bebe. I may have to take you up on your offer." Amelia places a hand on Bebe's shoulder. "One way or another, we'll get through this together."

Bebe smiles. "I see brighter days on the horizon."

"I don't know what I would do without you," Amelia says, leaning in to kiss Bebe's cheek.

"You would vanish into thin air," Bebe says. "Have you eaten breakfast yet?"

Amelia shakes her head. "But I'm not hungry."

Bebe gets to her feet. "With all this worrying, you need to eat to keep up your strength. How would you like your eggs? Scrambled? Poached?"

"An omelet, I guess." Amelia slides off the banquette. "If you don't mind bringing it to me in Daddy's study," she says and leaves the kitchen.

Seated at her father's desk, she clicks on Max's number. "Are you working tonight?"

"No," Max says. "Birdie is closed on Sunday and Monday nights. But I'm manning the coffee bar today. Why do you ask?"

"I was wondering if you could stay with me. Jonathan has a trial in Columbia. With my sister still on the loose, I don't want to be alone. And I thought you might like to have some breathing space. I have plenty of spare bedrooms."

"Sure, if you're looking for a warm body. But don't count on me to be very good company." Max tells Amelia about Ron's confession.

"But that's wonderful news. You've been exonerated of the arson charges. You should be ecstatic."

"I would be if I knew for certain the police were following through."

Amelia exhales loudly. "These things take time, Max. Or so I'm learning. I'm afraid I won't be a barrel of laughs tonight either. I have reason to believe my sister killed Mama. The police exhumed her body this morning. You and I should be great company for each other. I'll have Bebe make us a light dinner, and we'll drink a lot of wine."

"Count me in. The cafe closes at six. I'll come over then, if that works for you."

"Six is perfect."

Bebe enters the study with her breakfast tray. In addition to the omelet, there's a glass of freshly juiced orange juice, two slices of turkey bacon, and a small bowl of fruit. "I can't possibly eat all this, Bebe."

"Try," Bebe says, and bustles out of the study.

Much to her own surprise, Amelia devours every morsel of the food and drains the glass of juice. Pleasantly satiated, she spends the next couple of hours responding to emails from friends and acquaintances expressing sympathy over Nelson's death. Lying about what a wonderful person Nelson was and how much he will be missed is exhausting. And the distraction does little to take Amelia's mind off her mother. She leaves the study and climbs two flights of stairs. The attic is stifling in the midday heat. She opens the windows at both ends and turns on the whole-house fan, the enormous blades creaking to life. Sitting on the floor beside the trunk, she lifts the lid and explores the contents. Hidden beneath a soft crocheted baby blanket and several stuffed animals, she finds Robin's black leather jacket and lace-up boots. The items spark memories from screaming matches between her older sister and their parents, and she sits for a minute, allowing her mind to wander back decades. Digging deeper in the trunk, she discovers things her mother mentioned in the journal—the notebook with strange drawings and the knife with the silver handle. Buried at the bottom are two reports from private investigators. One is dated two years after her father's death. The investigator tracked Robin across the country to California where the trail ran cold. The second is more interesting. Ten years later, a different investigator out of Columbia unearthed an arrest warrant for the suspicious death of a newborn baby. The photograph of the accused woman is Robin. The name she used was Anna McCormick. The case never made it to court due to lack of evidence. Anna McCormick was never heard from again. End of report.

Amelia's gut is a churning pit of revulsion and fury. Her sister sacrificed her own child. Her sister killed their mother. Slamming the trunk shut, she hurries downstairs and locks the reports in her mother's jewelry safe. Changing into lycra shorts and a loose-fitting tank top, she goes in search of Bebe. She finds her sweeping the porch. "Bebe, I need some fresh air. I'm going for a walk on the beach."

Bebe looks up from sweeping. "I'm not sure that's a good idea, baby."

"I can't stay locked up in this house forever. Besides, I have my weapon." She pats her gun, hidden in her shorts at the small of her back.

"Now I'm really worried."

"I'll be fine. Just be sure to turn the alarm on when you go back inside."

"I will. Don't you worry. But be sure to take your keys. I may be in the basement, doing laundry, when you get back."

Amelia grabs her keys out of her purse on the kitchen counter and leaves the house through the front door. She trudges through the deep sand in the pathway cutting through the dunes. When she gets to the beach, she kicks off her shoes and walks at the edge of the surf. She senses someone following her, but every time she turns around, no one is there. Kids splash in the surf while their daddies drink beer and their mamas read romance novels. The women are hidden behind sunglasses and straw hats. Any one of them could be Robin.

When she returns home an hour later, she unlocks the front door and enters the house. She's greeted by an eerie silence, no pinging of the security system or hum of the vacuum cleaner. "Bebe!" she calls out, but Bebe doesn't answer. She remembers Bebe mentioning laundry. She passes through the kitchen to the basement door. She calls for the housekeeper again. This time, she receives a muffled response. She flies down the steps to find Bebe on the floor in the corner, her hands bound by rope and tape covering her mouth.

Before Amelia can comprehend what's happening, Robin

steps from under the staircase. Hooking an arm around her neck from behind, she snatches the gun from the waistband of Amelia's shorts and presses the barrel against her temple. "Scream, and I'll blow your head off."

Few customers enter the cafe during the afternoon. Around five, Max is wiping down an already-spotless counter when Birdie says, "Business is slow. Everyone headed for the hills when the storm came. I'll finish up here. You go ahead to Amelia's."

Looking up from her work, Max asks, "Are you sure you don't mind?"

"I don't mind." A wounded expression crosses Birdie's face. "I admit I feel left out. I'm jealous of the time the two of you have been spending together."

Max brushes a strand of Birdie's hair out of her face. "We haven't intentionally left you out, Birdie. You've been busy with the cafe and Stan. Once things settle down after Labor Day, the three of us will spend lots of time together."

Birdie's lips part in a soft smile. "I'd like that."

Max claps Birdie on the arm. "Look at you. You're practically glowing. I take it things are going well with Stan."

Birdie blushes. "He's so wonderful, Max. Slowing the progression of our relationship was the right decision. We know each other much better now. Because of our sacrifice, we have a strong foundation from which to grow."

"That's wonderful, Birdie. I'm truly happy for you." An image of Davis enters Max's thoughts. Maybe one day she can have the same with him. Max folds the towel and places it on the counter. "I'll grab some of my things and head out. See you tomorrow."

Upstairs, she throws a change of clothes and her cosmetics case into an overnight bag, and hurries back down the stairs and out the door. She's cutting through the park when her phone rings with a call from Toby. Accepting the call, she blurts, "Did you arrest Ron yet?"

"Not yet," Toby says with a sigh.

"Why not? I gave you the recording over twenty-four hours ago."

Toby ignores her question. "There's been a development, Max. Ron has checked himself out of the hospital."

Max slows her pace. "What do you mean, he checked himself out?"

"He left the hospital against his doctor's advice."

Max pauses a beat, letting this news sink in. "Please tell me Jared confiscated the evidence I told you about?"

Toby's silence is her answer.

"Great!" Max tosses a hand in the air and lets it fall against her thigh. "So now the evidence is gone. What is wrong with you? Why aren't you and Jared doing your jobs?"

"We've been busy on another case."

"Right. Amelia's. She's my friend, and I understand her situation is dire, but that's no excuse." Max paces in circles with head lowered and phone pressed to ear. "Tell me, Toby, how did Ron leave the hospital when his car is in the hotel parking deck?"

"That's why I'm calling *you*."

"What do you mean?" Max understands her nephew's insinuation, that perhaps she provided an escape vehicle for Ron, but she needs to hear him say it.

"Did you pick Ron up from the hospital? Are the two of you in cahoots? I'm thinking maybe you came up with the idea, and he started the fire."

She white-knuckles the phone. "You've been trying to pin this crime on me from the beginning. Even after I supplied evidence that proves Ron is guilty. You know what, Toby? You suck at your job," she says and hangs up on him.

Max enters the parking garage and takes the stairs to the second floor. She's tossing her bag into the back seat when a hand covers her mouth. She tries to scream, but the hand muffles her words.

A voice she recognizes as Ron's says in a loud whisper near her ear. "Quiet! Do as I say or you're a dead woman. Where are your keys to the hotel?"

She feels something jabbing into her back. Is that a gun? She removes the keys from her bag and dangles them in the air. Snatching them from her, he wrestles her over to the servant's entrance and unlocks the door. He drags her into the elevator cart. She tries to fight free, but his hold is too strong. They exit on the fourth floor, and he shoves her inside her apartment. She stumbles, and before she can right herself, he tackles her to the floor. Wrapping duct tape around her ankles and wrists, he picks her up off the floor and drops her in a straight-back chair. He secures her body to the chair with more tape, tearing off one last piece to cover her mouth.

"If you're lucky, someone will find you before you starve to death. But I'll be in Montana or Louisiana or Maine by then. By the way, where is your car key?" He dumps the contents of her purse on the floor. "Here it is." He pockets the key. "In case the police try to track your GPS . . ." He walks her phone across the room, opens the sliding glass door, and hurls it into the creek.

"Now then, I'll just pack up my belongings and be on my way." He disappears into the bedroom and returns minutes later with her rolling suitcase.

He crouches down beside her. "I didn't mean to hurt you, Maxie. Truly, I was only trying to help. But I can't take the fall for this. I'm not going to jail."

She screams at him, more muffled words, until her face turns red and tears stream down her cheeks.

"Sorry. I can't understand you." He kisses the top of her head. "Gotta run. Have a nice life. Or not." He slams the door on his way out, a reminder that no one is in the building to hear her.

She cries until her throat burns and rubs her wrists together until they bleed. She has to pee. Why did she drink the extra-large size cup of sweet tea? If help doesn't come soon, she'll have to wet herself to relieve her bladder. Rocking back and forth in her chair, she realizes if she crashes to the floor, she could crack her head open or break bones. Who will save her? Not Birdie. Birdie thinks Max is at Point Pleasant. And not Amelia, who isn't expecting her until after six. Which is thirty minutes from now. Will Amelia be concerned if Max doesn't show up? What about Davis? He stopped in for a coffee an hour ago. He told Max he'd left a message for the fire marshal and was waiting to hear back from him. Davis was going to press Reynolds to release the hotel so he can start renovations. He promised to call Max with an update. Will he worry if she doesn't pick up? And then there's her worthless nephew. Is Toby still wrapped up in Amelia's missing sister case or is he going after Ron? With any luck, he'll think to search the hotel.

Claustrophobia sets in and she thinks she might lose her mind. Closing her eyes, she calms her thoughts by envisioning herself on her paddleboard gliding across the water as the sun rises above the ocean.

THIRTY-ONE

R obin brandishes the gun at the housekeeper while shouting orders at Amelia. "Help her up! We're going upstairs to the study."

Amelia does as she's told. They have a better chance of being rescued on the first floor. One of the police officers might see them through a window. With Robin poking the gun in Amelia's back, they slowly climb the steps to the kitchen. As they make their way to the study, Amelia looks around for an object to use as a weapon against Robin. The fireplace poker in the living room is too far away. And the umbrella in the brass stand by the front door is just out of reach.

In the study, Robin shoves Bebe onto the sofa, and with gun still aimed at Amelia, she removes the tassel tieback from the curtain. "Here." She tosses the rope to Amelia. "Use this to tie her ankles."

When Amelia hesitates, Robin trains the gun at her head. "Don't make me shoot you, Mila."

Amelia drops to her knees and loosely wraps the rope around Bebe's ankles.

"Tighter," Robin yells. "And hurry. We haven't got all day."

Casting a sympathetic look at Bebe, Amelia binds her ankles tighter. She stands to face her sister. "Why did you kill all those people? Daddy. Mama. My husband."

"You should thank me for getting rid of your husband."

Amelia's mouth falls open. "How—"

"Did I know he was abusing you? Mama told me she suspected it."

"So, you saw Mama before you killed her?"

"Of course. I tried to make nice, but she refused to give me what I wanted. Let her death be a lesson to you, Mila. I intend to get what I want."

Amelia doesn't flinch. Being threatened is nothing new to her. "What about your child? Why would you murder your own baby?"

Robin's expression is anguished. "She died in childbirth. I gave her body to the gods."

Amelia wonders if her *god* is Satan. "What about my father?"

Robin shrugs. "He got in my way. That's enough of the small talk." With her free hand, Robin drags Amelia by the arm over to the desk, pushing her down in her father's chair. "Here's what I need you to do. You're going to transfer all the money out of Mom's account into this account." She removes a slip of paper from her front jean's pocket and places it on the desk. "Now access her account. I want to see the balance."

"I can't do that, not without her sign-on credentials."

Robin presses the barrel of the gun into Amelia's temple. "Do it, Mila! I know you have the password."

"Why would I have the password?" Amelia says, stalling for time while she thinks of a plan.

"Because I've been watching you through the windows at night. I've seen you tearing this study apart."

Amelia's ears roar. She didn't think it possible to hate anyone worse than her husband. "Now that you mention it, I think I saw a list of passwords in one of these drawers." In one quick motion, she opens the top drawer and rolls the chair sideways, catching Robin off guard. Stumbling backward, Robin's arms fly in the air and a shot rings out as the gun skids across the floor. Amelia leaps from the chair and dives for the gun. Robin pounces on her, and they roll about, pulling hair and clawing at each other.

Amelia hears footfalls in the hallway and someone yells, "Freeze! Roll over and place your arms over your head."

Rolling onto her belly, Amelia watches with one cheek pressed to the floor as two officers handcuff Robin and yank her to her feet.

Summers appears at her side. "Are you okay, Amelia?"

She smiles. "Yes. Finally. I'm gonna be okay."

Summers helps her to her feet, and they rush to Bebe's aid, untying her ankles and wrists.

Bebe removes the tape from her mouth. "Lord have mercy. I thought we were goners. You saved our lives, baby girl."

Amelia, sitting down on the sofa, pulls a shivering Bebe close. Looking up at Summers, she says, "Robin admitted to killing Mama."

He nods solemnly. "I was just coming to tell you. We got the results from the lab. Miss Dottie died from an overdose of Zolpidem. And Robin's prints were on the bottle."

Amelia falls back against the sofa cushions. "So, we have the proof we need to convict her."

"Yes, and there's more. Those prints also belonged to Anna McCormick. While in California, your sister was living under an assumed identity. Back in the late eighties, Anna, aka Robin, was arrested for the suspicious death of her newborn baby. The case was later dismissed due to lack of evidence."

"Right," Amelia says. "I learned about that earlier today from reports I found in Mama's trunk in the attic. Several years after

Robin disappeared, Mama hired investigators to look for her. Robin claims her baby died in childbirth. I guess we'll never know the truth."

"Maybe not about that case," Summers says. "But there's another active case. In early January of this year, Anna McCormick was arrested for killing the leader of her cult, a polygamist named Simon Lazarus. Anna convinced the judge that she wasn't a flight risk, and he released her on bail despite the mountain of evidence the prosecution has against her. Anna disappeared the next day."

"And she appears on Mama's doorstep seven months later." Amelia rubs her eyes with the palms of her hands. "I'm having a hard time wrapping my mind around all this. My sister is a real sicko."

"Yep. And she's going to jail for a very long time."

Max's neck is stiff and her muscles ache. The minutes on the clock on the table beside the sofa tick off like hours. She survives the physical pain and mental anguish by escaping in her mind to tranquil places like the beach at sunset and the mountains after a fresh snow. She's been tied up for about an hour when she hears the elevator coming to life. Someone's in the building. Does that someone know she's here? Her efforts to scream through the tape produce a guttural sound akin to a wounded animal. But she doesn't stop until Birdie and Davis burst through the door.

Birdie rushes toward her, but Davis calls after her, "Stop! Don't touch her yet. We need proof." Pulling out his phone, he snaps a dozen photographs of Max. "Okay, let's cut her loose."

Birdie retrieves the scissors from the kitchen, and they cut her body, hands, and feet free. Stripping the tape off her mouth, Max says, "My bladder is bursting," and races down the hallway to the bathroom.

When she returns to the living room, Birdie looks her up and down. "Are you okay? Are you hurt anywhere? You gave us quite the scare."

Max stretches her neck. "I'm a little sore. But mostly I'm freaked out. How did you know to look for me here?"

Birdie says, "About fifteen minutes after you left to go to Amelia's, I took out the trash and saw your car pulling out of the parking deck. I assumed you were driving, but the sun was bright, and I wasn't wearing my sunglasses. I didn't think anything else about it until Davis stopped by looking for you."

Davis nods. "I got worried when you didn't return my calls and texts."

"Ron threw my phone in the inlet," Max says.

"That explains it. Anyway, Birdie and I were trying to figure out where you might be when we heard on my police scanner app about a shooting at Point Pleasant."

Max gasps. "A shooting? Was anyone hurt?"

"We don't know," Birdie says. "Only that a suspect has been apprehended. I called Toby to tell him we were worried about you. He said you weren't at Point Pleasant, and he told me about Ron leaving the hospital. That's when I remembered about seeing your car earlier. And I figured maybe Ron was the one driving. Davis and I decided to check out your apartment." Birdie dangles a silver key. "Thank goodness I still have my key to the building from that brief period I lived here with you several years ago."

Max crosses the room to the door. "I need to check on Amelia. Can one of you drive me to Point Pleasant?"

"We can't leave. We have to wait for the police," Birdie says. "Toby is sending a unit."

"Forget the unit. I need to talk to Toby in person. Ron could've killed me. And it would've been Toby's fault for ignoring the evidence I found against him."

"I'll drive you." Davis flashes his phone. "I have the proof you need."

When Max and Davis exit the apartment, Birdie hurries after them. "Wait for me! I'm going with you."

Bebe, too shaken to drive home, calls her husband to pick her up. Amelia and Bebe wait for him at the end of the driveway. "I'm so sorry for dragging you into my family's mess," Amelia says, hugging her for the umpteenth time.

Bebe kisses her hair. "I've told you before, I *am* your family. I'm just upset. That was a scary scene in there." She points at the house. "I thought for a minute I might die. I just need to go home and have myself a stiff drink."

"I don't blame you. Take the day off tomorrow. Heck, take the rest of the week. With pay, of course. You deserve it."

Bebe stares at Amelia from under a furrowed brow. "You know me better than that. I'll be here at the normal time in the morning. I'll have Claude drive me."

When Claude arrives, Amelia hugs her one last time and helps her into the car. "Call me if you need anything. And please reconsider about taking the rest of the week off."

Bebe closes the door and rolls down the window. "Stop fussing, baby girl. You just get yourself some rest."

Amelia squeezes her hand. "You too, Bebe. And God bless you."

As Claude and Bebe are driving away, a white pickup truck pulls into the driveway. Max and Birdie pile out with a man Max introduces as Davis Watson, her contractor. The threesome surround Amelia as she recounts the events of the afternoon. "My sister is going to jail for a very long time. Maybe the rest of her life."

"I'm so sorry, Amelia," Birdie says. "You've been through so much."

"I'm glad you're okay." Max's gaze shifts to the porch behind

Amelia where a group of police officers are gathered. "There's Toby. I need to talk to him. I had my own share of drama this afternoon."

Max marches off across the lawn, and Davis goes after her.

"What on earth happened?" Amelia asks Birdie.

"Ron ambushed Max in the parking deck, tied her up in her apartment, and stole her car."

Amelia shakes her head. "Poor Maxie. She must have been terrified."

"I confessed to Max earlier that I'm jealous of the time the two of you have been spending together. But after what both of you have been through this afternoon, I've changed my mind. I don't need your kind of trouble."

Amelia laughs out loud. "Trust me, Birdie. I'm ready to get off this roller coaster ride."

"Toby!" Max calls out as she approaches the group of officers. "I need a word with you in private."

"Let's go inside where it's cool." Toby leads Max and Davis through the french doors to the living room. He motions them to the sofa, but Max remains standing.

She elbows Davis. "Show him."

Davis hands Toby his phone. Toby's jaw drops to the floor when he sees the photographs of Max tied up. "Ron did this to me," Max says, jabbing her finger at the screen. "I told you he was guilty. He tied me up and stole my car. I'm damn lucky he didn't kill me. If Birdie and Davis hadn't come along, I could've died. If you don't find and arrest him, I *will* have your job."

Toby's face turns white. "As of this minute, Detective Carlson is off the case, and I'm back on it. You have my word. I will apprehend Ron. What's your license plate number?"

She recites the plate number, and Toby steps away to make a

call. When he returns, he says, "I've put out an APB on him. Until we find him, I'm providing you with round-the-clock protection. Where are you staying?"

"Here. With me," Amelia says, entering the room with Birdie right behind her.

"No way," Max says, vehemently shaking her head. "Not after what you've been through today. The last thing you need is more trouble."

"On the contrary. We should all be together, *because* of what we've both been through today. That includes you, Davis, and you, Birdie." Amelia looks at each of them. "Jonathan called a while ago. He's on his way home from Columbia. We'll have dinner while we wait for word about Ron."

———

Amelia insists Birdie invite Stan to dinner, and Birdie, in turn, insists on bringing the food. Hours later, long after the sun has sunk below the horizon, the six men and women gather around a candlelit table on the porch. Police officers remain stationed along the perimeter of the property. Their presence offers a sense of security for Amelia, even though her abusive husband is dead, and her sister is locked behind bars in the city jail.

After Jonathan offers the blessing, Amelia taps her champagne glass with her knife. "I'm glad we could all be together tonight. I think it's important for us to discuss the traumatic events of recent days. Given the circumstances, I'm grateful Max and I came out relatively unscathed. I don't know about you, Maxie, but I'll be glad to see this week in the rearview mirror."

"Amen to that," Max says, and the table erupts into laughter.

"While I consider this an inappropriate occasion for a celebration, I think it's the perfect chance to reflect on the past and ponder the future." Amelia raises her glass. "To old and new friends. To childhood memories and carefree days ahead."

"Here, here." They all chime in as they clink glasses.

After several rounds of toasts, they dig into the feast laid out on the table in front of them—barbecue ribs, corn on the cob, a mixed green salad, and key lime pie for dessert. Multiple bottles of wine and champagne are consumed with dinner. Even Birdie, who's drinking sparkling water, appears tipsy.

Around ten thirty, Toby emerges from the house and whispers into Max's ear. A wide smile spreads across her face, and she announces, "Ron was apprehended at the Charleston airport while attempting to board a plane to New Mexico. He is on his way to jail as we speak. The arson charges against me have been dropped, and we can now begin the process of renovating the hotel." Turning to Davis on her right, she gives him a high five.

Max gets out of her chair and gives the chief a hug. "Thank you, Toby. I'm sorry if I was hard on you earlier."

"I deserved it. I trusted Jared to do his job. But he was taking the easy way out by blaming you. I hope you can forgive me."

She kisses his cheek. "Of course. We're family."

The chief salutes the table. "We'll be leaving now. It appears our services are no longer needed here."

Glasses are raised and a collective, "Here, here," comes from the table.

"Look at that moon," Max says of the full moon lighting up the night sky.

"Let's clean up and go for a stroll on the beach," Jonathan suggests with a mischievous glint in his eye.

Everyone pitches in to clear the table. The women rinse the dishes, placing them in the dishwasher, while the men store the leftovers in the refrigerator. Returning to the porch, they migrate as a group through the sand dunes. When they reach the beach, they stand together, staring up at the moon.

Max loops her arms through Amelia's. "I feel blessed to have you back in my life." She loops her other arm through Birdie's. "And to have shared so many wonderful years with you, Birdie.

I've been thinking a lot lately about my future, about what tomorrow will bring for me. For us. My future looks a lot more promising than it did a few hours ago."

"I ditto that," Amelia says under her breath.

"We've been given another chance at friendship. And at love." Max's eyes are on Davis. "Let's promise to make the most of the years we have left."

"That's a promise I aim to keep," Amelia says, and Birdie adds, "Let our golden years be our best."

They stand a moment longer before breaking off into couples. Amelia watches Birdie and Davis walk hand in hand, heading north up the beach. They make a cute couple, and while their relationship is in the early stages, Amelia predicts they'll be together for years. With her head resting on his shoulder, Birdie and Stan wander off in the opposite direction. Stan is a fun-loving guy, and Birdie obviously adores him. Amelia wishes her friends a lifetime of happiness.

Jonathan leans into her. "Penny for your thoughts."

"I was thinking about something Max said earlier. About the future. About making the most of the years we have left. After thirty years in an abusive marriage, the most important thing for me is my freedom." Amelia spreads her arms wide. "I'm free, Jonathan. My dream is finally coming true."

Jonathan places his arms around her from behind and rests his chin on her shoulder. "Tell me about your dream."

"I want to live out my days at Point Pleasant. To once again experience the seasons at the beach. The briskness of autumn. The quiet stillness of winter. The rebirth of spring. And the glory of summer."

Jonathan spins Amelia around to face him. "Is there room in this dream life for me?"

She touches the tip of her finger to his lips. "As long as you can be patient. I have a lot of healing to do, a lot of emotions to sort through."

"You're an amazing, beautiful woman, Amelia. You deserve a man who will put your needs first. Over time, if you give me a chance, I will prove to you I'm that man." He leans in, his lips close to hers. "May I kiss you?"

She smiles. "You definitely may."

ALSO BY ASHLEY FARLEY

Palmetto Island

Muddy Bottom

Change of Tides

Lowcountry on My Mind

Sail Away

Hope Springs Series

Dream Big, Stella!

Show Me the Way

Mistletoe and Wedding Bells

Stand Alone

Tangled in Ivy

Lies that Bind

Life on Loan

Only One Life

Home for Wounded Hearts

Nell and Lady

Sweet Tea Tuesdays

Saving Ben

Sweeney Sisters Series

Saturdays at Sweeney's

Tangle of Strings

Boots and Bedlam

Lowcountry Stranger

Her Sister's Shoes

Magnolia Series

Beyond the Garden

Magnolia Nights

Scottie's Adventures

Breaking the Story

Merry Mary

ACKNOWLEDGMENTS

I'm grateful to many people for helping make this novel possible. Foremost, to my editor, Patricia Peters, for her patience and advice and for making my work stronger without changing my voice. A great big heartfelt thank-you to my trusted beta readers —Alison Fauls, Anne Wolters, Laura Glenn, Kate Rock, Jan Klein, Lisa Hudson, Lori Walton, Jenelle Rodenbaugh, and Nicole Lau. A special thank you to Kathy Sinclair, criminal investigator with the Bartow County Sheriff's Office, and Captain Jessie Aliberti, Bartow County Fire and Emergency Services, for their arson expertise. And to my behind-the-scenes, go-to girl, Kate Rock, for all the many things you do to manage my social media so effectively.

I am blessed to have many supportive people in my life who offer the encouragement I need to continue the pursuit of my writing career. I owe an enormous debt of gratitude to my advanced review team, the lovely ladies of Georgia's Porch, for their enthusiasm for and commitment to my work. To Leslie Rising at Levy's for being my local bookshop. Love and thanks to my family—my mother, Joanne; my husband, Ted; and the best children in the world, Cameron and Ned.

Most of all, I'm grateful to my wonderful readers for their love of women's fiction. I love hearing from you. Feel free to shoot me an email at ashleyhfarley@gmail.com or stop by my website at ashleyfarley.com for more information about my characters and upcoming releases. Don't forget to sign up for my newsletter. Your subscription will grant you exclusive content, sneak previews, and special giveaways.

ABOUT THE AUTHOR

Ashley Farley writes books about women for women. Her characters are mothers, daughters, sisters, and wives facing real-life issues. Her bestselling Sweeney Sisters series has touched the lives of many.

Ashley is a wife and mother of two young adult children. While she's lived in Richmond, Virginia for the past 25 years, a piece of her heart remains in the salty marshes of the South Carolina Lowcountry, where she still calls home. Through the eyes of her characters, she captures the moss-draped trees, delectable cuisine, and kindhearted folk with lazy drawls that make the area so unique.

Ashley loves to hear from her readers. Visit Ashley's Website @ashleyfarley.com

Get free exclusive content by signing up for her newsletter @ ashleyfarley.com/newsletter-signup/

facebook.com/ashleywfarley

twitter.com/AshleyWFarley

instagram.com/ashleyfarleyauthor

9 781735 521282